The Girl I
Used to Be

BOOKS BY HEIDI HOSTETTER

The Shore House

Things We Keep
Things We Surrender
A Light in the Window
The Inheritance

Heidi Hostetter

The Girl I Used to Be

bookouture

Published by Bookouture in 2021

An imprint of Storyfire Ltd.
Carmelite House
50 Victoria Embankment
London EC4Y 0DZ

www.bookouture.com

ISBN: 978-1-83888-882-4
eBook ISBN: 978-1-83888-881-7

For Jersey Girls everywhere

Chapter 1

The only thing worse than arriving late for an appointment is arriving early.

Arriving early smacks of desperation, and Jillian DiFiore Goodman was *not* desperate. She was, however, beginning to perspire. She'd parked her car across the street from her appointment, in the shade of a leafy tree, and had cracked the windows, but the late September sun was merciless. Worse, the cicadas humming in the trees overhead meant the day would only get hotter. Jill shifted her position, feeling the cool leather seat underneath her, and breathed in the new-car smell, still a whisper in the air. She swatted a gnat from her face and glanced at the clock on the dashboard.

Twelve minutes more.

Across the street was the Brockhurst mansion, the site of her interview. Stately and imposing, it was one of the original homes in this upscale New Jersey neighborhood. A stone castle tucked behind sturdy iron gates, filled with mystery and old money. The front of the house was covered with ivy, a wall of boxwoods lined the front garden, and a lacy Japanese maple anchored the courtyard. The rumor was that the Brockhurst money came from the gold rush out west and had been brought east to buy respectability for an otherwise unremarkable family. Of course, no one would dare question their wealth now, because the Brockhurst money *had* bought respectability, and everyone wanted a piece of it.

Within the stone walls lived Georgiana Brockhurst, matriarch of the family. A formidable woman, she was said to be a generous philanthropist and noted patron of the arts. Her reach was wide, and her personal taste influenced much of the art world along the East Coast. She sat on the boards of the finest museums and galleries in the tri-state area. She'd promoted literacy and education programs too, but her passion was firmly within the arts. In fact, Georgiana Brockhurst was known to mentor emerging artists and that made Jill nervous. Because Georgiana Brockhurst was who Jill was scheduled to meet.

Jill glanced at her portfolio on the passenger seat again, if only to reassure herself that she'd brought it, that she had everything she needed. Then she placed her palms on her stomach to quiet the butterflies. They'd gotten worse in the minutes leading up to the interview and Jill had to remind herself to breathe.

At least Libby would be there.

Libby Brockhurst, the only granddaughter of Georgiana Brockhurst, was engaged to a man from an equally prominent family, and Jill wanted to photograph Libby's bridal portrait.

The wedding would mark the union of two of the East Coast's finest families. The planning alone had taken the better part of a year, and details had been mentioned in society pages in New York, New Jersey, and Connecticut at least half a dozen times. The affair would start at the Brockhurst mansion with a private party for family and close friends. St. Patrick's Cathedral in New York City had been reserved for the ceremony, and rumor had it that guests were expected to fill the pews to capacity. They'd booked the Plaza Hotel for the reception, where Jill had it on good authority that all three ballrooms had been reserved, with separate catering and entertainment in each. Afterward, family and close friends would return to the Brockhurst summer home in East Hampton for a final reception.

Jill's best friend Ellie Monahan had been hired to help and had inside information. Among other things, she'd told Jill that every wedding vendor within two hundred miles had been competing for a chance to work the Brockhurst wedding. Competition was so fierce, she'd said, that the Brockhursts had hired private security just to keep them away.

Jill wanted a chance too, but she knew better than to stand in that line.

She had another way in.

It was true that she and Libby Brockhurst didn't share the same social circle, but they did share a spin class. Three mornings a week they began their day on a stationary bike in an air-conditioned studio overlooking the Village Green. One day after class, had Jill plucked up her courage and invited Libby for coffee in a nearby café. Jill had done her research beforehand—she'd googled the wedding photographer the family had hired and visited his website to study his work. So when the time was right, over non-fat lattes, Jill proposed a unique approach for Libby's bridal portrait. She'd found an abandoned warehouse in Brooklyn, with crumbling brick walls and exposed pipes, where sunlight filtered from antique windows onto original hardwood floors. The texture and the setting would provide the perfect counterbalance to Libby's heirloom gown. Jill envisioned stark black and white for some portraits, then a transition to color, adding ferns and delicate ivy to soften the effect of the stark backdrop. Jill had concluded her pitch with a Pinterest board created especially for Libby, and Libby had loved it.

But they both knew the final decision—that all decisions—rested with her grandmother.

A few days after that coffee, Jill had been invited to the mansion to present her ideas for Libby's portrait to Georgiana Brockhurst. And that was why, at this moment, she sat across the street from the Brockhurst mansion, sweating through an ivory silk blouse and coordinating Marc Jacobs tweed blazer: for a chance.

With eight minutes until her interview, Jill turned the ignition on. After allowing herself a moment to enjoy a blast of blissful air conditioning, she drove across the street to the Brockhurst gates and was buzzed into the courtyard. She parked in the shade, then retrieved her portfolio and got out. Filled with purpose, if not yet confidence, she crossed the cobblestone courtyard to the front door and pressed the bell.

The carved mahogany doors were opened almost immediately by a uniformed member of the Brockhurst staff.

"Mrs. Goodman?"

"Yes."

"Mrs. and Miss Brockhurst are expecting you. If you'd follow me please, I'll let them know you're here."

He led Jill to a sitting room off the main foyer. It was bright and elegant, decorated in classic shades of French blue and pale yellow that reminded Jill of a jeweled Fabergé egg. The wallpaper was hand-painted in a soft blue that served as a canvas for everything else in the room, from the crown molding on the ceiling to the cherrywood bookcases flanking the windows on the far wall. Jill stepped closer to the windows, marveling at the panes of antique leaded glass and how they absorbed then softened the bright morning sun. Beside the windows were rich damask draperies in soft yellow, tied back with a navy tassel braided with gold thread. But the impressionist art on the wall was the most striking thing about the room, intricately framed and lit from below. Jill wondered if the paintings were original, then decided they likely were. In addition to her work with art museums, Georgiana Brockhurst was known to have one of the finest impressionist art collections in New Jersey.

Because she hadn't been told where to sit, Jill made her way to a chair covered in rich silk damask. The upholstery was so luxurious that Jill couldn't resist running her fingertips along the fabric. The pattern of deep yellow honeysuckle flowers and bright green hummingbirds was so intricate that it could only have been hand-embroidered. Curious as she was, Jill turned her focus to the door. It wouldn't do to have Mrs. Brockhurst enter the room to see Jill turning over the furniture to examine the quality of the fabric.

Instead, Jill sat down gracefully, crossing her legs at the ankle, as she'd seen on television. If Mrs. Brockhurst's office was wired with security cameras, as Marc's was, what the video would show was someone who knew how to conduct herself in polite society.

Suddenly the door opened, and two women entered the room. The first to enter was Georgiana Brockhurst, wearing an original Chanel suit, dove gray with a cream silk blouse and a layering of pearl and gold beaded necklaces that were probably worth more than Jill's first car. Mrs. Brockhurst looked older in person than she did in her pictures, though she was no less commanding. She had an air about her, a confidence about her place in the world. Jill rose from her seat immediately, resisting the temptation to curtsy.

Libby followed in her grandmother's wake. The smile she flashed Jill was wide and reassuring, and Jill felt herself relax. As Libby crossed the room, it occurred to Jill that she'd only ever seen Libby in bike shorts and the faded Radcliffe sorority T-shirt she wore to spin, and it was striking how different Libby looked outside class. She was a younger version of her grandmother, in a simple gray sheath dress and a single strand of pearls, and just as confident. It occurred to Jill that Libby might be training to take over her grandmother's philanthropy work in the future. She'd be good at it, Jill decided. Despite her wealth and influence, Libby was very down to earth. She'd listened to Jill's ideas, looked at Jill's work, and had arranged this meeting because she liked what she saw. For that, Jill was grateful.

Mrs. Brockhurst made her way to the chair behind the desk, and Libby sat beside Jill.

Libby leaned toward Jill and lowered her voice to a whisper. "You look nervous. Don't be. This will be so much easier than Dave's 6 a.m. class."

Jill smiled in return, reassured.

When Mrs. Brockhurst was settled, the meeting began.

Libby's tone changed, becoming more formal. "Jill Goodman, may I present my grandmother, Mrs. Georgiana Brockhurst?" Then Libby addressed her grandmother. "Grammy, this is Jill Goodman, the photographer I told you about."

"I'm honored to make your acquaintance, Mrs. Brockhurst." Jill winced at her awkward and stiff tone. The only part of this meeting she hadn't rehearsed was the greeting. Clearly, she should have.

"Jill Goodman." The older woman's gaze sharpened, though not unkindly, and Jill found herself wondering what Mrs. Brockhurst had been like when she was younger. Newspaper accounts mentioned that she wasn't born into privilege, but they didn't provide much background on her life prior to her marriage to the much older Franklin Brockhurst III. "Are you related to Marc Goodman, the developer for the Summit Overlook neighborhood? The one that borders the arboretum?"

Jill tensed. The neighborhood Marc had developed four years ago was divisive. The land had originally been a green space, a parcel the state no longer wanted and had offered for sale at auction. Most people had assumed it would remain a park and so there hadn't been much interest in buying it. Marc and his partners had snapped it up at a bargain price, and bulldozers had arrived almost immediately to clear the land, surprising local residents and sparking months of protests and lawsuits. Neighbors had hurled insults and accusations from their car windows as they'd driven by.

In the end, the land commission had apologized for the quick sale but insisted that no laws had been broken. Marc had won the fight, but he paid a price. Affluent clients who may have been interested in his custom builds were put off by the news reports, so Marc had had to work harder to find clients, and the development had taken longer to finish than he'd anticipated. In the meantime, the Goodmans had been pariahs in their own neighborhood.

"Yes, he's my husband," Jill answered, as neutrally as she could.

"Interesting." Her expression gave nothing away, cordial and polite, but not friendly. "I understand you'd like the opportunity to photograph my granddaughter."

"A wedding portrait, Grammy," Libby gently interrupted. "I mentioned this before."

"Yes, I remember, but I'd like Mrs. Goodman to speak for herself please," Mrs. Brockhurst replied. "I'm sure she knows how."

"I do." Jill ignored the butterflies and straightened in her chair. Libby Brockhurst may be the bride, but the wedding was very much her grandmother's to plan. "Libby and I share a spin class, as she may have mentioned. I showed her my work one day after class and shared an idea I had for her bridal portrait. Libby liked it and asked me to come here to meet with you."

"I see. That was very resourceful of you." Mrs. Brockhurst's gaze shifted, though it appeared to be more curiosity than judgment. "Tell me about your background. I'm sure you won't mind me remarking that you look quite young to have much career experience. How long have you been interested in photography?"

And because Jill had always met a challenge head-on, she decided to be truthful. "I'll be twenty-seven years old in November. I have a business degree from Rutgers—"

"A business degree? Not an art degree?" Mrs. Brockhurst pressed. "Why not an art degree, if photography is what you have planned as a career?"

In for a penny, in for a pound, as Jill's Aunt Sarah used to say. Jill squared her shoulders and answered this question truthfully as well. "I've always been interested in photography, but a business degree looks better on a résumé and back then my future was uncertain."

Majoring in art wasn't an option for Jill, though she would have loved it. The very idea of spending entire semesters abroad languidly studying the Old Masters was like a dream to her. Imagine, passing whole days doing nothing but wandering great cities, awaiting inspiration. But that wasn't in the cards for Jill; her reality was very different. She worked two jobs to pay tuition and cobbled together a patchwork of student loans and work-study to pay the rest. Work had always come before anything else, and unyielding budgets were a way of life for her. Opportunities to study abroad weren't for kids like her, and it was hard not to feel resentful at having missed them.

"So no, I don't have a formal art degree," Jill concluded. "What I *do* have is creativity—imagination and a fresh perspective. I think that's just as powerful."

"I'm sure you're talented," Mrs. Brockhurst allowed. "My point is that a formal art degree provides the foundation of one's craft. Technique is a difficult thing to learn on one's own."

"I agree. I've taken photography classes at the community college and workshops at Parsons School in Manhattan. But I believe the most important thing a good photographer can bring to her work is a critical eye, and I think I have it." She brought her portfolio to her lap. "May I show you?"

Mrs. Brockhurst inclined her head. "Please do."

Jill had spent three full days organizing—and reorganizing—the photographs she wanted to present in this meeting. Now was her moment. She unzipped her leather case and opened it to the first image. She rose to place it on the desk then reclaimed her chair. Other photographers might have elected to explain each piece, turning the pages as they went, but Jill purposefully decided not to. Mrs. Brockhurst knew enough about art not to have it explained to her, and Jill wanted her work to speak for itself.

Even so, the wait was nerve-racking. Jill sat quietly, squeezing her hands together in her lap while Georgiana Brockhurst flipped through the pages and examined her photographs. After what seemed like forever, she paused at one of Jill's very favorite ones.

"This one here." Mrs. Brockhurst tapped a neatly manicured fingernail on the image. "Tell me about this."

Mrs. Brockhurst had chosen the photograph that Jill had shown Libby, that day in the coffee shop. Libby had loved it, and the story behind it was the reason Jill was in the Brockhurst study now, interviewing for the job. So it was a very good sign that Mrs. Brockhurst had paused to notice that one.

"It was taken at the end of a week-long workshop at Parsons last year. The assignment was to bring a fresh perspective to a traditional composition. I chose bridal portraits because they've been photographed the same way for years and I knew I could do better. I wanted something that you might see on a runway or in an upscale fashion magazine. I found an old warehouse in Brooklyn and got permission from the owner to shoot there."

Jill straightened, remembering how excited she had been to find the space. While the rest of the class had headed for the lush green spaces of Central Park or to the gritty industrial tunnels of the subway, Jill had wanted something different. Even after the others had finished shooting and returned to the studio to develop, Jill hadn't found a place that spoke to her. When she finally did, her imagination sparked, and she worked straight through. Fueled by the euphoria of purpose and creativity, she finished a week-long assignment in record time. Finding that space and turning in the finished photograph was the happiest she'd ever been.

"Interesting composition," Mrs. Brockhurst murmured.

"The space inside the warehouse was absolutely amazing. It's a pre-war building so the windows are floor to ceiling, but the wind comes from the naval yards, bringing smoke. The soot on the windows filters the sunlight in the most amazing way. And the floors," Jill gushed, unable to contain her excitement, "the floors are *original* hardwood, warped and scuffed from almost a century of use. The woodgrain is beautifully layered, and the texture shows up with the right exposure. The brick walls are old and crumbling but the color of the brick is warm, and it *absorbs* the sunlight—that almost never happens." She breathed, then paused, suddenly aware of the flush on her face and the juvenile excitement in her voice. She pressed her lips closed and lowered her gaze, embarrassed by her enthusiasm. It was one thing to be excited in front of other students, but this was a job interview and she wanted to be taken seriously.

After taking a minute to compose herself, she raised her gaze. To her surprise, she was met with smiles from both Libby and her grandmother.

"Please, go on," Mrs. Brockhurst said, gesturing. "Genuine enthusiasm for one's work is refreshing and should be treated as the gift it is."

Encouraged, Jill steadied herself and continued. "The image you're looking at now is one of a pair I shot that day. There's another that I like even better. It's on the next page. May I show you?"

"Yes, please do."

Jill's favorite shot from that warehouse was honestly breathtaking. She'd taken it at a perfect moment, the elusive golden hour that comes just before dusk, when sunlight melts into honey tones and everything is bathed in magic. And just like magic, those moments were fleeting and you had to be ready for them. On that day, Jill's model had assumed the fading light meant they'd finished work for the day, so she'd relaxed her pose. In a completely unguarded moment, she'd buried her face in her bouquet, breathing in the scent of pink peonies, and the joy she'd experienced was reflected in her expression. Jill had been there to catch it.

"You can see here that I softened the brick hardscape by filling the space with delicate stephanotis flowers and a tumble of variegated ivy. I draped a sheer curtain panel across the broken window—see how the fabric billows in the breeze from the river? Do you see how the ivory material picks up the colors in the foliage and even the lighter shades of grout between the bricks? Here and here?" Jill pointed, then realized she'd been explaining amateur photography to one of the state's greatest art patrons, exactly the thing she'd told herself she wouldn't do. Her face flushed again as she drew her hand away from the print.

"You've quite an eye," Mrs. Brockhurst commented.

"Thank you." Jill's heart thumped in response. She might just get this job after all, and what a prize that would be! What a coup for her budding career. "What I imagine for Libby is something similar. Her hair color would be striking against the warm brick, but instead of an afternoon shot, I'd like to set up early in the morning. The sun rising over the river will wash everything in shades of pink and would pick up her skin tone. Libby's bridal portrait will be beautiful and completely original."

Jill was encouraged by Mrs. Brockhurst's thoughtful examination of the photograph. She followed the older woman's gaze as it swept the image, and when she noticed that Mrs. Brockhurst lingered on the same elements that Jill liked, she took it as a good sign. What if Mrs. Brockhurst took an interest in Jill's work? That might lead to other opportunities, and wouldn't that be wonderful?

Then, to her horror, Jill realized that Mrs. Brockhurst had noticed the very thing that Jill had hoped she wouldn't. A mistake. During the shoot, Jill had laid down old bedsheets to protect the bride's white gown, but she'd misjudged the amount of dust and grime that had accumulated on the floor from years of disuse, and a simple cotton bedsheet hadn't been nearly enough protection. If she'd gone back for something sturdier, she'd have missed the light—and her opportunity—so she'd decided to press on. After the shoot, there were a few smudges on the hem of the dress where it had dragged on the floor, and on the cuff of the sleeve where the model had placed her hand on the hardwood to steady herself. Blemishes in the otherwise perfect photograph were unprofessional. They were easy enough to digitally remove, but Jill hadn't noticed that she'd included the wrong prints until this morning. By then, it was too late to fix them.

She cringed at the sight of Mrs. Brockhurst's fingertip resting on the smudge.

The mistake.

"The dress is fine—the dry-cleaners got the dust off," Jill offered, unnerved as she sensed Libby stiffening beside her.

Mrs. Brockhurst shifted her attention from the portfolio and lifted her gaze to Jill. "How much do you know about my granddaughter's wedding?"

"Libby's told me a little bit about it," Jill answered, deliberately vague. Jill knew almost everything about the Brockhurst wedding. Everybody did. "I know both the ceremony and reception will be held in New York."

"It's more complicated than that, I'm afraid. I've allowed things to get quite out of hand. Libby is my only grandchild, you see. Regretfully, she bears the burden of family obligation. I've lost count of the number of guests we've invited, and truthfully, I'm not entirely sure that I know all of them." The diamonds on her wedding set flashed in the sunlight as she swept her words from the air. She straightened, her blue eyes sharp. "Libby's wedding gown has been in the Brockhurst family for more than one hundred years—has she mentioned that?"

"No, she hasn't."

"It's been altered of course, temporarily, to fit Libby, but the gown *is* an heirloom. Five generations of Brockhurst women have been married in that dress and it cannot be replaced."

"I'll bring something more substantial than bedsheets this time, and of course I'll pay for dry-cleaning afterward," Jill blurted, even as she felt her opportunity slipping away.

"My dear, one does not 'dry clean' a dress this old," Mrs. Brockhurst sighed. "I'm truly sorry but I'm afraid my answer is no."

Libby shifted in her seat, prepared to object, but her grandmother quieted her with a single glance.

"You have quite an eye, you really do," Mrs. Brockhurst continued, turning her attention back to Jill. "But it cannot start here. There's too much at stake. I wish you well, Mrs. Goodman."

"I understand." Jill pushed herself to her feet. "Thank you for your time."

Chapter 2

It was a short drive from the Brockhurst home to the shops on the Village Green, but Jill barely remembered it. The disappointment was heartbreaking, and Jill wasn't sure she could cope with it. There was one person who knew how hard she'd worked for this chance, one person who would understand her disappointment.

Jill pulled into a parking space and found her cell phone. She dialed the number, and as she waited for the call to connect, she adjusted the air-conditioning vent to blow cool air on her face. The tweed jacket she'd chosen had been a mistake—the whole interview had been a mistake. She should have removed the photograph from her portfolio the second she noticed the smudge. Including it was sloppy and unprofessional, not the impression she wanted to give. She yanked off her jacket and tossed it aside.

Ellie answered Jill's call almost before it had a chance to ring. "It's about time you called," she kidded, her familiar New Jersey accent as thick as ever. "You were there so long I thought you'd moved in. So tell me: how'd it go?"

Jill and Ellie had been best friends since fifth grade, ever since Ellie had rescued Jill from a series of horrifying packed lunches consisting of iceberg lettuce and rice crackers. When Jill turned eleven, Jill's mother had decided that if Jill were ever to attract the right boy's attention, she needed to lose weight. Every day began with a trip to the bathroom scale and her mother's disappointing sigh. One day, Ellie claimed a seat on the bench next to Jill, unwrapped her lunch and offered Jill half. The gesture almost made Jill weep and they'd been nigh on inseparable ever since.

"The meeting with Mrs. Brockhurst? Not great." Jill relayed the details as she waved the car behind her away. "I *knew* I shouldn't have included that picture, El, but honestly, it's my favorite. I didn't notice that I'd included the wrong print until this morning, and by then I didn't have time to fix it. I guess I was hoping she wouldn't notice."

"Still a great picture, Jilly."

"Thanks. I liked it too."

"Listen, you want to meet for coffee? I've got some time before I have to leave."

As one of the coordinators for the family at the Brockhurst compound in East Hampton, Ellie was expected in Long Island for training.

"What's the guest count up to now?" Jill asked, remembering an update she'd read in the newspaper. "Two hundred people?"

"Two twenty-five as of this morning. I don't know where they're going to put everybody." Ellie sighed. "And get this: they want servers to call the guests by name and memorize food and drink preferences too."

"It's a ton of work, Ellie—"

"I'll say."

"But," Jill continued, "I have complete faith in you. Imagine how great this will look on your résumé?"

After graduating high school, Ellie had gone straight to work. First as a server for a catering company, then as a team leader, then a supervisor. She had a talent for organization and an eye for detail, and promotions came quickly. Her dream was to start her own events company, and of course Jill wanted to help. She slipped Ellie's business card to Marc's friends' wives, who always seemed to be hosting a party or event. But when Marc had found out, he was livid, reminding Jill again that her friends and his associates would always be separate.

"Yeah, sure it will," Ellie agreed. "Anyway, what about coffee?"

"I can't," Jill said as she switched off the engine. "Marc's party is tonight, and I still have a few errands to run."

"Yeah, of course." Ellie's tone cooled, something only Jill would have noticed. But she did and it made her uneasy.

Jill's oldest and best friend and Jill's new husband had never warmed to each other. Back when Jill and Marc started dating, Ellie had accused Marc of coming on too strong. She didn't like that he expected Jill to fit into his world yet made no effort to fit into hers. Once, Ellie had hinted that she thought Marc might still be married while dating Jill, but the resulting argument was so fierce that she'd never mentioned it again. For his part, Marc accused Ellie of being crass and uninterested in bettering herself. He mocked her accent, made fun of the way she dressed, and he cringed every time she laughed. Jill refused to examine the fact that she and Ellie had practically grown up together and acted the same way until a few years ago. Until Marc took an interest in her.

"Hey—how about dinner when you get back?" Jill's heart sank at Ellie's dull acceptance of her second-place status in Jill's life. "Cheeseburgers and fries at Ruby Jacks?" Jill urged. "I'll meet you there at eight?"

Ellie snorted and all at once the tension between them was broken. "Better make it six, fancy girl. Some of us have day jobs."

"Deal." Knowing Ellie didn't have much money, Jill almost offered to pay, but that would mean poking another sore spot between them. So she didn't.

Jill's circumstances had improved since her marriage to Marc three years ago. She'd moved from sharing a dank apartment in a sketchy neighborhood with four other roommates to an 8,000-square-foot home in a posh neighborhood in Summit, New Jersey. Marc had been generous with credit cards and a clothing allowance, and he found ways to help her spend it. It was almost too good to be true that Jill would never again have to forage through clearance racks at Old Navy or scour the bins at Goodwill when she needed something to wear. However, despite her best efforts to remain in touch, many of her friendships had fallen away. Ellie was the only one left, and Jill had started to notice the threads connecting them were beginning to fray.

Chapter 3

Jill paid the lot attendant for her parking space and made her way to the shops. A tear in Marc's tuxedo had needed to be rewoven before the party, and Jill had paid a rush fee to ensure it would be ready. Marc was anxious to have it back so that would be her first stop. After the tailor's, it was on to the jewelry story to pick up Marc's watch. Finally, to the dry-cleaner for her own dress, a red backless number that required an extra month of spin classes and weeks of nothing but lettuce and rice crackers just to zip it up.

Jill rounded the corner, feeling her mood lift. She loved shopping and the Village Green was one of her favorite places to go. The streets were quiet, and sturdy oak trees cast the road in dappled shade. Despite the warm September days, the nights had cooled, and the leaves were just beginning to change. Bright spots of orange and yellow spattered the trees on the avenue, providing a preview of the glorious fall color to come.

As Jill turned the corner from the parking lot onto the wide sidewalk on the main road, she happened to remember a comment Ellie made once, about how all the women in Jill's world looked the same. Scanning the shoppers ahead of her now, Jill wondered if her friend had a point.

Most of the women here did look the same, wearing tennis whites or black leggings, with their blonde hair pulled back in slick ponytails. Their casual appearance gave the impression they'd come from the tennis court or the yoga studio. But it was their jewelry that gave them away: diamond stud earrings as big as acorns and wedding sets so polished that they practically glowed in the sunlight. These women wore expensive jewelry with a casual disregard that Jill had never understood.

Between the tailor's and the jeweler's was an authentic Italian deli. As Jill approached the open door of the shop, she was greeted with the unmistakable scent of real deli: spicy garlic and crusty bread, fresh parm, and marinated olives. She'd ventured inside once or twice when Marc was out of town, and the subs were the best she'd ever had. She paused for a moment to breathe it in and remember exactly the sandwich she'd ordered—salami and provolone with sautéed peppers and onions, dripping with olive oil and vinegar and dusted with oregano and red pepper flakes. Jill's stomach rumbled just thinking about it.

But now wasn't the time, so she kept walking.

Marc's birthday party was tonight, and she had a dress to get into. Months of hard work and deprivation wasn't going to be wasted on one deli sub.

The jeweler buzzed her in, and Jill approached the counter, feeling the deep pile carpet underfoot and the chill of air conditioning on her skin.

An older man emerged from the back office. "Mrs. Goodman, how nice to see you."

"Thank you, Joseph. It's nice to see you too." It still made Jill uncomfortable, addressing an older person by their first name. Aunt Sarah would have been horrified, but Marc said retail workers expected it. So she did.

"You've come to pick up Mr. Goodman's watch?"

"I have. Did you have any trouble with the inscription?"

Months before his birthday, Marc had picked out a watch for himself and tasked Jill with "running out to get it." But the watch was in demand and impossible to buy. Marc had placed himself on half a dozen waiting lists around the country, and his impatience grew as his birthday approached. So it was serendipitous that the little jewelry story in the Village Green telephoned to say they had secured one. Marc had texted the words he wanted engraved and asked Jill to pick it up in time for his party. She'd balked at the price—the watch cost more than the entirety of Jill's student loans—but Marc had insisted, and he'd always been sure of what he wanted. Who was she to deny him on his birthday?

"Trouble? Not at all," the man said smoothly as he offered her a chance to examine his work before wrapping it up.

The truth was that Jill had forgotten what inscription Marc had ordered, she'd been so busy with her portfolio and the Brockhurst interview. Even so, she nodded when she saw it and thanked the jeweler for his time.

On her way home, Jill chose a scenic route, through the leafy streets of the older neighborhoods in Summit, though it meant a longer drive. Traces of fall emerged here and there. In a few weeks, the canopy that shaded the neighborhood would be awash in deep red, bright orange, and golden yellow, and the afternoon sunlight filtering through would be bright pops of color. Maybe she could come back with her camera, photographing whatever looked interesting and adding the best images to her growing portfolio.

But she didn't have time.

Jill might not have a paying job, as Ellie pointed out, but that didn't mean she was any less busy.

Too soon she came to the stoplight that marked the boundary between the older neighborhood and the development Marc had created, and the effect was still jarring. She remembered what the land had looked like before Marc developed it, and if she were honest, she had preferred it before. Marc had ordered bulldozers to raze old growth trees and dump trucks to fill in the duck pond. They'd brought in heavy machinery to scrap away the topsoil and laid down ugly gray gravel and parked construction trailers where flowers once grew. Neighbors hated it and threatened to sue. As a peace offering, Marc had promised to plant new trees, double the number his company had removed, and that seemed to satisfy them. But three years later, the seedlings he'd planted still required regular watering, and Jill suspected it would be decades before they grew tall enough to cast shade.

The light turned green, and Jill continued to the home she shared with Marc.

The house was built on a hill, above the rest of the neighborhood, and was clearly visible from the front gates. She'd been stunned when Marc first showed it to her, overjoyed to call such a place home. Eight thousand square feet. Seven guest bedrooms, each one en suite and all guest-ready, though they'd never been used. Downstairs was the foyer with its marble floor and double staircase, designed to give visitors a lasting first impression. Beyond that was what Marc called "a statement kitchen," with quartz countertops and professional-grade appliances. The formal dining room comfortably sat twenty-two and was used often to host Marc's friends. The library, the media room, and Marc's office were also on the first floor, in the east wing. Down one level was a home gym with a sauna and spa showers. Outside, just past the rose garden, was an oversized pool with a detached pool house that

Marc's grown children were very fond of. The oversized trellis was threaded with climbing roses and provided shade for daytime parties.

Jill had heard the real-estate pitch so many times she could recite it herself.

The house she and Marc shared was called a showcase home, meant to demonstrate the level of quality that buyers could expect in one of Marc's custom builds, and it was impressive. But what agents didn't mention during showings was almost as important. That the appliances in the kitchen were bought on close-out, dented in the back, and their warranty was nearing the end. That the dramatic curved staircase wasn't genuine mahogany, just stained to give that impression, and the wool runner on the stairs was actually a poly-blend bought from a liquidation sale.

Agents' exaggerations made her so uncomfortable that she'd questioned Marc about it, shortly after they'd married. Marc's reaction had been harsh and unexpected. He had said she couldn't possibly understand, given her background, and that she should leave the real world to him. He'd had a point, so Jill had never brought it up again.

She slowed the car as she approached the driveway. She'd planned a simple but elegant party for her husband's fifty-first birthday, and she found herself looking forward to it. Because she wanted to get to know Marc's friends better, she'd kept the guest list small and the setting casual. An outdoor party near the pool house, cold beer and wine on ice, and burgers on a charcoal grill might be just the icebreaker they needed to become friends. When the sun set, she'd light the tiki torches and the floating candles, and they'd all retreat to the pool house to chat.

So when she pulled into the driveway, she was a little surprised at the commotion that greeted her. A maze of box trucks and catering vans lined the driveway, though she hadn't expected anything delivered today.

She slipped into a spot behind a truck and got out of her car.

Someone came to carry in her packages and Jill gave instructions to hang the clothes up to prevent wrinkles.

"Mrs. Goodman?" A young man jogged toward her dressed in khakis, Top-Siders, and a white polo embroidered with Marc's company logo. "Mr. Goodman told me to keep an eye out for you. Says he wants to see you."

"Okay. Who are you?"

"I'm Kyle. New intern," he said as he thrust his hand forward for her to shake. "Mr. Goodman hired me to assist with the presentation tonight." His smile revealed a neat row of perfect teeth. "One good sale and I'll have earned next year's tuition."

Jill frowned in confusion. "I think you might have your dates mixed up. Mr. Goodman's birthday party is tonight. I arranged it myself and it doesn't include sales presentations."

"Um… I got the call from Mr. Goodman himself, this morning. We all did," Kyle said as he pointed to a battered white van near the garage, back doors open. "Support staff got called in too. Even Mr. Garcia."

Standing behind the van was an older man whom Jill recognized as Manny Garcia, the best electrician in the company. Manny scowled at an assortment of tangled wire and circuits. At his feet was a bucket filled with hardware.

"He doesn't look happy about it," Jill remarked.

"He's not," Kyle agreed.

"Well, it's nice to meet you, Kyle," Jill said smoothly. "Can you tell me where I can find Mr. Goodman? I think we can straighten this out."

Kyle gestured to the backyard. "He said to meet him out back. I think he's supervising the tent."

"The what?" Jill turned back to Kyle but was interrupted by Marc, striding toward them.

At fifty-one years old, Marc still had the power to make her heart flutter. Tall and lean, he was desperately handsome, and he knew it, which was part of his charm. Jill watched him approach, moving with a powerful confidence that she found intoxicating. Years of consultations with personal shoppers had taught him the type of clothing he looked best in and he rarely wavered from that formula: a neatly tailored dress shirt with the cuffs folded back exactly three inches along the forearm, dark silk trousers, and handmade leather loafers, worn without socks.

"Hello, Jilly." He leaned in for a quick kiss. Jill noticed the ends of his hair were damp and his skin was smooth, as if he'd recently shaved. Both seemed unusual for this time of day because Marc was a creature of habit. His days started early and followed an unwavering routine: showering, shaving, and dressing the moment he got out of bed. But maybe he was excited for the party and had wanted a fresh change of clothes.

"Kyle, can you make sure Garcia has what he needs for the screens?" As Marc gestured toward the van, Jill detected a hint of Marc's spicy cologne, also odd. The scent had usually faded by now.

"Sure, Mr. Goodman." Kyle nodded and jogged across the driveway to the electrician.

"What's this about a presentation?" Jill asked as she fell into step next to Marc, moving toward the backyard.

"You'll see."

"Marc…" Jill came to a full stop at the edge of the yard, struck by the transformation. An oversized party tent had been erected near the rose garden. Someone had rigged a DJ station on the patio of the pool house. And on the lawn near the pool, carpenters pounded together parquet sections that looked suspiciously like a dance floor. But the worst part was the television monitors mounted by the entrance.

"It's not a big deal." Marc lifted a shoulder in a dismissive half-shrug.

The pieces fell together, and Jill was stunned. She pointed to the screens. "Is that why Manny's here? Are you hosting a work presentation? This isn't the party I planned for you. I sent a guest list and bought decorations; we were going to have a cook-out. What *is* this, Marc?"

Marc sighed as if he were dealing with an errant child, a habit Jill loathed.

Jill's anger sparked, though she tried to keep her tone even because anger would get her nowhere now. "Did you call in a *sales team*? Is that what Kyle meant by 'earning his tuition'? This isn't anything like the birthday I planned for you, Marc."

"It's a slight change of plans. And it's good for business so I hoped you would be supportive."

"But—"

Marc ended the discussion with a single look. "It's my birthday, Jilly. I should be able to do what I want." His voice was calm, but Jill understood the warning.

Jill looked away because he had a point. She was doing it again, taking over. If he wanted to celebrate his birthday with a work party, he should do it. But was it too much to ask that he at least recognize the effort she'd made to arrange a party in the first place?

"Don't pout, Jilly." She felt his arm on her shoulder and heard his voice soften. He'd won—they both knew it. "More important right now is your meeting at the Brockhurst mansion. Did you get the job?"

"She hasn't decided," Jill lied, still annoyed with how he'd changed the party.

"Jillian." Marc's voice deepened. "I hope you realize how important a connection to the Brockhurst family would be for my company. I've been trying to break into that circle for years, and it hasn't been easy. A wedding invitation would offer a tremendous opportunity to network with other guests."

"A wedding invitation? Is that what you want?" Jill glanced up at him. "Marc, the interview was for a *job*, for Libby's bridal portrait. It's nothing to do with the ceremony or the reception."

"You're already friends with Libby, aren't you? That spin class I pay for?" Marc frowned. "I'm sure you'll find a way to get invited. Hundreds of couples are going—why can't we be one of them?"

"Because it doesn't work that way."

"The *world* works that way, Jillian," Marc pressed. "A simple wedding invitation isn't a lot to ask in exchange for the thousands of dollars I've spent on photography equipment and classes. An investment in a hobby that has yet to return a single dollar, I might add."

Jill stiffened. It was an old argument, but it seemed to be gaining more traction lately—how much Jill's "hobby" had cost him. It was true that her camera was one of the best, but Jill had bought it used. The classes she'd taken over the years were just a fraction of the number she'd wanted to take. She loved photography, being behind the lens, bringing forth an image that may have gone unnoticed before. The whole process felt like alchemy to her and there was so much more to learn, but Marc didn't believe in pursuits that didn't recoup their investment.

"I'll try again," she conceded, but only because she didn't want to spoil his birthday.

He leaned in to kiss her forehead. "That's all I ask."

Kyle jogged back across the lawn toward Marc, so Jill turned her attention to the activity in the yard. This was nothing like the party she'd arranged. The pool house, where she'd planned to serve Marc's cake, was closed, the curtains drawn tight. A catering van had pulled up and workers were unloading supplies. A florist rolled a cart overflowing with centerpieces toward the entrance of the party tent, and behind him a row of workers hauled crates of wine glasses and silverware.

"I can't believe this," Jill muttered, her heart sinking. Marc's parties always came with strict rules, for dress and for conversation, and that wasn't what she wanted. It had begun to feel as if she were expected to become another person altogether.

Marc tensed beside her and Jill followed his gaze across the yard toward the rose garden to the cause of his distraction. There, a young woman in a too-short black dress and too-high stiletto heels stood by the pool. She'd arrived too early to be a party guest and she wasn't dressed like one of Marc's staff, so Jill couldn't place her. She watched as Kyle moved toward her and saw the woman laugh a moment later at something he'd said. As the woman tossed her long blonde hair off her shoulder, she turned, aware that someone had noticed her. When she saw that it was Marc and Jill, she froze.

Marc gestured for her to join them—no doubt she'd be warned about her dress and behavior. As the woman walked toward them, Jill recognized her from the summer before.

"Is that Brittney?" Jill asked.

"It is."

"Dewberry Beach Brittney?"

"Yes." Marc's answer was curt.

The Dewberry Beach house was a remote project, finished before she and Marc were married. One of Marc's largest builds, it was decidedly upscale, built right on the beach in a quaint New Jersey shore town. It was perfect for entertaining, and she and Marc had hosted several client parties there. The house itself wasn't Jill's taste and it seemed that buyers agreed because it had been on the market for years. Marc's solution had been to hire a live-in property manager, the idea being that she'd be available for immediate showings. Her name was Brittney and she'd graduated college just a few weeks before Marc put her in charge of marketing the million-dollar home. She hadn't been able to sell it either.

"Why is she dressed like that?" Jill asked.

She watched Brittney, who was not much older than Marc's eldest daughter, pick her way across the lawn, her spiky heels sinking into the soft earth. As she approached, Jill noticed that her dress had been tailored to fit her body. Odd choice for an employee to wear to a work party.

Marc offered a steadying hand as Brittney transitioned from grass to gravel, which she accepted with a shy smile.

"Brittney, it's nice to see you again," Jill began, because Marc didn't. "I believe the last time we spoke was at the summer clambake?"

"Yes. Hello, Mrs. Goodman."

"Brittney's come to field offers for the Dewberry Beach project," Marc offered, and that was the end of it.

Across the driveway, Kyle staggered under the weight of two cardboard boxes. It didn't look like he was going to make it to the table.

"Brittney, go help Kyle. He's supposed to be putting pamphlets on the welcome table."

When they were out of earshot, Jill turned to Marc for a further explanation of Brittney's dress. There was a time when Jill would have chosen something similar, but Marc had made it very clear what he thought of that.

To her surprise, Marc shrugged it off. "I'm sure she just made a mistake. She's young."

So was I, Jill thought as she tracked Brittney's progress across the driveway. Her heels wobbled on the gravel, and if she tripped, Jill predicted that she'd fall out of her dress completely.

"Do you have something nice Brittney can borrow? Like a necklace or something?"

The question was so jarring that it took a moment to process. "What did you have in mind?"

"I don't know." Marc swirled his hands in the air. "Something. She looks… plain. I'm sure you can find something." He shrugged absently as if the details didn't matter, but Jill didn't believe him. For Marc, details always mattered. Marc was a man who lived in details.

"Don't you think it's weird to ask me to lend my personal jewelry to an employee?"

"Her dress is missing something," Marc said again.

"I see that. Maybe a sweater would help."

He frowned. "Don't be like that."

"She shouldn't be dressed like that in the first place," Jill countered, confused by Marc's obvious double standard. "Kyle's part of your sales team and he's wearing khakis. Your whole sales team is dressed appropriately. So why isn't Brittney?"

"The Dewberry Beach house is unique… it needs a different touch," Marc said. "Besides that, she's a property manager and he's an intern. She doesn't need to wear the uniform."

"What's wrong with the Dewberry house?" Jill asked, steering the conversation back because she didn't want to talk about Brittney.

To her surprise, Marc seemed to take the question seriously. He frowned as he considered it. "I thought the clambake Brittney organized would have generated new interest in the house. It didn't. Things aren't progressing as well as I'd hoped."

Jill had attended Brittney's party and she hadn't been impressed. The theme was "A New England Clambake" and, properly executed, clambakes were one of the joys of summer. In fact, the highlight of childhood summers spent with Jill's Aunt Sarah and Uncle Barney had been the clambake. It was an all-day event and it started early, with a walk to the beach with Uncle Barney to prepare the site. As the men dug a pit in the sand, the kids were charged with gathering seaweed to steam the food and collecting twists of driftwood to feed the fire.

When the fire had burned to embers, the women arrived with food: ears of sweet New Jersey corn, baskets of tender red potatoes, buckets of clams, mussels, lobster, and shrimp, all of it dotted with butter, wrapped in foil and ready to steam. The trick to layering the food was to alternate the packets with handfuls of seaweed and strips of burlap soaked in seawater, and techniques were a closely held secret.

As they waited, the men gathered around a battered radio to listen to the Sunday afternoon baseball game while women chatted and yelled at kids who had wandered too far into the surf. When the food was ready, the men dug it up, unwrapped the foil and laid everything out on enormous platters, placed in the middle of the table. And that's when the magic happened. For Jill, the best part of a clambake was sitting with your neighbors and sharing the treasure.

Jill couldn't imagine that kind of party would be welcomed by the upscale crowd who had been invited, though it turned out she needn't have worried because the party Brittney had arranged wasn't a clambake at all.

Engraved invitations were sent to guests, complete with suggested attire. The guests, almost all from the Hamptons, arrived in a predictable uniform. Seersucker sports coats, slim linen pants and driving moccasins for the men, and breezy black silk dresses, summer tans and perfect blow-outs for the women. Jill remembered dressing differently for those earlier clambakes, in cut-off shorts and summer tees.

Brittney had arranged for valet parking, a bartender on every floor, and a string quartet on the rooftop. The caterers had "re-imagined" traditional New Jersey Shore food. Instead of steamed lobster, there was puff pastry filled with lobster mousse. In place of fresh corn dripping with butter, there were shot glasses filled with chilled corn chowder. But worst of all, at least to Jill, fresh garden tomatoes had been pureed to "reveal their essence" and served as a paste. Guests were visibly disappointed, and if Jill had been in charge, she would have fired Brittney on the spot, but Marc had let it go, calling it a "learning experience."

"Why is Brittany here at all? This isn't her market," Jill asked.

Marc's gaze cut back to Jill, then he frowned. "She's young and needs guidance, that's all. Cush and I both think she's got potential."

Jill scoffed but said nothing. She didn't like Cush, never had, but now wasn't the time to open that can of worms. Her annoyance lay firmly with her husband. He'd changed the party without consulting her and had allowed one of his employees to dress as if she belonged in a red-light district.

Marc had been watching her and his expression hardened. Jill lifted her hand in surrender. She'd made her point and nothing good would come from pushing it.

She turned to leave, but Marc called her back. "Wait."

She turned back, hopeful.

"Are you still planning to wear the red backless dress tonight? The one from Saks?" Marc's gaze swept from her head to her feet and the question was clear: *was she* able *to wear the backless dress—as in, could she zip it up?* Jill reflexively pressed her palm against her stomach as she felt a flood of shame rise from her chest. She'd worked hard, forcing her naturally curvy size-twelve body down to a size six because she knew that's what Marc preferred, but every day was a constant battle. And this dress had been particularly challenging.

Because she couldn't find the words, she simply nodded before turning to make her way to the house. She'd wear what he wanted her to wear. After all, wasn't that what she'd always done?

Inside, the house was the explosion of chaos that always preceded one of Marc's business parties. People were everywhere—caterers, florists, servers. The kitchen floor was a maze of boxes and every inch of countertop space was crammed with platters and linen. Jill had hoped for space to assemble a quick lunch, but a team of caterers had completely taken over and Jill had learned that it was best just to stay out of their way. So she grabbed a bottle of juice from the refrigerator and headed upstairs to run a hot bath.

In the tub, the hot water and the lavender scent worked its magic. She was still annoyed at what Marc had done, how casually he'd dismissed the party she'd planned, but, as the water in the tub cooled, so did her temper. She'd married a man who was confident enough to change things that didn't suit him. That, in fact, was one of the things she'd admired most about him, that he knew exactly what—and who—he wanted. A man like Marc could have chosen anyone and it was still thrilling that he'd chosen her. Everything else could be worked out.

After her bath, Jill stood before the bathroom mirror wrapped in a towel, wondering what to do with her hair. Typically she would arrange a salon blow-out before Marc's events, but today she hadn't. She swiped the fog from the mirror and studied her reflection. Besides encouraging Jill to lose weight, Marc had taken an odd interest in her hair. When they met, Jill had worn her naturally brown hair cut short and liked it that way. But Marc had persuaded her to grow it out, and when the length reached her collarbone, he'd arranged for blonde highlights at an expensive salon. Jill had never liked the color, thought the shade wasn't flattering against her olive skin, but she kept it because Marc wanted her to. To be honest, sometimes she caught a glimpse of herself in the mirror and was surprised at her own reflection.

With her hair and make-up done, she padded across her bedroom to her closet, her favorite part of getting ready. As she opened the door, the overhead lights flicked on, revealing racks of dresses, boxes of shoes, and shelves filled with cashmere. She paused to take it all in—the smell of new clothes, the abundance, the possibility.

Growing up, her parents didn't believe in wasting their money on children, so they didn't. Jill's clothes were thrifted and her toys were used. The year Jill turned seven, Aunt Sarah had gifted her a brand-new Barbie doll and it had changed Jill's life. She'd immediately set to work creating a wardrobe for the doll: fashioning dresses from strips of paper towel, embellished with poofs of stretched cotton and wraps of scrap yarn. That Barbie had ignited a life-long interest in fashion, and even now, twenty years later, she had to pinch herself when she entered her closet because she couldn't believe her good fortune. She owned racks of the most beautiful clothes ever created, and every one of them made her feel glamorous and important.

What difference did it make if fitting into them meant skipping a few meals?

The red backless dress was another story though. The cut was all wrong for her body, and the shade of red wasn't flattering. When she'd first tried it on, she'd rejected it, telling the personal shopper that no amount of alteration would make it fall right. But it was delivered to the house anyway and now Marc had asked her to wear it. She would, but she didn't want to.

They hadn't started out this combative, she and Marc.

In the beginning, they'd shopped together, and it was thrilling. He'd sat outside the dressing room and Jill had modeled outfits for him. She'd twirl, barefoot on plush carpeting, delighted to have found a man who wanted to spoil her. He'd insist that she have whatever she wanted. And she did. She bought cashmere and tweed, and dresses that cost more than she made in a month, and Marc paid for everything. Afterward, he'd take her to lunch at the Boathouse in Central Park, then back to his Greenwich Village apartment to watch the sun set over the city. She'd loved that time with him, and she missed it. Now, he ordered her clothes from a personal shopper's checklist and had them sent. And it had been a long time since they'd gone to lunch.

After everything he'd given her, it was a small concession to do as he'd asked.

As she reached for the dress, she stumbled over a pair of strappy silver sandals on the floor. The shoes were meant to be worn with the dress, but they pinched and were all wrong for an outdoor party. The heels were too high and the straps were too tight. If she wore them, she'd looked ridiculous, like Brittney had.

Jill slipped on the red dress but reached past the sandals for a pair of flats she liked better. It was a small, petty victory but one she allowed herself anyway.

Chapter 4

The Summit house was designed for parties and they'd hosted quite a few, but Jill had never enjoyed them. Invited guests were invariably Marc's friends, not hers. Worse, most of the women had been Dianne's friends first, and Jill could feel the weight of their judgment from across the room. Once, she'd overheard a coven of them blaming her for ruining Marc's "perfect marriage" and "traumatizing the girls," but that wasn't true. He and Dianne had been legally separated when they began dating, and Jill knew their marriage had been difficult from the start.

But if Marc's friends didn't like her, it wouldn't be for her lack of trying. Jill had worked to soften the edges of her personality—the swearing, the loud laughter, facets that Marc had called "unrefined." She restricted her beloved Spice Girls and Wham! songs to earbuds only and even pretended to appreciate jazz when Marc was home. She'd slipped once in three years, a story Ellie still teased her about.

One night, early in their marriage, Jill and Marc had met another couple for dinner and a show on Broadway. When the show let out, Marc and his friend had trouble hailing a cab because the sidewalk was crowded and the rain made taxis scarce. Jill thought she'd help them out. Pressing the tip of her index finger and thumb together, she'd hailed a taxi the only way she knew how—with a whistle. The sound was so piercing that two cabs had screeched to a halt and Jill turned to Marc, triumphant. She'd never forgotten the look of horror on the other couple's faces or the twist of distaste on her new husband's.

Still, Jill was determined that her marriage to Marc would be a happy one, and everyone knew that good marriages required compromise. In the end, what did it matter if the parties they hosted were for Marc's circle instead of hers? Or that she never seemed to be quite good enough for his friends? Or that she felt a little bit of herself falling away with every "improvement" Marc suggested? The point was that she'd married the man of her dreams. She'd get through tonight with a benign smile and small talk, just like she got through everything else.

She checked her reflection one last time in the mirror. Satisfied that Marc would be pleased, she added a spritz of the French perfume she knew he liked.

Then she went downstairs to find her husband.

As Jill descended the front staircase to the marble foyer, she heard a soft clatter of dishes as caterers worked in the kitchen and a murmur of voices as they coordinated dinner service. The new flower arrangement on the foyer table suggested guests might be invited into the house after the party, which made Jill uneasy. Because the house had been used as a model, it was available for showings. It wasn't unusual for minivans filled with property agents to arrive unannounced or for potential buyers to knock on the door and request a tour. The unexpectedness of it was unnerving, and Jill had never got used to the intrusion. Now the development was finished, Jill had looked forward to their space becoming a bit more private.

She heard Marc's voice coming from his office. She crossed the short hallway, pausing outside his door to wait for him because Marc preferred they greet his guests together. They'd be arriving soon, and it wasn't like him to keep them waiting, so she wondered what was keeping him. The door was ajar, and she peeked inside. Marc was seated at his desk, hands clenched, and his expression twisted into a sneer, as if he were arguing with someone he loathed.

Dianne. It had to be Dianne. No one got under Marc's skin faster than his ex-wife.

Jill remained where she was, shamelessly eavesdropping on his conversation. She knew very little about their relationship and she was curious about what Dianne wanted.

"It doesn't matter what she wants or what your overpriced divorce attorney says," Marc hissed into the telephone. "All I'm required to pay is tuition and I have—four years of Ivy League college for all three girls. Now Rebecca wants me to pay for grad school? Not happening." He paused to listen, then his words sliced the air. "Don't you threaten me, Dianne. Put her on, I don't care. I'll tell her myself."

This was a side of Marc she'd rather not see. Despite what Dianne had done, it was unsettling to witness how vindictive her husband could be. Jill was about to retreat into the kitchen when she heard the change in his voice, the tone he reserved for his girls.

"Rebecca, honey, I don't think—" Marc shifted uneasily in his chair. "Yes, that's true. I did say that." He listened and after a moment, his shoulders sagged as he closed his eyes. "Of course I meant it, but I'm not sure you appreciate the cost of three tuition payments at once. What if you took a gap year until Sinclair graduates? You can come work for me, and we'll talk about grad school a year or so from now."

Jill knew how the rest of the conversation would go without even hearing it. Whatever the issue, if Rebecca didn't get her way, she'd pout until Marc gave in. He might argue the cost, but he'd eventually give her whatever she wanted. Despite his feelings toward Dianne, he could be a very generous and loving father, which made his decision not to have children with her all the more disappointing. Jill had always wanted a large family, a house filled with loud chaos—matching flannel PJs at Christmas and family summer vacations at the beach. Intellectually Marc's decision made sense, especially considering that he would be more than seventy when their first child graduated high school, but Jill's heart didn't care. Sometimes, she would come across the social media post of a friend starting a family, or adding to it, and the pain of what she was missing almost felt physical.

But to be with Marc meant no children. He'd made that very clear. And she wanted to be with Marc.

Marc's conversation ended abruptly. Jill nudged the office door open in time to see him throw his cell phone onto his desk and watch it skitter across the surface. He heaved a sigh then motioned for her to come closer.

"You look good," he said finally, nodding with satisfaction. He seemed not to notice that Jill had sucked in her stomach as his eyes lingered on her neckline. "I knew that red would be a good choice."

"I'm glad you like it." She stepped closer and felt his arm circle her waist. She held her breath and dropped her voice, hopeful. "Your guests are waiting."

But Marc didn't notice the change.

"Dianne's a nightmare," he groaned. "I'm glad I never have to worry about you."

She leaned against him as they walked toward the party, uneasy at how harshly he'd spoken to Dianne but taking comfort in the stability of their own relationship.

They walked outside together to discover that the yard had been transformed, and Jill's mood brightened. It wasn't what she'd chosen, but it was pretty. The bright afternoon sun had given way to the cool blue of dusk. The day's humidity had lifted, and the air held a whisper of glorious fall weather to come. Lighted hurricane lamps at the tent's entrance glowed a warm yellow, matching the pinpricks of tealights scattered on tables inside. The pool's backlit fountain cast the water in shades of soft pink as it splashed over the rocks, adding a gentle wash of color. Inside the tent were tables set for an elegant dinner. Music softly played from inside as the guests made their way across the yard.

"Not bad, right?" Marc glanced at her for approval.

She leaned into him. "Not bad."

Only the humming video screens near the pool house hinted that Marc's party might be, in fact, a sales presentation instead of a birthday celebration. Jill ignored them.

Marc had always made a point to greet his guests formally before every event, to note who had come. And who had not. He'd ordered the caterers to set up a receiving line near the rose garden, so that's where Jill and Marc headed to greet their guests. The line was long, but it moved quickly. After offering birthday wishes, guests were escorted to the hosted bar and served. Jill hoped the sales presentation would start much later, well after dinner.

It was a beautiful setting, but still her annoyance lingered, resurfacing to remind her that her party hadn't been good enough. The idea stung no matter how much she tried to push it away.

Jill gestured to the pool house, to a sales table staffed with agents from Marc's company. "That looks new. Is that for the Berkshire development?"

The Berkshires was where Marc and his company were headed next, though it seemed an odd choice to Jill. The land he'd bought was miles away, in rural Massachusetts, far from their home in Summit and even further from the unsold house in Dewberry Beach. Jill wondered about the expense of managing projects two hundred miles apart. But maybe his business was doing well.

But he didn't answer, so Jill repeated her question, this time nudging him. "Hey? Are you guys looking to sell the Berkshire lots already?"

A flicker of disapproval crossed Marc's face and Jill knew immediately what she'd done wrong. She'd slipped. Marc had told her many times that the New Jersey slang term "you guys" was crass and he wanted her to drop it.

But he didn't correct her, probably because there wasn't time. His attention was on the trio of approaching party guests. Jill watched her husband's social mask slip back into place as he greeted them. To be honest, Jill envied Marc's ability to talk to anyone about any subject; he was smooth where she was awkward, urbane where she was clumsy. But she tried and that had to count for something, didn't it?

Forty minutes later, they were still greeting guests, and Jill wondered how her husband could possibly know this many people. Her own social circle was considerably smaller. She shifted her weight as her stomach growled and felt a trickle of perspiration slide down her back. The reception line seemed endless, but thankfully Marc seemed to bear the brunt of it. After speaking with Marc, most people only managed a quick hello and air kiss for Jill, which was fine by her.

To distract herself, Jill imagined what Ellie would think of a party like this, a tent filled with fancy people she didn't know talking about things she didn't understand or care to learn about. If Ellie had planned this party, there would be beer on ice in coolers, cannonballs into the pool, hot dogs on the grill, and probably noise complaints from the neighbors about the stereo speakers they'd dragged outside. It would have been fantastic, and even the thought of it made Jill smile. But her smile faltered, just a bit, when she remembered that she'd left that life behind three years ago when she married Marc.

An hour later, Marc decided they had greeted the guests that mattered and were allowed to leave the receiving line. Official hosting duties over, he made a beeline for his best friend Cush, and Cush's new wife Nadia, as expected. Cushman Lawrence's official title in Marc's company was Lead Staff Attorney, and their friendship went all the way back to college. The story was that Marc and Cush had met as fraternity pledges freshman year, and although they'd parted ways after graduation, they'd kept in touch. Cush went on to law school while Marc joined the family business, but the minute Cush passed the bar exam, Marc offered him a fancy title and fired the man who'd held the position for years.

"Cush!" Marc grabbed his friend's hand and thwapped him on the shoulder. "How was Freeport?"

Cush groaned as he threw up his hands, as if he couldn't possibly put such an incredible experience into words. "Construction is booming down there, if you know what I mean. So much going on that you need to come down, take a look."

"Yeah?" Marc lifted his chin. "Better than the Berkshires?"

Cush grinned. "Let's just say that the regulations down there are much more flexible."

"Did you get the other thing done?"

"I did."

"Okay then. Business trip before the end of the year?"

"You know it." Cush clapped his hands together. "I'll bring my clubs. You bring your wallet for all the rounds you'll lose." Then he hooked his arm around Marc's shoulders and led him away, calling over his shoulder, "Jillian, you don't mind if I steal your husband for a second?"

Jill lifted her hands in mock surrender and watched them cross the lawn, leaving her alone with Nadia.

Nadia was Cush's second wife, and they'd been married just over a year. She carried herself with an easy elegance that Jill envied. Nadia had had a successful career as a model before marrying Cush. Because she'd come into the marriage with money of her own, she did exactly as she pleased. Nadia hadn't known Dianne, but Jill hoped that even if she had, she and Nadia might still be friends. There was something genuine in Nadia that put Jill at ease.

Nadia rolled her eyes at their retreat, her long silver earrings dancing against her dark skin. "Put those two together and they're like little boys on the playground."

The women watched the men cross the yard then Jill returned her attention to Nadia. "Did you have a good time in Freeport too?"

"Not especially, no." Nadia's lifted a flute of champagne from a passing waiter's tray.

"Really? Why not?"

Nadia's expression flickered just before she changed the subject. "For one thing, when we returned, Cush was served. It seems that his ex-wife Angela is dragging him back into court—that put him in a mood."

"Why would she do that? What happened?"

"No idea." Nadia sipped her drink. "The curse of the second wife is never to ask questions about the first wife, so I don't." She lowered her voice. "But I do overhear things."

"Really?" Jill had heard whispers of husbands traveling out of the country, to Freeport specifically, just before a divorce settlement. She had a theory that those men were hiding assets, but she didn't know for sure. It wouldn't be a stretch to imagine Cush doing it too.

"Who goes to Freeport in August? I'll tell you: the heat was unbearable." Nadia brought the champagne to her lips and sipped. Her diamond tennis bracelet glinted in the late afternoon sun as she gestured toward the pool. "What's happening over there?"

Jill followed Nadia's gaze to a quiet corner of the pool house, where Brittney stood and where Marc and Cush were headed. Brittney looked different than she had earlier, more relaxed. She'd put her hair up in a messy bun and one long tendril rested on her ample cleavage. Her lipstick seemed brighter, too—a different shade of red, more vibrant. She looked up and smiled as she waited for Marc to approach.

"No idea."

"You'd better watch that," Nadia warned. "This is how things get ugly."

"I think she's about to be fired."

"Yeah?"

"Makes sense. Dewberry Beach hasn't sold and she's in charge of selling it."

Nadia eyed her with a critical gaze. "She doesn't look that worried."

Chapter 5

Two weeks after Marc's party, Jill had good news of her own. To celebrate, she was attempting to recreate Aunt Sarah's magnificent stuffed shells from memory. But it wasn't going well. The dish that Aunt Sarah could whip up in a few minutes had taken Jill most of the day and even now she wasn't sure she'd gotten the recipe right.

She peered into the pot, at the red sauce that was far more complicated that she remembered. Jill had driven to the fancy organic market across town for the last of the summer tomatoes because Aunt Sarah always used Jersey tomatoes. Jill had heated the pan and added a healthy pour of olive oil, just like Aunt Sarah always had. And when the oil shimmered, Jill had added the chopped tomatoes, diced onions and fresh oregano all at once. But she hadn't expected the ingredients to pop and burn like they did. Or the smoke alarm to go off so quickly.

It took three attempts and a second trip to the store, but the effort had paid off. Now, the aroma of softened onions and rich garlic threaded the air, and Jill was transported to summers in Aunt Sarah's tiny kitchen. Clad in an apron and standing on a chair, Jill's job had been to add ingredients when instructed, but it was always Aunt Sarah who'd provided the magic. Later, Aunt Sarah, Uncle Barney, all the cousins and their friends would gather around the table and dinner would become a free-for-all of conversation, interruptions, and, eventually, an epic battle waged over the last meatball.

Those were the best memories of her life—summers at Aunt Sarah's beach house.

Even if Aunt Sarah would have been disappointed with how long it had taken Jill to recreate her red sauce, she'd celebrate the occasion. Mrs. Brockhurst's personal secretary had telephoned earlier that morning. Mrs. Brockhurst wanted to meet with Jill to discuss ideas for the upcoming family Christmas portrait. Jill managed a cool "of course," as if that sort of thing happened every day, and they'd arranged a date. But the moment she'd hung up, Jill had *shrieked* with glee. Her moment had come. And it was this news that she planned to share with Marc tonight before he left for the Berkshire property. The new project had ramped up quickly and Marc now spent much of the work week at the construction trailer on site.

Jill listened as the front door opened, then closed. A few seconds later she heard Marc toss his keys onto the foyer table.

He entered the kitchen with a stack of mail. He must have noticed the delicious smell because his expression changed from concentration to bemusement.

"What's all this?" He lifted a brow in query.

"I *happen* to be cooking," Jill announced happily as she leaned in to kiss her husband. He smelled like the spicy aftershave she liked, the kind he used after a fresh shower. Oddly, the scent seemed to have once again lasted all day. "We have something to celebrate."

"Oh yeah? What's that?"

"I heard from Georgiana Brockhurst today. She wants to talk to me about ideas for her family's Christmas portrait." Jill sprinkled salt into the pasta water, feeling almost professional. "Isn't that *wonderful?*"

"Christmas?" Marc repeated as he lowered the stack of mail. "I thought you were still working on getting me an invitation to the wedding. I'd expected that we'd be going."

Jill turned to face him, honestly confused. "I told you this before, Marc. Libby's bridal portraits were not part of the wedding. Even if they were, I'd be a vendor at the wedding, not a guest. We were never going to be invited."

"So you said." Marc frown deepened. "But I thought *you* understood how important an invitation is to me, to my company. I told you I'd been trying to break into that social circle for years. If you had brought an invitation home, *that* would have been something to celebrate."

On the stove, the tomato sauce plunked against the skillet lid and Jill adjusted the flame. Marc had been short-tempered lately and Jill had assumed the reason was lack of sleep. She imagined him spending restless nights on a cot at the construction trailer on the Berkshire site, working extra hours just to get the project off the ground. For the past few days she'd been choosing her words carefully and had ignored most of his moods, but not this time. The Brockhurst phone call was too important.

Jill straightened to meet his scowl. "Marc, this is big news for me. Georgiana Brockhurst has seen my work and likes it enough to consider me for another project. I'm really excited about this."

"We'll celebrate when you do something worthy of celebration," Marc muttered as he tore open an envelope. "Until then, you're wasting your time. And my money."

The pasta water rolled to a boil. It spattered on the grate, hissing as it touched the hot metal. Jill let it burn.

"This is the second time you've said that and I'm beginning to think you might really believe it." Jill drew a steady breath, though it took effort. "So now I'll ask you directly: do you think my photography is just a hobby?"

He ignored her, focusing instead on sending a text from his phone.

"Marc, I asked you a question." Jill planted her hand on her hip, her South Jersey temper flaring. "I would appreciate an answer."

"Just a minute," he snapped, his face flushed as he typed.

She watched him receive and send not one but a flurry of texts, his expression appearing more desperate after each one. Clearly whoever he was texting wasn't cooperating and Jill felt her anger soften just a little. He looked so utterly exhausted. Of course he hadn't meant what he said…

When he was finished with his texts, Marc lifted his gaze and blinked, as if he'd forgotten Jill was in the room. It took him a moment to pick up the thread of their conversation, but when he did, his expression cleared.

"No, of course I didn't mean that." He reached for her and Jill felt her anger melt. But then he added. "You know I don't care that much about your pictures."

That was worse.

Jill shook him off and turned her attention back to the skillet, though the sauce had long since finished cooking. "Why don't you go upstairs and take a hot shower?" His comment hurt and she wasn't ready to let it go so easily, no matter how exhausted he might be. But neither was she ready to fight. Her day was too good to be ruined.

"Fine." As he left the kitchen, he unlocked his phone.

She used to forgive casually hurtful remarks like this one. But this felt different, purposeful and targeted. As Jill added pasta to the salted water, she wondered what had changed.

A few minutes after Marc left the room, Jill's cell phone vibrated with an incoming message. Ellie had promised to send pictures of the Brockhurst compound in East Hampton and Jill looked forward to seeing them. As she rinsed her hands, her cell phone vibrated again. And a third time as she dried them on the towel. She retrieved her phone and swiped at the screen to open her mailbox. But the messages were not from Ellie. They were from Brittney. Three new emails, each with attachments and blank subject headings. Jill tapped the icon to open the attachments and as she flipped through the pictures, she felt the floor dissolve beneath her.

The attachments were selfies.

Pictures taken by Brittney.

Photographs of Brittney and Marc together… in bed.

Jill sank into a chair as her breath left her body. She flipped through the images again and felt her world crumble. This had to be a mistake.

She forced herself to look at the pictures, to zoom in on the details. One looked as if it had been taken on a cot in a construction trailer—had to be the Berkshires. Two others, graphic images of Marc and Brittney together in the master bedroom at the Dewberry Beach house. Another on the couch in the pool house, just fifty yards from where Jill now stood. The last one taken in the bedroom Jill shared with her husband on the night of his birthday party.

So many of them.

It occurred to her, in an odd, detached way, that this explained Marc's afternoon showers and the reason she had smelled his cologne just now.

The phone burned in her hand and she flicked it away. It skittered across the table and crashed to the floor.

After that, time melted into memory. Fragments of memories that didn't quite make sense on their own suddenly arranged themselves in a surreal game of Tetris and the picture became whole. That August in Dewberry Beach when Marc's hand had grazed Brittney's shoulder as he'd passed her in the kitchen. Marc's unwavering confidence in her work, despite her inability to sell the Dewberry Beach house. And finally, his bizarre request for Jill to lend Brittney "something nice" from her jewelry case. Like a cyclone gathering strength as it spun, the images came, clawing her with unexpected force. The whispered phone calls taken in another room. Routine work meetings that suddenly ran late and required an overnight stay in the Greenwich Village apartment. The renewed interest in the Dewberry Beach property and the trips to check on it.

All of it came together in one picture, a truth that struck her like a physical blow.

Marc was having an affair.

Jill gripped the edge of the chair as she felt the room spin. She closed her eyes and forced herself to breathe, though she'd forgotten how. They'd only been married three years.

"Hey, dinner ready?" Marc entered the kitchen, freshly showered.

She heard him pause at the doorway and she opened her eyes.

"You good?" Marc asked casually as he lifted the skillet lid to inspect the contents underneath.

Jill stared at the man she'd married.

She'd been twenty-two years old when she'd accepted a temp job in Marc's office, commuting into Manhattan because city jobs paid two dollars more an hour and she needed the money. Their first date began with a casual invitation to lunch. Marc had said he'd meet her outside but when she'd seen him standing beside a sleek black limousine, she'd been sure she'd mistaken the dates. Their "simple lunch" date had included a carriage ride through Central Park to the Boathouse restaurant where Marc had reserved a table overlooking the water. After a two-hour lunch, he'd taken her to Bergdorf's and told her to choose anything she wanted from the jewelry case, something that would remind her of their first date. It was an outrageous offer, and Jill had suspected that Aunt Sarah would have disapproved, but Jill had just ended a terrible relationship and Marc's attention had been precisely the balm she'd needed. When she'd shyly asked for a charm bracelet, Marc had bought it without hesitation, even though it was outrageously expensive. And when the clerk had suggested a horse and buggy charm to go with it, Marc had laughed and added several more. For the next two weeks, he'd taken her out every night and gifted her a different charm before the start of every date.

Idly, Jill wondered if Brittney had received a charm bracelet too.

"Jill?" Marc's voice felt like a stab.

"You're sleeping with her." Saying it out loud made it real. The accusation was explosive, and the resulting mushroom cloud floated on the air like poison.

Marc cursed softly under his breath and she knew it was true. Jill felt her heart shatter, her soul splinter. A part of her hoped he would deny it—wanted him to deny it. She wanted to believe that there would be a reasonable explanation for the pictures.

"Then it's true?" she asked again, just to be sure. Maybe there was an explanation, something she could hold on to. Something that would make things right again.

"I told her not to send the pictures," he sighed, as if the worst part was that Brittney had disobeyed him.

Jill unlocked her phone and turned the screen toward him without looking at it herself, because seeing them together again would break her.

"How long?" she managed to ask. Of the million questions that bubbled up, this one seemed the most important.

But Marc refused to look, refused to abandon his place by the stove. Would not accept the evidence of his betrayal. In a surge of rage, Jill hurled her phone at him, but she missed. It ricocheted off the fancy quartz countertop and clattered to the floor once more.

"How. Long?" Her shriek filled the room, absorbing the air and smothering what was left of their marriage.

Marc let the question hang in the air, unanswered. They locked eyes, and when he understood that Jill would not back down, his own widened in surprise. She'd always backed down before.

He raked his fingers through his hair and shrugged. "I don't know. A few months, maybe more."

Jagged emotions swirled and churned, erupting in questions that pelted her like scattershot, each one inflicting a wound that would fester. How could Marc so casually toss aside a marriage that had meant everything to her? Was Brittney his only affair or had there been others? Others that may have begun and ended with Jill blissfully unaware. And, most importantly, had Marc ever loved her or was she just a placeholder? The last question almost brought her to her knees, but she steeled herself because right now, she needed to know.

"At the Dewberry Beach house." Jill sagged against the countertop. "That's why you traveled there so often."

"Yes."

His easy admission surprised her. It gave her the courage to ask another question, though it felt as if she were pressing on a bruise. And the pain was cumulative; she wasn't sure how much more she could bear.

"Your birthday party. You left me alone with your guests while you were with—" The room spun, and she drew breath to steady it. "You were with Brittney. You slept with her that night, didn't you? That last picture was taken in our room. In our bed."

"Yes."

"Where is she now?"

"What?"

"I assume you've set her up in her own apartment. That's what you did with me. Or is that why the Dewberry house hasn't sold? You're keeping it for her? A house that big is quite a step up from the apartment you offered me, I must say."

Even as she asked the question, Jill knew the answer. All of this was so unimaginable that it had to be a dream. It must be a dream. Jill grabbed the metal spoon from the skillet and squeezed the handle as hard as she could, hoping for pain. If it didn't hurt, that meant she was dreaming—that what was happening now wasn't real.

Marc straying from her had been Jill's deepest fear from the very beginning. The gap between Marc's official separation from Dianne and the start of his relationship with Jill was razor thin, something that had always bothered her. If it were true that Marc had cheated on Dianne with her, Jill had always suspected he would do the same to her. And if she were honest, that was part of the reason she did everything he wanted, so that she would be good enough for him.

She increased the pressure on the spoon, willing the stress of the party or the intensity of the Brockhurst interview to explain away the nightmare.

All at once, a shock of pain radiated across her palm. She released her grip and the spoon clattered to the floor, spattering an arc of red sauce into the air.

"You're being ridiculous." Marc moved from his spot at the stove. "I can't talk to you when you're like this."

"Why, Marc? Why would you do this to me?"

"To you?" Marc's eyes widened with genuine surprise. "This has nothing to do with you. I admit Brittney crossed a line when she sent those pictures and I'll talk to her about it, but nothing's changed between us. We can go on as we always have."

Time slowed as she considered what he'd said. Outside, Jill heard the air conditioner click on and felt a trickle of cool air rise from the vents. She glanced at the stove, oddly aware of a stray noodle clinging to the side of the pot.

"No. We can't," Jill said, and she knew it had to be her answer.

"We can," he pressed, misunderstanding her. "To prove it, I'll cancel the next few days of meetings and we'll go away, just us." He reached for her shoulder. When she flinched, he withdrew.

"This is how it happened with Dianne, isn't it?" Jill said, almost to herself. "She didn't know about us, did she? You told me that you didn't want your girls to meet me until you were sure, but the truth is that you didn't want Dianne to find out. We weren't 'dating' at all, were we? You were cheating on her too."

"You're being ridiculous—" Marc began, but Jill cut him off.

"I'm being ridiculous? *Me?*" Jill howled at the absurdity. You're the one who cheated on your wife."

"It's a little too late to claim the moral high ground now, Jillian DiFiore." Marc's laughter was edged with venom. "You slept with a married man too." Marc's expression changed and Jill braced for whatever was coming. Marc never backed down, even when he was wrong. He misdirected, honing his replies until they drew blood. She'd seen him do it but never thought he'd turn on her. "I wonder what dear Aunt Sarah would think of you now. The perfect girl she had such hope for."

Jill fingers tightened against the corner of the granite countertop as the barb hit its mark. It was a vicious thing to say, but what if he was right? What if Aunt Sarah could see her now? Could see what Jill had become? The answer was clear: she would have been disappointed.

It was Marc's smug expression that jerked her back to reality. *How dare he?*

"So why did you propose?" Jill asked, feeling anger surge forth when the sharp pain of betrayal had dulled. "You asked me to marry you at the Boathouse, *three hours* into our first date." It was the one thing that didn't make sense to her—Marc had pursued her. Jill had refused that proposal and all the ones that had followed, until he'd finally presented her with a diamond ring too big to ignore. "If all you wanted was an affair, why the proposal? Why the ring?"

Marc shrugged, crossing the room to pour himself a measure of Scotch. "I thought you had potential. I guess I was wrong."

Jill watched the man who had been her whole world lift the glass to his lips and sip, as if none of this mattered. As if their marriage, their entire world wasn't falling away from beneath their feet.

Then she realized it wasn't. *Their* world wasn't collapsing at all.

Hers was.

Marc would move forward, unscathed. Even now, he seemed completely unaffected while Jill struggled for breath.

"I grant that finding out about this wasn't ideal," Marc continued, as if they were discussing a business project instead of facing the end of their marriage. "I intend to speak to Brittney about what she did. Sending those pictures to you was childish, and she should know better." He finished his drink and set the glass on the counter. "As for us, I'll tell you again that I'm willing to put this incident behind us but know that my patience isn't unlimited."

"Get out."

Marc laughed, a reaction so surprising that Jill gaped. The Marc she'd known, married, and loved was gone, and in his place was someone she didn't recognize. Unmasked, his expression was evil, and his eyes were soulless.

"I suggest you reconsider what you're saying, Jill," he sneered. "You're not the same girl you used to be. How are you going to support yourself and your new fancy tastes? What will you do for money?" His lip curled as he leaned against the counter. "Are you going back to temp work? You wouldn't last a month behind a desk."

"Get out of this house. *Now.*" Jill grabbed the skillet from the stove and hurled it at him. The pan grazed his shoulder and hit the wall, spraying a bloody arc of tomato sauce across the kitchen.

Marc glared at her with naked hatred. "I guess I was wrong about your potential." He turned to leave, calling over his shoulder as he made his way out of the house, "No matter how you dress or act, you'll never be anything more than trash from South Jersey."

She met his insult with the same strength she'd used to stand up to playground bullies when she was a kid. She stood, her back straight and her eyes clear, as if nothing he did could touch her. She watched the man she'd loved open his car door and turn on the engine. And it wasn't until Jill heard his car pull out of the driveway and watched it disappear from view that she allowed herself to fall apart.

Chapter 6

The punch of regret came on the heels of her fury.

Would he come back to her if she asked? Could they salvage their marriage if he did? When she realized she could never forgive him for what he'd done, her regret melted into an overwhelming sadness. She'd loved Marc with her whole heart and thought he loved her too. Retreating to the couch, she cocooned herself with a soft blanket and sobbed until there was nothing left.

Hours later, her anger returned, but this time it landed on Marc for casually discarding a marriage that had meant everything to her. And when the anger was finished with Marc, it turned on Jill. It accused her of abandoning the woman she used to be, rough-edged and loud, in favor of the plastic shell of a woman that Marc preferred. And when her anger was satisfied with the damage it had done, it stilled, leaving her feeling hollow and afraid.

Panic filled the space that anger had carved out, reminding Jill that everything in this house, from the shoes in her closet to the pepper mill in the pantry, had been purchased by Marc. The income from Jill's photography business was barely enough to pay for the newspaper delivery. To support herself, she'd have to find a job—and quickly. Not that she was afraid of hard work; she wasn't. She'd come from nothing, earning her place in college with grades and paying her way with work-study and student loans. The life Marc provided was easier, but it came with a cost, and Jill refused to pay it. Not anymore.

When she realized she could right herself again, the panic receded, leaving her feeling utterly exhausted and alone. She felt a wave of despair and almost buckled against it.

And in that moment, a memory of Aunt Sarah presented itself.

Aunt Sarah had been a gentle presence during a difficult childhood and was a master of untangling painful situations. She was the one who had taught Jill to manage and control her anger, gently explaining that those emotions only served to cloud rational thought.

The memory gave Jill the strength to push aside the blanket and rise from the sofa. Shards of broken pottery crunched under her feet as she made her way to the sink and filled a glass with water. The liquid cooled her throat and cleared her head as she found her way to Aunt Sarah, her voice as clear and distinct as if the woman herself were standing in the kitchen, and Jill felt tears of longing collect behind her lids. She closed her eyes and let the tears fall.

"Chin up, sweet pea," Aunt Sarah said, her voice as gentle as the rustle of fall leaves. "This is not a disaster, though it may seem like one now. This is a correction, and there are valuable lessons in upheaval."

Jill felt a bittersweet smile tug at her lips. Aunt Sarah was all about great life lessons.

"I see you, Jillian DiFiore," Aunt Sarah continued, her voice as warm as Jill remembered. Jill let it wash over her. "I know what you've overcome, and I know what you can do. The fight's not over and you cannot give up now. You have to remember what's important."

"I thought my marriage was important." Jill's croak broke the silence.

Instead of an answer, Jill felt the softest caress across her brow and she froze, knowing it was Aunt Sarah and wishing the moment would last forever.

"I miss you, Aunt Sarah," Jill whispered.

And the moment was gone.

Sometime later, Jill watched the headlights of Ellie's car slice through the darkness as she came up the driveway. Ellie had called to chat on her way home from the Brockhurst compound in East Hampton, and when Jill had told her what Marc had done, she'd insisted on coming over right away.

Jill met her outside. "You didn't have to come right away, Ellie. I'm okay."

"Is he still here?" Ellie demanded as she glared over Jill's shoulder toward the house.

"No. I threw him out." Jill straightened.

Ellie turned her attention back to Jill, her gaze steady but gentle. "And tomorrow?"

Jill winced, though the question was reasonable. Jill's track record for relationships wasn't great and Ellie had seen the worst of them. But this time it was different. Marc wasn't a boyfriend; he was her *husband*, and he'd betrayed her, more than once. Then he'd laughed it off as if it were nothing. Jill wanted to tell Ellie all of that, but she couldn't find the words, so she pressed her lips together and shook her head.

"Okay then." Ellie slipped her arm around Jill's shoulders. "We can work with that."

Jill leaned into years of friendship as they crossed the driveway to the house. At the first sign of trouble, Ellie was the friend who grabbed a pitchfork and lit the torches on her way to storm the castle. She was encouraging when she needed to be, tough when the situation called for it, and she *always* took Jill's side, no matter what. Having her here made Jill feel as if what she faced was not insurmountable. As if it was possible to salvage the life that Marc had so casually tossed away.

They entered the house through the side door. When they came to the kitchen, Ellie stopped in her tracks and gaped at the mess Jill had left: broken dishes scattered across the floor, red sauce splattered on the wall, and bubbles in the drywall where it had been hit with boiling pasta water.

"Wow." Ellie whistled. "I missed some fight. You must have been pissed."

"I was. I am." Jill slid onto a chair, completely drained. She felt Ellie take a seat beside her and they sat in silence.

"You'll get through this, Jilly," Ellie offered. "I'll help you, whatever you need."

"Aunt Sarah was here," Jill said finally.

That got Ellie's attention. "Tell me."

"There's not really anything to tell. She wasn't here long."

"Did she say anything?"

"It wasn't so much talking as it was a feeling. That everything's going to be okay, eventually." Jill rested her head on her arm. "I miss her, El."

"I do too."

"She would have known what to do."

"We'll get through it."

"I don't want to be here if Marc decides to come back."

"Whatever you want. You can stay with me. I just moved into a two-bedroom and I have lots of space."

With a jolt, Jill realized that Ellie had moved into the apartment they'd looked at months ago. This was a big deal for Ellie, to finally get her own space, and Jill had yet to congratulate her. Ellie, who was supposed to be her best friend.

Misunderstanding Jill's disappointment, Ellie's expression changed from concern to surprise. "I don't have to *invite* you to come over, do I? You know you're welcome. I even had a spare key made for you. We can go right now."

In response, Jill squeezed Ellie's arm. "I've been thinking. Remember Ricky Tremont?"

"Ricky from high school? That's a stretch." Ellie wrinkled her nose. "Sure I remember, but what made you think of him?"

"I dated him for—what? Three weeks, a little more, a little less?" Jill glanced at Ellie, and when she nodded, Jill continued. "And do you remember the music I listened to back then?"

"The Ramones." Ellie sagged dramatically as she rolled her eyes. "On repeat."

"We even tried to dye my hair black, remember?"

"Yes, I do." Ellie groaned. "You drove us all nuts."

"Remember when I tried to convince you to sneak up to Queens to see their show?" Jill laughed. "We were going to take the commuter rail? But we couldn't figure out the tickets?"

Ellie smiled, then asked, "Whatever happened to them? You used to love them, then all of a sudden you didn't."

"Ricky Tremont said their music was stupid." Jill shrugged. "And because I was desperate for him to like me, I threw away all my posters and never listened to their music again."

"You didn't. Oh, Jilly."

"Yep. And the boy after him…" Jill squinted as she tried to recall the boy's name. When she couldn't, she swirled her free hand around the top of her head. "The one with the hair? Took me to prom senior year?" Jill straightened, steeling herself against the memory of what she'd done. "Aunt Sarah made a prom dress for me. Picked out a pattern and bought the material. She made it because she wanted me to have something nice and she knew I probably wouldn't otherwise. And she wrapped it in white tissue and mailed it to me. The card inside said she knew I'd look like a princess and all she asked for in return was a picture."

"I remember. It was blue."

"Ice blue satin," Jill corrected. "The boy I went with, the one with the hair, happened to see it before the prom and he called it tacky. Said only hookers wore ice blue satin. So I stuffed the dress into the back of my closet and never looked at it again." She frowned, feeling a stab of regret at what she'd done. "That boy picked me up wearing a rented tux and a neon-green cummerbund but had the nerve to call blue satin tacky." She paused to catch her breath. "I don't even know what happened to that dress. I wish I did. I wish I had it now. I'd wear it every day."

"Everyone knows you have to date a lot of toads before you find a prince," Ellie offered, as consolation.

But Jill shook her head. She slid from her chair and began to pace the room. "When Aunt Sarah asked about it later, about the prom, about the dress, I lied to her. And when she asked for a picture of me wearing the dress she'd made, know what I told her?"

Ellie shook her head.

"I said I couldn't afford to have them taken."

"Oh, Jilly."

"Know what she did?" This time Jill didn't wait for a reply. "She sent me twenty dollars. And she offered to help me find the photographer."

"Oh no." Ellie sighed.

"Yeah." Jill drew a ragged breath. "My whole life I've changed myself to be whatever the guy I'm with wants me to be, no matter the cost. Ricky with the posters, Neon-green Cummerbund, and the one after that, whose name I will *never* utter. And now Marc." Jill felt her breath catch. "I've lost myself, Ellie. Somewhere, I've lost the girl I used to be."

"You're being *entirely* too hard on yourself. Marc's the one who cheated, not you."

"You asked me to lunch, week before last, do you remember?"

Ellie frowned so Jill filled in the details, striding across the floor and chopping her hands through the air as she spoke. Marc hated when she used her hands to talk. She did so now freely.

"The new Italian bistro in Westfield. You said the eggplant parm reminded you of Aunt Sarah's and that the garlic bread alone was worth the drive." She whirled around and threw up her hands. "And what did I tell you?" When Ellie opened her mouth to speak, Jill answered for her. "That I would only go if I could have a plain green salad without dressing, which is ridiculous if you think about it. I never even *tasted* the eggplant parm." She closed her eyes, pushing past the lump in her throat. "I miss Aunt Sarah every single day and when you found a place that might bring me a little closer to her, I ordered a green salad. Do you know why?"

"Tell me."

"Because I had a dress fitting later that afternoon—hours after lunch—and I needed to be a perfect size six. That's the size Marc wanted me to be and that's the size the saleswoman had ready. But, El, I am *not* a size six—never have been." Jill shifted her gaze because she couldn't meet her friend's eye. "So I don't eat and I exercise too much.

And I force my body into a six because that's the size Marc decided I should be. What kind of person does that?"

"That's a lot to put on yourself, Jilly, and it's not fair," Ellie said, finally finding her voice. "Do *not* blame yourself for Marc's affair."

"Oh, I don't. He did that all by himself." Jill stopped, grounded to the spot. "My point is that somewhere along the way, I've lost myself. I've changed into someone I don't recognize. None of this…" She swept her arm in the air for emphasis. "None of this is me."

"That's sounds harsh, Jilly," Ellie pressed. "People change for their partners all the time."

"Maybe so, but my point is that Marc didn't change for me. The parties we had were for *his* friends—mine were never invited. The fancy restaurants we frequented were the ones Marc liked to be seen in. You know I'd rather watch *I Love Lucy* reruns in my PJs eating from a tube of cookie dough, but I went, without a word of protest." As her words gained speed, she swiped her hands through the air to emphasize every point. "I used to have a *million* friends, before Marc. The apartment the five of us shared was heaven to me—loud music, good friends, and cheap beer. I *liked* that life, but I abandoned it the second Marc told me to. You're the only friend I have left from that time."

"I think we may be getting a little ahead of ourselves here," Ellie said. "You shouldn't bring your entire life into question over something Marc did."

"You've never liked Marc." The realization stopped Jill in her tracks. "I should have paid attention to that. Why didn't I?"

"Jillian—"

"There's something wrong with me, El. I just know it." Jill dropped back to the chair next to her friend, physically exhausted and emotionally spent. "Tell me anyway: why didn't you like Marc?" she asked finally.

"I didn't like the way he treated you."

"You never said. How long have you not liked him?"

"Forever."

"Yeah, well." Jill leaned her head against the chair and closed her eyes. "I don't like him anymore either."

Chapter 7

A sugar hangover can be a powerful thing, and Jill woke recoiling against the sunlight even before she opened her eyes. At some point the night before, Ellie had suggested ordering food, and Jill had pounced on the opportunity to order everything she'd ever denied herself. Three different deliveries from three different restaurants had resulted in a mountain of food: pasta heavy with cream, double-cheese pizza, and gallons of real ice cream. So, when Ellie had found a forgotten stash of ice cream toppings in the catering kitchen, it seemed serendipitous. As they ate, they'd talked about everything and Jill had started feeling a tiny bit better. And when Ellie had pulled out her phone and put together a playlist, piping the songs through Marc's whole-house sound system, the mood had shifted and Jill had known she'd be okay. Not right away, but eventually.

It was Ellie who'd reminded her that Aunt Sarah had said there were great life lessons in the lyrics of songs from strong women like Linda Ronstadt, Dolly Parton, and Aretha Franklin. Women she called "The Greats." When Ellie began the playlist, Jill had been transported back to Aunt Sarah's kitchen on Cape May the summer Bobby Collins broke her heart. Then Jill and Ellie had grabbed soup ladles from the drawer and began to sing, loudly and mostly off-key.

The old songs had been like a balm on her heart, and Jill had felt a pinhole of light shine against what she was afraid would be a very dark future—like there just might be a path forward now, though she wasn't sure of the terrain or direction. Still, it was something to hold on to.

But that had been last night. This morning felt very different. With her head pounding in the sharp morning light, Jill pushed aside the cashmere throw and rose from her place on the couch. Ellie had stayed most of the night, but she couldn't stay forever; she had her own life to tend to. Lewis the cat would be waiting for her and she had to work. After Ellie left, Jill had made her way to the couch, curling up because she couldn't bring herself to return to the bedroom she'd shared with Marc.

Eventually Jill stumbled to the kitchen to brew some much-needed coffee and spied the soup ladles they'd tossed in the sink. The one good thing to come from all of this was that she and Ellie had reconnected friendship bonds that never should have been allowed to splinter. By the time Ellie left, they'd cobbled together a loose plan that felt like progress. Even if she'd wanted to—which she definitely did not—Jill realized the impossibility of living in the Summit house. Financially she couldn't afford it, and emotionally she couldn't bear it, so she accepted Ellie's offer to stay with her. She'd find a job and figure the rest out.

She'd just started the coffee maker when the front doorbell rang, startling her.

It couldn't be Ellie; she'd left only a few hours before and she wasn't one to use the front door—or ring the doorbell. Jill couldn't imagine that any of the women in Marc's circle would be inclined to drop by. They'd always viewed Jill as an extension of Marc, the plus one on every invitation that required couples. And except for Nadia, they only spoke to her when absolutely necessary.

Jill brushed the fuzz from her yoga pants, straightened her T-shirt, and went to answer the door. The moment she opened it, she regretted doing so.

"Cush." Reflexively self-conscious about her appearance in front of Marc's friend, Jill crossed her arms in front of her chest. There were many reasons not to like or trust Cush and she didn't appreciate him showing up uninvited. "What do you want?"

"Is that any way to greet a friend?" He cocked his head, offering a slick frat-boy smile that may have worked with those who didn't know him. But Jill *did* know him, and she wasn't fooled.

"Marc's not here," Jill said, though of course Cush would know that better than anyone.

"Yeah. He sent me a text asking me to come over because he's not sure you'd want to see him." Cush leaned against the doorframe. "Marc doesn't want this, Jilly." His voice was heavy, regretful. Fake. "You're the one who asked him to leave."

"I did," Jill countered as she crossed her arms across her chest. "Did he happen to mention that he'd been sleeping with a woman young enough to be his daughter?"

Cush looked away and for a moment Jill imagined she saw something like genuine regret, until she realized that both he and Marc were master manipulators.

"Yeah." Cush grimaced. "And that was wrong. It was incredibly stupid, but it was a mistake—one he deeply regrets."

"It wasn't just *one* mistake. He's been sleeping with her for months."

"He wants to make it right, Jillian. He knows your situation and wants to—at the very least—see that you're taken care of."

She eyed the briefcase he carried and was curious as to what Marc thought could possibly make this better. Then, from the kitchen, Jill heard the coffee machine sputter to a stop. She inhaled the heady scent of fresh coffee that had wafted through the air. At that moment, all she wanted was a cup.

"Five minutes," she said as she stood aside to let him in.

He followed her down the hall and into the kitchen. Jill gestured to a place at the table. As he settled in, she saw him take in the mess she'd left—the spatter on the wall, the dented pot on the floor, the melted ice cream on the counter.

He didn't ask and Jill didn't explain.

She reached past the sink, piled with dirty dishes, into the cabinet for a pair of mugs. "You take it black, right?"

He nodded, though she knew it wasn't true. He drank his coffee with generous amounts of both cream and sugar. She used to like the taste of creamy coffee too, before Marc side-eyed every pour of half-and-half and she gave it up. Forcing Cush to drink the same black coffee Marc had encouraged her to drink was petty, but she enjoyed it anyway.

Jill set his coffee down and took a seat opposite. She glanced at the briefcase and arched an eyebrow, though it aggravated her headache. "So what's in the briefcase? A payoff?"

His eyes widened in surprise and she regretted her comment the moment it left her mouth. Needling him was childish and counter-productive. Her argument was with Marc and she was taking it out on Cush. She drew a breath and apologized, which also seemed to surprise him. He'd clearly expected her to be angry and seemed thrown to discover that she wasn't.

Jill sipped her coffee, feeling knots of tension loosen as the warm liquid spread across her chest. She hoped Cush would leave soon, so she could lose herself in a hot shower. She had packing to do.

The tap of Cush's coffee mug as he set it on the table pulled Jill from her thoughts. She brought her attention back to him, saw him sitting with his hands folded and an expression of grave concern on his face.

"As you know, Marc and I go way back. He's the best friend I've ever had so I want you to think of me as your friend too—"

Jill's response was immediate—laughter bubbled from her chest so quickly she couldn't stop it. Cush looked so affronted that she only laughed harder.

"You can't be serious," she snorted. "You've never been my friend."

Cush opened his mouth in shock, then closed it again.

"Don't worry. I've never told him. Though I should have."

"I don't know what you mean."

"Last Christmas at the Weingolds' party, you *propositioned* me with your new wife not three feet away."

"I would never—"

"At the fundraiser last spring at the Summit Club, just outside the coat check. Then again, at the Dewberry Beach house not two months ago. Don't you remember? The 'best friend you've ever had' went to get you a drink and you used that opportunity to corner me in the butler's pantry." She glared at him. "We're not friends, Mr. Lawrence. We never have been."

It was then that his mask slipped, and the change was chilling. He looked away to hide it, but Jill saw the transformation, the hardness of his expression, the flint in his eyes. It was gone by the time he looked back, replaced by an icy calmness that seemed worse somehow, unpredictable. It made her wary.

"I told him not to marry you." His voice dripped with contempt. "But he wouldn't listen to reason. He was crazy about you."

Cush's eyes were wild, and it occurred to Jill that the two of them were alone in this house. Even so, she held his gaze, refusing to back down.

"There were others before you, and others after," he sneered. "But *you* were the one who got under his skin. You were the one he wanted." He pushed the mug away and coffee sloshed over the side, pooling onto the table. "*I* reminded him you were nothing but a tramp from South Jersey. That all he had to do to keep you happy was rent a crappy two-bedroom in Paramus. But no. He insisted on giving you the very best of everything. And look what a *mistake* that was."

"You don't scare me." Jill leaned back, recognizing him for what he was. "We're the same, you and I, as much as you pretend we're not. And I know you're terrified to be sucked back to where you came from, so you do whatever Marc tells you. You're a lackey, Cushman. Nothing more. Without Marc to give you a job and a fancy title, you'd be just another ambulance chaser."

Cush's jaw clenched and for a moment, Jill was afraid that she'd gone too far. When he spoke again, his voice was even, though rage simmered beneath it. "Marc made me promise to ask you directly if you would consider taking him back—"

"No."

"What if he offers to give up Brittney?"

Jill sighed. They were so far beyond the Brittney problem that she seemed almost like an afterthought.

"If your final answer is no, then he's asked me to tell you that he's sorry. That he wants to give you some money to help you start your new life." With crisp efficiency, Cush pushed a folder and pen toward her.

"What's in there?" Jill gestured to the folder without touching it.

"A check for $25,000."

"Why?"

"Because Marc wants to help you move forward if that's what you want."

Jill pushed aside the pen and opened the folder. Inside was a check clipped to a legal document. She glanced at Cush for explanation, though she wasn't sure she could trust what he told her.

"The paper is just a formality. A simple receipt."

Jill drew the paper closer and skimmed the first few paragraphs. The language was complicated, and she understood none of it. "This looks like more than a simple receipt."

"It's a lot of money, Jillian," he countered.

It was true, and it was more than Jill would make as a temp in a year. The reality was that she had a tiny bit of money in a personal account and not much else. All the credit cards were in Marc's name. The investment accounts, the savings accounts, the household accounts: all in Marc's name. She'd quit her temp job after he'd proposed and hadn't held another in the three years they'd been married. Everything she had came from Marc.

"If you're holding out for more, you won't get it." Cush misunderstood her hesitancy. "The prenup you signed before the ceremony was rock-solid. I drew it up myself."

"I just bet you did," Jill replied, returning her attention to the paper.

Although Cush insisted the document was a receipt, it didn't look like one. It didn't read like one. The money, however, was tempting. With it, she'd be able to pay rent to Ellie and share living expenses while she looked for a job. That kind of money would relieve a lot of pressure.

Still, something was off.

So she read it again.

The language in the document was heavily padded with lawyer-speak and Jill hadn't had nearly enough coffee. Finally, she gave up and settled her gaze on Cush. "If Marc regrets... if Marc is truly sorry, then why do I have to sign this? We can stop pretending it's a receipt, by the way, because it's clearly more complicated than that. If he's sorry, why does his check come with strings attached?"

Cush flinched at her directness but recovered quickly. "Because offering you this money goes against the prenup. Your signature says you won't use his generosity now against him later, in court," Cush said smoothly. "Standard practice."

What Cush said made sense, but the oily earnestness of his tone set off every internal alarm she had. His explanation sounded rehearsed.

She hesitated.

Cush sighed heavily, sagging in his chair. "Fine. I'll tell you the truth, though you don't deserve it. Marc wants his business protected so he can leave the company to his girls, intact. That's all this document says—that you agree not to come after his business."

That sounded more reasonable. Marc's father started the business and Marc had always intended it to go to his girls.

"I have no intention of taking his business," Jill said, because it was the truth. "It's a family business and of course the girls should have it."

Cush pushed the pen toward her, and she reached for it.

The chirp of an incoming text on Jill's cell phone was startling. Three texts in quick succession, after days of silence. Thinking it might be from Ellie and that it might be important, Jill rose from her place and moved toward her phone, still plugged into the charger.

The messages were sent from a number she didn't recognize. A number that wasn't in her contact list.

Don't sign anything.

I know Cush is there. Don't trust him.

Don't sign that paper.

Jill's heart beat faster. She felt Cush's stare as she read the messages on her screen, and her skin prickled in warning as goosebumps rose on her arm. Not knowing what else to do, she locked the screen and docked her phone. When finished, she looked up to see that Cush's expression had changed again.

"Who was that?" His tone was wary.

"Reminder for the dentist." Jill shrugged, with forced nonchalance.

Nothing in this situation made sense—not the visit, not the money, not the texts. Jill needed time to think. So instead of returning to the table, she collected the coffee mugs and brought them to the sink.

It was just the break she needed.

"Okay." She turned from the sink to face him.

"Okay what?" Cush asked.

"If Marc is willing to admit that things may have gotten a bit out of hand, then I am too. I'll go with you, right now, to wherever he is, so we can talk things through. Where is he? The Berkshires? We can leave now—right now."

Caught unawares, Cush spluttered. "He's not at the job site. He and Brittney are at the apartment in Greenwich Village."

The information sizzled in the air like a lit firecracker.

"Really?" Jill mused. "It appears that he's not quite as broken as you led me to believe, is he?"

Cush's expression hardened as his face flushed with anger. He pressed his lips together in a thin white line, and when he spoke again, his voice was menacing. "Listen to me, Jillian. I'm finished playing games with you. You want this money, you sign the paper."

"No," Jill refused, though she very much wanted that check. "I don't think so."

"You're being childish."

"You need to leave now."

"You're making a mistake."

"I've made them before."

He rose. "You're going to regret this."

"I regret a lot of things, Cushman." Jill escorted him to the front door. "Add this to the list."

He stepped outside and she closed the door behind him.

Chapter 8

After Cush left, Jill rushed back to the kitchen to retrieve her phone. She pulled up the anonymous text messages and read them again, but they still didn't make sense. Too detailed to be a wrong number, they didn't contain enough information for Jill to identify the sender. She thought about calling the number, but what if it was Marc? Or Brittney? They were the last people she wanted to talk to. Eventually, curiosity won and she tapped the text and connected the call.

It was answered on the first ring. "Jill?"

"Who is this?"

"Is Cush still there?"

"No, he just left." The voice sounded familiar. "Nadia? Is that you? What number are you calling from? My phone didn't recognize it."

"Yes, it's me. This isn't my phone. Cush has been monitoring my calls so I bought a disposable. Listen, I don't have much time before he comes back." Nadia's voice dropped to a whisper, low and urgent. "Did you sign that paper?"

"No. No, I didn't."

"Good. Listen to me—"

But Jill had had enough of people telling her what to do. She had questions of her own and she wanted answers. "Did you know about Marc and… that woman?

Nadia hesitated for just a moment. "Yes, I did. We all did."

"Why didn't you tell me? I thought we were friends." Even if Nadia wasn't what Jill would consider a real friend, like Ellie, she was the closest thing she had to an ally in Marc's circle.

"I thought this time was a phase. Like the last time."

"Last time? You mean he's done this before?"

"Twice."

Jill felt the breath leave her body and she wasn't sure how to take another. She steadied herself against the counter as her legs threatened to give way.

"Listen to me, Jill," Nadia continued. "I'm trying to help you, and I don't have long. I can't be a part of this anymore. The money Cush offered means nothing. What's important is the Dewberry Beach house. There are things you don't know about it."

"How long, Nadia? How long has Marc been cheating on me?"

"Jillian—you're not listening. And if you don't listen to me now, you'll be in trouble. Marc has already filed for divorce. The papers Cush wanted you to sign are meant to distract you."

"Divorce?" Jill drew herself up. "What do you mean, divorce? Cush told me that Marc wanted to work things out."

"He lied. The divorce papers have been drawn up for weeks."

"You can't be—"

"Jillian." Nadia's voice was sharp. "I know this is a lot, but you have to keep it together. They've had a substantial head start, orchestrating an outcome that's best for Marc. Things are happening, even now, and you have to be ready when it hits."

Jill sucked in a breath. "Tell me."

"I've listened at the door—the two of them meet in Cush's office. I don't know everything, but I'll tell you what I've heard as long as you promise not to think badly of me."

"Think badly of you?" Jill parroted. "Nadia, that doesn't make sense. None of this makes sense."

"You'll find out." Nadia hesitated. "And when you do, know that I'm sorry. But right now, I can't have Cush know I'm talking to you. So promise you won't call me again."

"What— Okay. I promise."

"You've refused his check, and they didn't expect that. From now on, things are going to happen fast." Nadia's words were a rush. "You signed a prenup. Find it."

In the background, Jill could hear Cush's voice call out for Nadia. Nadia muffled the phone and called back to him, "Be right there.

"I have to go. They're back." Nadia's voice dropped to a whisper. "The house in Dewberry Beach is not what you think. Start with the mortgage... I'm sorry, Jilly—about everything."

Before Jill could respond, Nadia ended the call.

Jill stood in the kitchen, staring at her phone, unable to understand what was happening.

Two weeks ago, she'd stood beside her husband at his birthday party. She'd greeted his guests and laughed at his jokes, being exactly who Marc wanted her to be. Though parts of it were challenging, Jill had thought her marriage was rock solid and she was happy.

But all of it had turned out to be a lie.

Marc had betrayed her. He'd slept with another woman and returned to the party as if nothing had happened. He'd stood beside Jill, draped his arm around her, as if he hadn't just betrayed her. And now it turned out that Marc had been planning to divorce her for months.

Jill made her way to the sofa and collapsed, resting her head on the upholstery, and closed her eyes. The life she'd thought was perfect had imploded, utterly and completely, and she was afraid the destruction would break her. Dazed, she lifted her head and glanced at the doorway to the kitchen, almost expecting someone to jump out and shout "surprise." Even that would make more sense.

It was all just too much.

Jill woke sometime later, sprawled across the couch, her head foggy from an anxious sleep. Outside, the bright morning sunlight she remembered had shifted and dimmed into dusk. An entire day had passed, and she'd slept through it. Pushing the tangle of blankets from her legs, she rose from the couch, badly in need of fresh air to clear her head.

Outside, the evening air was sharp and crisp. The last of the summer crickets chirped as the streets quieted. From the hill of her driveway, Jill could see the entire neighborhood, the warm glow of lights in the homes below. She listened to parents calling their children inside from their play. And she imagined families gathered around the dinner table. After dinner, there would be baths, bedtime, stories. And in the morning, the cycle would start all over again. Kids would be sent off to school with a packed lunch and a kiss on the cheek, knowing they were loved.

That rhythm. The rhythm of everyday was what she wanted to build a life on.

It was all Jill had ever wanted: a home, a family, children. How did she end up here, so far from that?

She turned to look at the house that she'd shared with Marc, the one she'd moved into on the afternoon of her wedding. The biggest in the neighborhood, it stood perched on this hill like a king on his throne. Suddenly, the opulence didn't impress her as much as it used to. The house was apart from the things that mattered to her. Neighbors never dropped by for coffee or to chat, as they had at Aunt Sarah's house. When she and Marc did entertain, it was an organized occasion, with printed invitations, party clothes, and company manners.

Curated.

All the choices, big and small, that Jill had made over the years added up to a life she didn't recognize and one she no longer wanted.

With a sigh, she returned to the house to find her prenup. Whether or not she wanted it, a fight was coming, and she'd best be ready.

As she made her way up the stairs to the master bedroom, it occurred to her how different she and Marc were when it came to storing important papers. It was funny, in a twisted sort of way. Marc was fastidious, obsessive even. Current projects were organized into neat files, older projects archived and tucked away from view. By contrast, Jill stuffed everything worth saving in a shoebox, newest on top, oldest on the bottom, and stored it in the back of her closet.

She crossed the master bedroom quickly, without looking at the bed.

There were two master closets in the bedroom, each a mirror image of the other and combined were larger than Jill's first apartment. Inside were enough clothes, shoes, and accessories to supply a small boutique, many of them still unworn. Marc had insisted she have the best of everything, and to a girl who used to make Barbie clothes from paper towels and cotton balls, that seemed like something out of a fairy tale. So she'd accepted and spent lavishly. Sometimes she came to her closet just to sit there, because the sight of what she owned—the abundance of it all—would remind her of how lucky she was.

This time, Jill ignored everything except the lumpy shoebox in the far corner.

Inside, it smelled musty, of old paper and memories of the life she'd had before Marc. On the bottom was a copy of the lease for the apartment she'd rented. There was a faded picture of Jill and her roommates taken at a pub crawl one weekend. And a twist of tin foil that had once decorated a spindly Christmas tree. A letter from Rutgers congratulating her for making the dean's list, for the third time in two years. And the coupon book she'd used to repay her student loans, with the date and check number carefully marked on each stub. After their marriage, Marc had paid the entire balance as if it were nothing. Now, Jill wished that she'd insisted on making the payments herself, because scribbling "paid" on each stub had been so satisfying. And finally, an overexposed Polaroid of her and Marc on the courthouse steps, newly married. Cush and his now ex-wife Angela had borne witness. There had been no other guests, which was strange, given how fond Marc was of entertaining. Her friends were not invited. His children didn't come. There had been no reception afterward, no toasts, no dancing. At the time, Jill had been too timid to ask for more. She was twenty-three years old and thought that Marc, at forty-eight, knew better.

Jill tossed the picture back into the box, then unearthed what had brought her to the closet in the first place—her prenup. She hadn't understood the document Marc had asked her to sign, so she'd been hesitant to do so. But then he'd explained that his marriage to Dianne had been abusive, that she was difficult and unpredictable, and that her outbursts scared the girls. He'd told Jill that when he'd decided that he couldn't live as he had been, he'd asked Dianne for a divorce and she'd flown into a rage, threatening to take the only thing that mattered to him: the company his father had founded. She'd threatened to break it up, to sell it. And without a prenup in place, he was vulnerable.

All he wanted, he'd said, was to protect his girls. The prenuptial agreement he wanted Jill to sign was no more than a promise to his daughters. Proof that Marc had meant to pass along the company that his father had given him. Marc had said that after everything Dianne had put them through, he owed them a secure future.

And Jill had believed him.

She'd led with her heart, barely skimming the document before putting her signature at the bottom of it. Afterward, she'd dropped her copy into the shoebox and stepped into her new life, confident of the future Marc would provide. It was wonderful to be taken care of; Marc provided a lifestyle she could never have afforded on her own. She hadn't even known what a personal shopper was until Marc had arranged that first appointment. And what an experience. Jill could barely wrap her head around the fact that a gum-snapping chubby girl from South Jersey would find herself sipping chilled Prosecco as she decided between outfits that cost more than her car.

But how things had changed.

She settled onto the floor of her closet, folding her legs underneath her, and read the agreement for the first time.

An hour later, she'd read it through twice and still couldn't understand it. The phrasing was awkward, the meaning obscure. The first part seemed to say that if she and Marc divorced within the first five years of marriage, Marc would retain ownership of all his business assets. That part was fine. Harder to understand was the definition of a business asset. Further down was a section that seemed to say that if either of them wanted a divorce, it would happen quickly. Their case would be sent to mediation and heard by the first available judge. The goal, the paper said, was mediation within ten days and a final divorce within thirty.

Jill returned everything to the shoebox and pushed herself up from the floor. With the box firmly under her arm, she snapped off the light on her way out of the closet. She wasn't naive enough to think she could fight this on her own. She knew Marc's measure of success came from not only winning but from utterly annihilating his opponent. And right now, she was the opponent.

It was time to hire an attorney.

Chapter 9

After an extensive search, Jill and Ellie found a divorce attorney who seemed as though she wouldn't shy away from a brawl, which was exactly what they needed. Her name was Phyllis Jessup and her website said she specialized in contentious divorce, which was what Jill suspected was heading her way. The website also promised a free consultation, which she needed because money was tight. The best part was that Phyllis happened to have a cancellation for that very afternoon, so Jill snapped it up.

Ellie drove them to a squatty brick building that required a key-code for entry. After the receptionist buzzed them in, they climbed a set of grungy stairs to a dank outer office. The receptionist escorted them to Phyllis's office, and announced that their consultation time had started before shutting the door firmly behind her.

Phyllis Jessup was not the kind of attorney Jill had expected. Instead of a dark suit, silk blouse, pearls, and heels, Phyllis wore a rumpled pantsuit and kept an unlit cigarette in the ashtray on the desk. Jill would learn later that Phyllis had quit years before and kept the cigarette as a reminder. She had a sturdy build, a sharp expression, and looked as if she could hold her own in a bar fight. Best of all, Phyllis was competent and direct, exactly the sort of person you'd want in your lifeboat. Jill liked her immediately.

"Does Prince Charming have a police record?" Phyllis asked in a gravelly voice.

"Why? Is that important?" Jill asked.

"Not really, not unless he's violated parole. Then he can be arrested, and sometimes a few days in a holding cell brings them to their senses." Phyllis shrugged. "I have a friend connected with the state police—locking him up could be a good thing for you. You want me to check?"

Jill shook her head and Phyllis reluctantly returned her attention to the document.

"Mediation, huh?" she muttered to herself as she flipped the page. "Unusual choice." She pursed her lips as she glared at the last page. "You signed this?"

"Yes."

"Willingly?"

"Yes."

"Were you of age?"

"I was."

Phyllis heaved a disappointed sigh, then leaned back and folded her arms across her chest. "Remind me again how long you've been married to Mr. Wonderful?"

"Three ye—" Jill's voice cracked unexpectedly so she tried again. "We were married three years ago."

Phyllis's eyes narrowed as she took Jill's measure. Her chair creaked loudly as she leaned across her desk to lock eyes with Jill. "You always this mousy?"

"No." Jill's spine snapped in place and she returned the attorney's gaze with one of her own. "No, I am not."

"Good."

"She's been through a lot in the past week or so," Ellie offered.

"She's about to go through a lot more." The pages of the document fluttered as Phyllis tossed the packet across her desk. "Whoever drafted this contract wrote it with divorce in mind. Did you *read* it before you signed it?"

Jill shook her head.

"How old were you when you signed this contract?"

"Twenty-three."

"That's out then. Thought I could work the minor angle, but you're right, you were of age. Signature's legal." Phyllis puffed her cheeks with air then let it out in a steady stream. She swiveled her chair away slightly and stared out the window.

"Should I hire you to help me through this? Marc has an attorney, and I don't. I'm worried." Jill glanced at the clock. The free consultation was almost over, and Jill didn't want to lose Phyllis's help. She had no idea where the money would come from to pay her, only that she'd find it. "It looks like this hearing might be difficult."

"Yeah, I think so too, but I couldn't represent you even if I wanted to. This prenup says defendants must represent themselves. It's almost as if Prince Charming expected this outcome," Phyllis answered, almost to herself. "There's a clause that says you both agree to the first available judge in the pool—which is always a crapshoot—and agree to be bound by his ruling, whatever it is. Usually judges give each party a chance to respond and to amend their complaint. This one specifically forbids it, which is concerning." Suddenly, Phyllis swiveled back. "Where you from?"

"South Jersey. Asbury Park."

"Thought so. I can see a tiny bit of that in you." Phyllis nodded, the beginning of a smile spreading across her face. "Despite your fancy clothes, you look like you might know from scrappy. Like you won't back down from a fight. Is that accurate?"

"I think so."

"You need to *know* so. This prenup is an issue." Phyllis jabbed her finger at the contract. "I'm willing to bet that the guy who wrote this is used to dealing dirty and that you can expect more of the same when you meet with the judge." She pursed her lips as she thought. "The judge'll do his best to stop anything blatantly unfair, but he can't reverse time. If he could, I'd tell you not to sign that thing in the first place."

Jill glanced at the clock. They were seventeen minutes into the twenty-minute consultation and there were still so many questions to ask.

"Should we arrange a longer appointment? I'm happy to pay." She'd find the money somehow.

"Wouldn't help you." Phyllis pointed to the registered letter Jill had brought to the meeting. "According to that little beauty, the judge has been selected and mediation is scheduled for the end of this week. Even if I wanted to help you—and I do—I couldn't pull anything together in time. I have other clients who need my help too." She leaned forward, a scowl etched on her face. "When a divorce is pushed through quickly, it gets me thinking, and this one seems to be going at light-speed. I'd be willing to bet the farm he's got something to hide. Something big."

"There's got to be something Jill can do," Ellie pressed. "It can't be that hopeless."

"That's why I needed to know if your friend was a fighter." Phyllis tossed a fresh legal pad across the desk. "Write this down."

Jill retrieved a pen from the cup.

"First thing—most important thing." Phyllis leveled a gaze at her. "Do *not* get emotional. Emotion is a distraction, and my guess is that Prince Charming knows what buttons to press to get you flustered. Then he'll use whatever tactics he needs to make you seem…" She waved her hand in the air as if to gather the right word. "Crazy," she said finally.

"But he's the one who cheated, not me," Jill blurted, her face flushed with indignation.

Phyllis jabbed her finger at Jill. "That right there. You can't do that. Even if Mr. Wonderful brings his side piece to the arbitration meeting and sets her up in the chair right next to him, you act like you don't care. Emotion is drama, and judges hate drama. Pisses them off."

"Okay," Jill murmured. That Marc might bring Brittney to their divorce arbitration had never occurred to her.

"I'm not kidding," Phyllis warned. "I've seen husbands bait their wives into the most spectacular meltdowns and all it does is serve their own purpose. Prince Charming already knows what gets to you, and my guess is that he'll use all the tricks. Don't let him."

Jill nodded, underlining what she'd written.

"And this may seem like a small thing, but it's not," Phyllis said. "Twenty-eight years of divorce law has taught me this little gem and now I'll pass it on to you, free of charge. Pay attention to who the judge looks at first, after he introduces himself. Judges are supposed to be unbiased but they're not always—they're human, just like the rest of us. The person he looks at first is the one he thinks has the strongest case. Whoever's left has to work harder just to be heard."

"You're kidding."

"I wish I were."

Then, for the better part of an hour, Phyllis navigated them through the jungle of divorce law in the state of New Jersey and Jill never received a bill. When the meeting was over, Jill's head was swimming with precedent and process. Written across four pages of legal paper was a list of tasks she needed to accomplish in just a few days' time.

But she would do it.

She would do whatever it took. Marc would not take advantage of her again.

On a Friday afternoon in mid-October, exactly one week after Jill discovered Marc's affair, she reported to the county judicial center to dissolve the marriage. As she made her way up the stairs, it occurred to her that her marriage to Marc had begun in this very building, in a gray courtroom on the ground floor. The ceremony had lasted less than ten minutes and was a disappointment, truth be told. It had taken Jill longer to decide what dress to wear than it had to recite her vows, which seemed appropriate, given where she was headed. At the time Marc had been anxious to be married, and now he was equally anxious to be divorced.

They both were.

The conference room was empty when Jill arrived, stark and cold with air conditioning flowing from an overhead vent despite the chilly fall weather outside. The walls had been hastily painted a dingy institutional beige and were flecked with chips, the windows streaked with grime. Three places had been set at the conference table, two opposite and one at the head, where Jill assumed the judge would preside. At each place was a fresh yellow legal pad and a cheap ballpoint pen. In the center of the table sat a stack of cracked plastic cups and a pitcher of stale tap water.

So this is how it ends, Jill thought, marriage to a man who swore he would love her forever.

Moments after Jill settled into her seat, the conference room door opened and Marc sauntered in, well-rested and confident as if this were just another meeting in a typical day.

By contrast, Jill's nerves were frazzled. She was anxious and exhausted and couldn't remembered a time when her head didn't pound. Since Marc left, it had become painfully clear that he was the one with money, not her. The reality was that Jill was very nearly broke. So she had been looking for work, calling on every temp agency in the area, asking for whatever they had, but hadn't found anything yet. At night, she worked on the list of tasks that Phyllis had given her, but checking them off was harder than she'd expected, especially when it came to their financials. Bank branch managers who had known Jill for years, had even cashed checks without asking for identification, suddenly refused to provide her with basic account information. They were sorry, they'd said, but Marc Goodman was the account holder, not her.

Now, as Marc eased into his chair, his chunky silver cufflinks tapping against the conference table, he appeared completely unaffected by the events of the past week. His navy suit looked new, his hair was neatly trimmed, and his shoes were polished to a high shine. The unfairness of it all shook Jill to the core. She wasn't the one who'd cheated; Marc was. After today, Marc's life would go on as it always had while Jill's entire life had imploded. Nothing would ever be the same.

At that moment, Jill realized—fully—that she meant nothing to him and that she probably never had. Right now, she was a loose end, something for Marc to see to before he returned to his wholly unaffected life.

Well, she wasn't going to let that happen. Jill pressed her back against the vinyl chair as she felt a swell of anger. She leveled her gaze across the table at the man she'd been stupid enough to marry and promised that she would *not* go down without a fight.

The door opened again, and the judge walked in. He was an older man, stoop-shouldered and weary, as if he'd overseen the end of too many marriages and this was the last in a particularly trying week. His robes fluttered as he crossed the room; his thick framed eyeglasses sat heavily on his face. A tuft of white hair clung stubbornly to its position on top of an otherwise balding head, while a full beard and sideburns seemed to make up the difference. As he rolled out his chair, Jill shifted in hers, remembering what Phyllis had said and hoping to catch his attention.

But he seemed not to notice her.

"Good afternoon. I'm Judge Atkinson." The judge set a folder on the table and opened it. As he smoothed his hand across the first page, he looked at Marc and Jill tensed. "You must be Mr. Goodman?"

"Yes, sir." Marc leaned back in his chair, as if he'd already won. Apparently he'd heard the same bit of advice. "I am."

"And I'm Jill Goodman, your honor," Jill offered quickly, refusing to be ignored. An older male judge who seemed to favor Marc was exactly what she didn't want, but she wasn't about to give up.

"I imagine you are," the judge replied dryly, his face devoid of expression. He took off his glasses and placed them on the table, then slipped on an almost identical pair and scanned the first page in the folder. "And we're here this afternoon to facilitate the dissolution of your marriage?"

"Sadly, that's true, Your Honor." Marc's voice dripped with manufactured regret so extreme that Jill wanted to jump across the table to smack him.

But that would be a show of emotion that Phyllis had warned her about. Instead, she squeezed her hands together on her lap as she nodded. "We are."

The judge paused to peer over the frame of his reading glasses. "You've both agreed to binding arbitration. So unless the record shows bias on my part, which it won't, or fraud on your part—and it'd better not—my judgment here today will be final. Do you both understand and agree to that?"

"Yes, Your Honor."

"Yes, Your Honor."

"Good. Then we'll proceed." Returning his attention to the folder, he turned the page. "To review the basic facts in this case." He picked up a fat silver pen and unscrewed the cap. "Mr. Goodman, you are fifty-one years old, healthy and capable of work to support yourself?"

"That's correct." Marc reached for a cup and filled it with water.

"Mrs. Goodman, you are twenty-six years old, and also healthy and capable of working to support yourself?"

"Yes," Jill said.

"And there are no children from this marriage?"

"Sadly, we have none together." Marc managed a frown that almost looked genuine.

Jill grit her teeth but said nothing. She simply shook her head.

The judge looked down at the folder. "I understand there is a prenuptial agreement in place, and this is a copy of it?" He flipped to the last page and tapped the signature block. "Is this your signature, Mrs. Goodman?"

"Yes."

"And Mr. Goodman, is this your signature above?"

"It is, Your Honor."

The judge turned his attention to the document, flipping the pages and skimming the contents with the tip of his pen. "Prenuptial agreements usually make my job easier, but this one seems a bit… unusual." He scrutinized Marc, who shifted in his chair. "Mr. Goodman, the accompanying financial declarations seems to be incomplete." He held up a single page. "Do you have an updated packet? Nothing's been added to your balance sheet since your marriage. Is there, perhaps, a page missing?"

"No, sir, it's all there." Marc's expression was guarded. "The past three years have been challenging for my company. The housing market has shifted dramatically so we've been forced to pivot to a new business model. We're yet to turn a profit."

"No profit for the past three years," the judge repeated. "Is that what you're telling me?"

Marc nodded.

"Interesting timing." The judge replaced the document and folded his hands together on the tabletop. "Your company's 'pivot' seems to coincide with your marriage to Mrs. Goodman."

"Completely coincidently, sir."

"I hope so, for your sake, Mr. Goodman. The courts take a very dim view on hiding assets. The penalties are most severe."

Seeing that Marc intended to object, the judge held up his hand. "I'm not accusing you, Mr. Goodman, just reminding," Judge Atkinson finished smoothly.

He turned his attention to Jill. "Mrs. Goodman, do you have any objection to entering Mr. Goodman's list of business assets into the record?"

"No, sir, I don't." Jill shook her head. Despite everything she'd learned, Jill still had no interest in taking any part of Marc's company.

"Then we'll move on to marital assets." As he read the page, his frown deepened. "Here, too, there seems to be information missing. Mr. Goodman, what is your explanation for this? Do you really have no shared assets?"

"My personal assets are tied to the business, Your Honor. Mrs. Goodman was fully aware of this," Marc said smoothly. "As I said, the construction industry isn't doing well, and as a result, neither am I. Regretfully, we've been living off investments and savings."

The judge stared at Marc for what seemed like a long time. Then he turned to Jill. "Mrs. Goodman, you have the right to object to Mr. Goodman's statement if you don't believe it to be true. Your objection will be entered into the record and arbitration will end right now."

Jill had no idea what that meant. "What happens if arbitration ends?"

"Typically, your case will be reassigned to a New Jersey court. You'll have the opportunity for representation and your case will be litigated in front of a judge."

"Reassigned? How long does that take?"

The judge drew a deep breath and let it out slowly. "Well, the courts are a bit overloaded at the moment, but I'd say no longer than twelve months."

"But when we leave this room we'll still be married?"

"Legally separated," the judge corrected. "But yes, you'll still be married in the eyes of the law."

It was tempting, if only to see Marc on the witness stand and be there when Phyllis questioned him. But the price was being tied to Marc for another year and Jill didn't want that. All she wanted was out.

"Forget it," Jill decided. "I don't object."

"If you're sure? We'll proceed." The judge nodded, then returned his attention to the pages in front of him. "All of Mrs. Goodman's personal possessions, clothes, jewelry, shoes, accessories, will be hers to keep—"

"Excuse me, Your Honor," Marc interrupted.

The judge raised his gaze and arched his brow. "Yes?"

"Mrs. Goodman's clothing was purchased for business functions so they're company assets. Many of the items are unworn and still have value. I intend to return everything with a price tag and deposit the refunds to my business accounts."

"Are you telling me that you wish to keep your wife's clothing?" The judge's eyes narrowed in concern. "This is a very unusual request, Mr. Goodman."

Marc gestured calmly to the folder. "This very thing was addressed on page three of the prenuptial agreement, which Mrs. Goodman signed without coercion—"

"Take them," Jill snapped, unable to control her temper. "If this is what three years of marriage has come to—bickering over clothes with price tags—you can have them. Take everything. I don't care. All I want is my camera equipment."

"Your camera equipment?" The judge slipped his reading glasses on and flipped the page. "I don't see any camera equipment listed here." Marc opened his mouth to speak, but the judge quieted him with the raise of his hand. "Let Mrs. Goodman answer the question."

Jill continued. "I started taking photography classes on the weekends, before I met Marc—"

"Before you were married?" The judge raised his brows as he cut in.

"Yes. When Marc and I met, I was working as a photographer's assistant on my days off because I wanted to start my own photography business."

"And have you had success?"

"I've had a few freelance jobs," Jill answered honestly. "But it's a hard field to break into. I'm still working at it though."

"And you want to continue this business?"

"I really do."

"And you need your camera equipment to continue?"

"Yes."

The judge turned to Marc and frowned. "Mr. Goodman, I fail to see how you or your company would have a use for Mrs. Goodman's photography equipment, so I'll ask you plainly: Is it your intention to prevent Mrs. Goodman from accessing gainful employment? Because if so, that will influence my final decision."

Marc looked away, his jaw tight. "No, Your Honor. Of course not."

"Good choice." The judge smoothed his hand across the pad and began to write. "I'll note that Mrs. Goodman will be awarded all her personal possessions, shoes, bags, jewelry, and clothing—those items without price tags," he added wryly. "And all her camera equipment."

He jotted a few quick notes. When he finished writing, he slipped off his reading glasses and reached for the pitcher of water. No one spoke as he poured himself a cup, the sound of water and the whoosh of the air conditioner the only noise in the silent room.

"Would either of you like a break before we continue?" the judge asked as he set his cup down.

Jill shook her head. "I don't need a break." The rest of her life would begin the moment she walked out of this conference room. True, it would be different from the one she'd had with Marc, but it would be hers to shape however she wanted. And she wanted it to start right away.

Marc shook his head as well, his expression unreadable.

The judge appeared not to notice. "Alright then. Let's move on to the largest shared asset, the house in Summit. The report says you've lived there for the duration of your marriage?"

"We have, Your Honor, but I'm afraid the Summit house is also not a shared asset." Marc leaned forward in his chair, deliberately casual though his eyes had darkened. She'd seen that look before and it never ended well.

He rested his hands on the table and laced his fingers together as if he had all the time in the world. A cat playing with a mouse. "The Summit house is strictly a business asset. It was designed and built as a model for the neighborhood we were developing at the time. But the development has been completed and the house has served its purpose. We sold it just last week. The new owners take possession at the end of the month."

Jill attempted to smother her gasp but couldn't quite pull it off.

"Judging from your wife's reaction, I assume this is news to her?"

"I never kept anything from her, Your Honor," Marc lied. "She's never been interested in my work, but if she had been, I would gladly have shared the details. She knew the development was a business venture and that the house was part of it. I honestly don't see how she can claim not to know. Buyers often toured the house, and I entertained business clients on the property. The whole site was maintained by my company."

"Even so, if that house was your primary residence, Mrs. Goodman may be entitled to half the proceeds at closing. I don't see the selling price in the financials."

"Sadly, the house was sold at a loss," Marc replied without emotion. "So I'm not required to disclose it."

"This seems strangely one-sided to me, Mr. Goodman."

"As was our marriage, Your Honor." Marc looked away as he produced a frown.

Jill's fingers curled around the edge of her seat as she remembered Phyllis's warning to stay calm. Judges don't like drama, she'd said, but even Phyllis would have taken a shot at Marc by now she thought.

"Mrs. Goodman didn't care for young children because my own are grown and we have none between us. She didn't cook or clean because I have staff to do that. Other than a vague interest in photography, she expressed no interest in a career that would produce income. Mrs. Goodman was content to spend the entirety of our marriage shopping, enjoying the luxuries I provided. In short, Your Honor, she'd contributed nothing to our marital assets during the entirety of our marriage, so she deserves nothing from it."

Jill drew her hands to her lap and squeezed them together so tightly that they cramped. He'd twisted the truth and made her sound awful, but if she objected, it would be part of the record and mediation would stop. Their case would be sent to trial and that was the last thing she wanted.

"Interesting sentiments from someone who is essentially a newly-wed," the judge mused as he turned his attention to Jill. "What do you have to say to this, Mrs. Goodman?"

Jill gathered her strength and replied, taking care to keep her tone even. "I didn't have a job because Marc didn't *want* me to have a job. He said that my place was by his side. As for children, Marc said he had three of his own and didn't want more."

"I see." The judge sighed. "I'll ask you again. Do you want your objection to be part of these proceedings?"

"No," Jill answered firmly. "I do not."

"Alright then." The judge nodded and consulted his list. "The final item on the list is a house in Dewberry Beach. Tell me about this house, Mr. Goodman."

"There's nothing to tell, Your Honor." Marc drew himself up and his tone changed again, as if he'd been coached. "The Dewberry house was built as a model for a development, similar to the Summit neighborhood. Unfortunately, the Dewberry Beach project didn't catch on."

It was then that Jill remembered what Nadia had said on the phone the day Cush visited her.

"That's not right, Your Honor," Jill blurted, then glanced at Marc. She was on to something, she just didn't know what, so she stalled. "The house in Dewberry Beach—there's a mortgage."

"There's nothing to see, Your Honor." Marc shrugged, projecting a coolness that seemed off to her.

Jill ignored him. "We need to look at it."

"I don't see how this—" Marc began.

"There's no harm in looking." The judge shuffled through the papers for the Dewberry Beach house. "Especially since this is Mrs. Goodman's first objection." He scanned a page in front of him, then paused, his finger holding his place. "This bank, Mr. Goodman—Sunshine Trust. I'm not familiar with them."

"They're based in Freeport, Bahamas."

A sprinkle of goosebumps rose on Jill's arms as she remembered Cush's trip there just weeks before Marc's birthday party. An unusual vacation choice for August.

"And do you do much business with this bank?" Judge Atkinson asked.

"Not yet, Your Honor. We're exploring the idea of a partnership. I'm not sure anything will come of it."

Was it Jill's imagination or had Marc tensed? His face was utterly expressionless, but his body seemed coiled.

"I see." The judge flipped through the documents on Dewberry Beach with polite efficiency until he came to the final page. Then he stopped and raised his gaze to Marc, his expression hard. "And is your wife part of this new endeavor? Because I suspect she might not be, given your previous testimony. You did say she had no interest in your company's business, didn't you?"

The judge pushed the packet toward Jill and pointed to the signature block at the bottom of the last page. "Mrs. Goodman, is that your signature?"

It looked very much like hers, but it wasn't.

Jill glanced at Marc to see his face had drained of color.

She turned back to the judge. "I'm not sure. Can you tell me what this is? It's been a while and I may have forgotten."

"This document is a mortgage, a loan on the house in Dewberry Beach. The mortgage is in your name, with your husband and Cushman Lawrence as witnesses." The judge laid down the paper. "It's interesting that you don't seem to remember. Mortgages are a serious undertaking. Documents are finalized in person so you would have to have been there. Do you remember taking a trip to Sunshine Trust in Freeport, Bahamas?"

Nadia. This was what she had meant when she said Jill might never speak to her again when she found out what she'd done. She'd gone to Freeport with Cushman. It was Nadia who had forged Jill's signature on the mortgage.

"Forging signatures on banking documents is a serious federal crime," the judge continued. "If this is *not* your signature, Mrs.

Goodman, these divorce proceedings will cease immediately. Your husband and his friends will be investigated for banking fraud. All company records will be audited and years of transactions will be re-examined. The process could take months, longer if the investigation uncovers evidence. During that time your husband's company assets will be frozen. It will not be business as usual, I'm afraid."

Jill looked at Marc, then back at the judge. "May I have a moment, sir, to speak with my husband?"

"Yes, I think that's a good idea." Judge Atkinson rose. "I'll be back in a moment."

As the door closed behind him, Jill watched Marc collapse against the back of his chair. If she could freeze one moment in her life to relive over and over, it would be this one. Just for the look on Marc's face when he'd realized the power she held over him, over his company. Part of her *wanted* him to be investigated and punished. But the bigger part of her just wanted to be rid of him.

"Now, Jilly." Marc regrouped, softening his gaze and offering a tentative smile. "You know this is all a misunder—"

That might have worked before, but it didn't work now. Jill held up her hand and Marc paused, assuming she was willing to bargain. She wasn't.

"Pay it off," she said.

"Pay what off?" Marc echoed. He seemed honestly confused.

"The mortgage, Marc. The mortgage you and your stupid friends took out in my name. Pay it off right now and I'll let it go. I won't press charges."

"Okay, fine. As soon as the house sells—"

"No. Not when the house sells—now. That house has been on the market for so long that I don't think it will ever—" Jill gasped as the realization struck her. "You never intended to sell that house, did you?

That's where you meet Brittney. That's why you still have it. You don't *want* to sell it."

"Jillian."

"No." Jill reached for her cell phone and opened her banking app. "We're done. Transfer the money to my account and I'll pay it off myself. Everything you need is right here." She turned the screen toward him.

But Marc spluttered, "I'm afraid the company is a little short on working capital right now."

"You don't have the money?" Jill lowered her phone. "How can you not have the money? Five hundred thousand is nothing to you." She flicked her hand dismissively through the air. "I don't care how you get it. A line of credit, a loan, I don't care. I want it paid off and you need to figure out how to do it."

"I'm not willing to—" Marc began, but she cut him off.

"Then the judge should know about this, shouldn't he?"

"Jill." Marc's voice was stern. "This isn't funny."

"No, it's not funny at all." Jill folded her hands on the table's surface. "You called me a Jersey Girl, implying that I'd never be good enough for you—"

"Fine," Marc snapped. "You want an apology? Will that make you feel better?"

"No, I don't. I want you to remember that *this* Jersey Girl holds the fate of your entire company in the palm of her hand. That I was gracious when you didn't deserve it." Jill leaned forward, locking her gaze with his. "So lemme tell you what happens now."

Several minutes later, the conference room door opened, and the judge poked his head in. "Are we all finished here?"

"We are." Jill straightened in her chair.

"And what have we decided?" The judge settled into his place and opened his folder.

"Marc has decided to sign the house over to me. I intend to sell it." Jill's voice was clear and strong.

The judge glanced at Marc. "Is that true, Mr. Goodman?"

"Yes, sir."

"He's also transferring the balance in a small investment account to me, Your Honor," Jill added. "To cover expenses for the sale."

"That house comes with quite a bit of equity, despite the sizable mortgage. Is it your intention, Mr. Goodman, to assign that equity to Mrs. Goodman as well?"

"Yes, Your Honor." Marc's voice was tight, and it was all Jill could do to keep from cheering.

The judge nodded. "I think we can make that happen right now. We have a notary on staff who will be happy to help." He made a note and closed the folder.

"So we're finished here?" Marc pushed his chair back from the table, like a petulant child.

"Not so fast, Mr. Goodman." The judge's voice was stern. "It's not my job to rule on morality. If it were, the outcome of these proceedings would be very different. Even so, I suggest you think about what you've said, what you've put forth as fact. These proceedings may take place in a conference room, but they are still legally binding. Is there anything you've said, or any evidence you've submitted, that you care to reconsider?"

"No."

When Judge Atkinson turned to Jill, his expression softened. "I'm sure you're pleased with Mr. Goodman's decision to assign you ownership of the Dewberry house, but don't forget that you face challenges ahead. The terms of the prenup are very clear. The Summit house has been sold, and you are ordered to gather your things and vacate it within forty-eight hours."

"Yes, Your Honor."

"Mr. Goodman, you are not to set foot in the Summit house until Monday morning, do you understand?"

"Yeah," Marc sighed.

The door opened and the judge motioned for his clerk to enter. He handed her the folder. "Please make these orders your priority."

After the clerk left, the judge addressed Marc and Jill with his final ruling. "Mrs. Goodman, you are awarded full ownership of the house in Dewberry Beach. You are hereby awarded all your clothes—those without price tags attached—your jewelry, *and* your camera equipment. You have until Monday morning to collect your things and vacate the Summit house. At which time Mr. Goodman may take possession and ownership. The closing can proceed after Mrs. Goodman leaves. I will sign the order and file it with the court by 5 p.m. today. If there are no further objections, you may consider this marriage dissolved one month from today."

Marc rose from his chair abruptly and left the room, not bothering to mask his disgust.

The door closed behind him and Jill turned her attention to the judge. "Sir, may I ask one more thing?"

"So you own a beach house now?" Ellie raised her beer bottle in toast later that night. "*And* you're divorced. Congratulations on both."

"It appears I do." Jill tapped her bottle against Ellie's. "Officially, as of a couple of hours ago, although the divorce won't be final for thirty days."

Flush with a bit of cash, Jill had driven to Ellie's apartment after the meeting with the judge. On the way, she'd bought the double-cheese pizza that Ellie loved and a six-pack of beer. She'd bought groceries too, to repay Ellie for her hospitality over the past week. They sat on the couch in Ellie's small apartment, sipping beer and making plans.

"What are you going to do?"

"Sell it—as soon as I can," Jill replied quickly. "No way can I afford to live there." She tossed the crust back into the open box, then leaned into Ellie's faded purple couch. "For practical reasons if nothing else. It comes with a hefty mortgage."

"What about after the sale?" Ellie asked. "Do you get to keep the profit?"

"Yeah, anything beyond the mortgage and closing costs, I get to keep."

"Shouldn't you be happier? That house is worth a fortune."

"I'm worried, El. The house has been on the market for years and it hasn't sold. What if there's something wrong with it and it *never* sells? I have a colossal mortgage payment at the end of the month and another after that. I'm just…" Jill reached for another slice, then changed her mind.

"Is that something you know for sure, or are you guessing?"

"I don't know for sure."

"So don't go looking for trouble, as Aunt Sarah said. You might be surprised at how easy that house is to sell."

"Maybe." Jill rested her head against the cushion, her head swimming with details. "I still need to research agents this weekend and reach out to them. You know the weirdest part? I never wanted the house in the first place. I lost my temper and now I'm stuck with this thing."

"Jilly, I think we're missing the bigger picture here." Ellie rose to retrieve two fresh beers from the refrigerator. She snapped the lid and passed a bottle to Jill. "You just shed two hundred pounds of useless, overblown, cheating man-weight; you've got to feel better about that. Let's celebrate that first and worry about the beach house later."

Jill held her bottle up and Ellie clinked it. "You're right."

"Of course I am." Ellie flipped the lid of the pizza box closed because Lewis looked a little too interested in the pile of crusts, despite the pieces that Jill had already slipped him. Then she settled onto the couch, crossing her legs, a position she took when she meant business. "What about the Summit house? Did you say you have this weekend to get your stuff? Is Marc going to be there?"

"No. He gets it Monday morning and the new owners take possession a week after that."

"You okay with that?"

"Yeah, I really am." Jill pulled a blanket from the basket and draped it over her legs. "It's a pretty house, elegant, but cold, you know? With so many people coming and going, it never felt like home."

Home to Jill was watching Aunt Sarah pour pancake batter into a sizzling frying pan on a Saturday morning. It was holding the flashlight exactly right while Uncle Barney changed the spark plugs in his battered pick-up truck. Home was the first cold spray of water in the outdoor shower and the warm towel afterwards. It was waking up before dawn to go fishing with Uncle Barney, just to be with him. In Aunt Sarah's kitchen there'd been a leaky green refrigerator and a temperamental gas stove that required a lit match and a steady hand just to cook dinner. Would Aunt Sarah and Uncle Barney have wanted a stainless-steel refrigerator with a smart screen or an eight-burner gas stove with a pot filler, like the one in Marc's kitchen? Possibly, but it wouldn't have made their home any better. They hadn't cared about money. Their home had been perfect the way it was.

"And you're okay with tomorrow on your own? Because I can cancel—"

"Absolutely not," Jill replied. "Don't cancel anything. I'll be fine."

"Okay then. I'll be over on Sunday morning." Ellie raised her bottle. "Here's to moving forward."

"To moving forward." Jill raised her own bottle to meet Ellie's.

The clink echoed in the cozy room.

Chapter 10

The judge's order allowed Jill the weekend to collect her personal things before leaving the Summit house for good. Forty-eight hours to pack up one life and begin another.

After unlocking the door and disabling the alarm, she made her way to Marc's office. She'd taken the Dewberry Beach house from him in the heat of anger and she was becoming more and more convinced that it was a mistake. That house had been on the market for years and no one wanted it. That alone was concerning. Even though the bank had allowed Jill to assume the mortgage payments, the first payment was due in just two weeks and the amount she was responsible for was staggering. Worse, after adding up every bit of cash she had on hand, Jill had been horrified to realize that she had only enough for three mortgage payments. Just three.

So the clothes in Jill's closet could wait.

Right now, the contents of Marc's office were more important.

Jill's plan was to sell the Dewberry Beach house as quickly as possible, and for that to happen, she needed to know everything about it. Marc had told the judge that the Dewberry property was supposed to be part of a neighborhood development, similar to the one he'd built in Summit, with the house itself being the model. He'd bought a large oceanfront lot at a bargain price and started construction. But Marc had said that buildable lots in Dewberry Beach were impossible to find so they'd expanded their search to include neighboring towns. The model home had remained where it was, with the rest of the development planned for a less expensive parcel of land further inland, though Marc had told the judge that managing the two properties was too costly so they'd abandoned the project entirely. The house in Dewberry Beach was all that remained.

Although Marc hadn't confirmed it, Jill still suspected that he'd had little interest in selling the house because it was where he met up with Brittney. But as painful as that was to consider, it would actually be good news. The house might be easier to sell than she thought.

When Jill reached his office, she pushed open the door with a bit more force than necessary. This room had been Marc's little kingdom, which Jill hadn't been allowed to enter. Things were different now. Jill plopped herself into his chair and spun it around. And when it slowed, she leaned back and propped her feet on his desk.

"Where did you put the Dewberry stuff, you little weasel?" Jill's gaze swept the contents of his office.

It was possible that she wouldn't find anything here at all. If Marc had been trying to sell a prime piece of oceanfront in the hottest real-estate market in the state and couldn't, he wouldn't have kept a reminder of his failure. In that case, all information on the Dewberry house would be in his city office, or in the shredder.

She pushed back from the desk and began her search in a filing cabinet.

Because she didn't know what she needed, Jill examined all of it. She opened up his cabinets and flipped through his property binders. She considered every scrap of paper inside every file folder in every drawer, lifting out whatever might be relevant. And when she was satisfied that she'd left no stone unturned, she gathered everything and left.

She dumped it all on the dining-room table and sorted through it.

What she found was a strange mismatch of things. There were drone shots of the property and the beach. Interior photographs of every room, expensively staged. And marketing copy that described the town of Dewberry Beach as an "upscale shore experience," with a rich nightlife, shopping, and restaurants. To be fair, Jill had only driven through town, but her impression was that Dewberry Beach was a family town with not much to do apart from visiting the beach. Anyone expecting more than a quiet day would be disappointed.

However, it was possible she was mistaken.

To make sure, Jill opened her laptop and pulled up information about Dewberry Beach. Her search showed that the town was small, bordered on the east by the Atlantic Ocean and on the west by Barnegat Bay. There was a tiny train depot on the edge of town, a salt pond a few blocks from the ocean, and a walking path beside a creek. In town, shopping seemed to be limited to a few blocks along the main road, which wasn't what Marc's ad copy suggested at all.

Jill went to the town's website and liked what she saw. It had a small-town, friendly feel that was inviting. The pictures of the October farmer's market showed wheelbarrows piled high with fat orange pumpkins, and baskets of apples, and drums of fresh kettle corn. An announcement in the corner proclaimed that money earned from the pancake breakfast at the fire department would fund new equipment. Further down, a blurb congratulated the Fish Shack on winning Best Lobster Roll for the third consecutive year. And finally, there was a notice that the ice cream stand next to the beach would be closing for the season but that containers of black licorice were still available for sale, at a discounted price. Apparently, there was quite a bit left.

The real Dewberry Beach was nothing like Marc's description.

Closing her laptop, Jill returned her attention to the papers on the table and found something interesting. Brittney had been put in charge of marketing the house and grounds, and had been given a very generous operating budget. She'd hired a real-estate firm who specialized in vacation homes in the Hamptons to consult. A bizarre choice, it seemed to Jill, given that the look and feel of Dewberry Beach wasn't anything like the Hamptons. It appeared that Brittney had been in way over her head, completely unqualified for the job.

So maybe things weren't as bad as they first appeared.

Maybe this house just needed a reset.

Jill continued her research, feeling a bit more optimistic. She still needed to hire someone to list the house and handle the sale, someone willing to work hard and start right away. They had to be familiar with small towns on the New Jersey shore, and given the price of the house, they had to understand upscale clients. Those requirements narrowed Jill's list considerably, from more than a dozen to just three. Jill composed an email to each of them, introducing herself as the new property owner and expressing her desire to sell quickly. She sent them off and closed her laptop.

She'd taken the first step and it felt good.

The next task would be sorting out her closet.

Chapter 11

With the office sorted, Jill climbed the stairs to the master bedroom, her anxiety rising with every step. Jill couldn't forget the selfies Brittney had sent. She remembered every detail of every picture. One of them had been taken in the master bedroom, in Jill's bed. She'd known her marriage was over the moment she saw the pictures, but her heart was slower to understand. It did not want to revisit the scene of her husband's betrayal.

But she had to.

Jill opened the door and stood at the threshold, steeling herself for the task at hand. As she crossed the room, she happened to glance at her reflection in the full-length mirror and she slowed, as if seeing herself for the first time. Three years of monthly salon appointments had transformed her hair to a perfect blonde. Regular keratin treatments had taken her curls, and she'd never gotten used to the longer length. Marc preferred blondes so that's what Jill became, even though it didn't feel right. Even though she never felt like herself.

Jill's attention turned to the clothes she was wearing, the type of outfit she'd worn a million times before. She pinched a bit of the pants fabric between her fingers. Tweed. Expensive tweed, if Jill remembered correctly. And the twinset she wore so casually was cashmere, the cost of which would have fed her for a month in college. On her feet were a ridiculous pair of branded ballet flats that made her look as if she were on her way to the country club, which she decidedly wasn't.

She used to live in slouchy jeans and sweatshirts. She was only twenty-six years old. When was the last time she wore jeans? Did she even own a pair anymore?

Jillian Marie DiFiore was born in South Jersey. She used her hands when she talked, frequently chopping the air in conversation to make her point. She could swear like a sailor—and often did—whenever the situation called for it. She drank beer from a can and ate cold pizza for breakfast. She blasted her music loud enough to feel the thumping in her body. She had friends. She had fun. But most of all, she would not have been caught dead in a pair of fussy tweed pants or an overpriced cashmere twinset. And her body would have rebelled at the idea of branded ballet flats instead of scuffed sneakers.

She'd changed herself to fit into Marc's world, to the point where she didn't recognize herself anymore.

But that stopped now. All of it stopped now.

Jill turned on her heel and left the bedroom. Outside, she locked the house and got into her car to drive across town.

She knew exactly where she was going, and she hoped they were open this early in the morning. A New You, a hair salon on the back side of the Village Green, looked edgy and interesting. The lobby was a tumble of green vines and flowering plants. The walls were hung with work by local artists, and the music inside flowed out to the sidewalk. It was vastly different from Jill's regular salon, where the staff had been instructed to greet clients by name, with a benign smile and a chilled glass of Chardonnay. Jill hated Chardonnay.

Behind the reception desk was a woman with cropped hair and a lace of delicate tattoos across her shoulders. As Jill approached, she looked up from her work and offered a smile that couldn't quite hide the surprise of seeing someone who looked like Jill in this salon.

"Can I help you?" She posed the question as if she were expecting Jill to ask for directions or coins for the meter.

"I want to make a change and I hope you have an opening."

"I'm not sure. We're pretty booked up today, but it's early so let's see…" The woman ran her finger down the page of her appointment book. "Wow. Okay, that never happens." She offered a bewildered shrug. "Shasta came in early today and her first appointment isn't for another hour or so. If you want a change, she's your girl."

Delighted, Jill took the appointment.

Shasta projected an air of self-confidence that won Jill over right away. Dark and petite, her braided hair was swept into a colorful wrap. A delicate silver nose ring and a swipe of blue lipstick provided the perfect finishing touch.

Jill settled into the chair while Shasta snapped open an apron and secured it.

Then she stood behind Jill, frowning at her reflection in the salon mirror. As she lifted a piece of Jill's hair, her brow furrowed in confusion. "Chemical?"

"Keratin."

"Interesting cut. Not one I would have chosen for you." Her frown deepened as she lifted more sections of Jill's long hair and let them fall. With a benign smile, Shasta asked, "So what are we doing today?"

"Cut it off," Jill said simply. "All of it."

Shasta's brows lifted. "You sure?"

"Absolutely."

"How short are you willing to go?"

"I don't care. I just want to look like myself again."

"How old are you?"

"Twenty-six."

Shasta's smile widened as she practically cackled with glee. "Oh, this'll be fun."

The process was expensive but worth it. Shasta had worked Jill in between clients, excited to be part of her makeover. When Shasta finally turned the chair and Jill looked in the mirror, she recognized herself looking back. The cut was short, the color a more familiar auburn, and Shasta had even been able to recover a bit of curl. Jill left the shop feeling hopeful, as if she just might be strong enough to find her way back to the girl she used to be.

A few doors down, Jill spied a thrift shop and a display window filled with warm clothes perfect for the changing weather—soft flannel shirts, cozy sweaters, faded jeans. And it occurred to her that her hair wasn't the only thing that needed overhauling. With a closet filled with cashmere, tweed, and silk, she dressed more like a matronly senator's wife than a young woman who hadn't yet turned thirty. Impulsively, she ducked into the shop and left an hour later carrying a shopping bag filled with clothes that felt authentic.

Chapter 12

Sunday morning found Jill and Ellie in the bedroom of the Summit house. Ellie had arrived to help early that morning, armed with bagels and coffee. She'd nearly dropped both when she spied Jill's transformation. Even now, after Ellie'd had a few hours to get used to Jill's look, she still had something to say.

"I can't get over it." Ellie lowered the bundle of hangers she'd been holding and paused to stare at Jill yet again. "You look so different. I mean, you look like yourself again. I hadn't realized how much you'd changed until today."

"Yeah?" Jill brought her fingertips to the back of her neck, still getting used to her new cut. "You don't think it's too short?"

"*Absolutely* not." Ellie shook her head for emphasis. "It's exactly right. You look like yourself."

"Thanks, El."

As Ellie returned to work, Jill allowed herself a smile. It was good to be back.

Packing up Jill's old life was easier, and faster, than she'd thought it would be. Marc had made it very clear that everything in the house—apart from her clothing and camera equipment—belonged to his company so there wasn't much she was permitted to take, though even if she'd had the option to take anything, there wasn't much she wanted.

Within a couple hours, they'd sorted everything in her closet—things she thought she couldn't live without—into three piles: keep, give away, and sell. The first pile was the smallest, fitting neatly into a few suitcases. The donation pile was larger, boxed, taped, and loaded into Ellie's car, headed for the women's shelter. Accessories and cast-off clothing made up the last pile, things Jill had no use for but knew thrift shops would love, so they were off to be sold.

Jill stood, pushing the sleeves of her sweatshirt to her elbows, and surveyed what remained. "There's still so much here."

"I had no idea you were a real-life Cinderella. This, for example, is the most exquisite dress I've ever seen." Ellie held up a navy tea-length from Jason Wu. The sleeves and the neckline were a delicate mesh that melted into a sumptuous cloqué fabric, embossed with a darker navy pattern.

"You'd look amazing in that dress, Ellie. It's perfect for the Brockhurst reception."

"You think so?" Ellie replied airily as she held the dress against her body and swished the skirt around her calves.

"I do. And if I remember correctly, the dress has shoes to match…" Jill quickly located a shoebox and opened the lid. Inside was a pair of black T-straps with a gold buckle at the ankle, unworn and perfect for the dress. She laid the shoes at Ellie's feet. "We're the same size. Try them on."

As Ellie slipped them on, Jill remembered that the outfit came with a bag as well—a navy satin Kelly bag with a delicate gold-button closure. She pulled it from the shelf and handed it to Ellie, whose face was bright with excitement.

"Oh, wait—one more thing…" Jill retrieved a box and presented it to Ellie. Inside was a pair of twenty-four-carat filigree earrings.

"Jilly… they're stunning." Ellie's breath was a sigh. She held them to her ears and turned toward the mirror. "Just *look* at how they sparkle." As she examined her reflection from a dozen different angles, a price tag worked itself loose and fluttered into view. Ellie's expression faded as she lowered the dress. "What are we doing? We can't take any of this. What about what the judge said? You can only take clothes that don't have a price tag.

Jill reached for the tag and snapped it from the dress. "I don't see a price tag."

"Jillian," Ellie gasped. "The judge—"

"Said not to take anything that had a price tag *attached*." Jill's voice muffled as she bent down to rip the tags from the rest of the outfit. As she straightened, she stuffed them into her jeans pocket. "I don't see one, do you?"

"Jill—" Ellie began, but Jill stopped her.

"Wait." She pulled a branded leather suitcase from the top shelf. "This very definitely doesn't have a tag, do you agree?"

"Jilly, it's—"

"If you like it, then you should have it. Cinderella magic should be shared."

"I don't know…"

"Well I do, and I'll tell you why." Jill leaned against the doorframe. "Marc has no idea what's in this closet, so he'll never miss anything we take. But more important is that clothes this beautiful should be worn and appreciated. It's like wearing art, El. You feel different. You move different. It's wonderful and probably the only thing I'll miss from this life—the clothes."

"Then why aren't you keeping them?"

"Because I need to remember the girl I was before all this. That's why."

"Okay, then." Ellie's excitement returned. "Let's box it up—but only one outfit."

"Great. Just one more outfit—maybe two."

Completely ignoring Ellie's protests, Jill gestured to the rest of her closet with the sweep of her hand. "See anything else that looks good to you?"

"This is the last of it," Jill said as she slid a box into the trunk of her car.

By mid-morning, they'd finished sorting through Jill's closet. Ellie would drop the donation boxes off at the women's shelter on her way out of town, and Jill would take the rest to a consignment shop on her way to Dewberry Beach. The extra cash would be a nice cushion after the salon visit.

Ellie followed with the suitcase Jill had given her. She laid it carefully on the back seat. "Are you sure you want to go to that Dewberry house all by yourself? I'll be back soon. If you want to wait, we can drive down together."

"I can't afford to wait. I have to sell this house as fast as I can," Jill reminded Ellie. "I'll be fine—just a quick trip down to sign with the listing agent and I'll be back."

"Did those real-estate agents reply already? That was quick."

"I have a meeting the day after tomorrow. I need a day to open the house and make it appear lived-in."

Ellie sighed. "If Brittney really has been trying to sell the house for so long, that's worrying. If she can't sell it, I'm afraid you won't be able to either."

"First of all, Brittney's a moron."

"Noted."

"And second, I don't care who buys that house. I plan to sell it at a bargain price, clearing just enough to pay off the mortgage and closing costs—I don't want anything else."

Ellie slid the key into the ignition but didn't start it. "You're coming back right after?"

"That's the plan. I don't want to stay there any longer than I have to." Jill paused to dust her hands on her jeans. "Besides, I still have to find a job."

"Okay then." The engine clattered to a start and Ellie winced. "You have the key to the apartment. I'll be back after the wedding."

Jill reached inside the car to squeeze her friend's shoulder. "I'll be fine, El. I'm strangely okay about leaving. I'm strangely okay about all of this."

"Are you sure?"

"I'm positive." Jill waited while Ellie snapped her seat belt, then she laid her hand on the car door and smiled. "Oh, I almost forgot to tell you—I saved the best for last: I changed my name back. At the hearing, after Marc flounced off, I asked the judge if I could and he signed the order right then. Had his clerk file it. I think he was pretty happy about it, to be honest. He didn't seem to like Marc very much."

"Well, well." Ellie smiled. "Look at you, making things happen. I may have underestimated you, Jillian DiFiore." She jammed the car into gear. "It's nice to have you back."

After watching Ellie drive off, Jill returned to the house for the last time. There was one thing she had to do before she left. Something she should have done a long time ago.

Inside, Jill paused briefly to gather an armful of supplies then continued to the master bedroom. It was strange to see the room now, as if she'd never been here. Her vanity table had been cleared of make-up, the bathroom empty of her things—all trace of her had been boxed up and taken away.

Almost everything.

Jill seated herself on the cushioned bench of her vanity table. Tucked away in the back corner of her jewelry box was something Marc had given her but she'd never had the courage to wear. Something that never should have been hers. She removed the case, careful of its contents, and placed it gently on the bedroom floor.

Then she went to work.

She padded the inside of a sturdy box with bubble wrap and lined it with tissue. When she was sure that nothing she placed inside would jostle or break, she carefully opened the case and removed the items inside. One by one, she wrapped each piece in tissue and then in bubble wrap before tucking it securely into the box. Then she added a final layer of bubble wrap and brought the box downstairs.

Writing the note would be the hardest part, explaining why she'd kept the items in the first place. She needed to ask forgiveness for her arrogance in thinking these things ever belonged to her. Somehow Marc had taken possession of heirloom jewelry that had rightfully belonged to Dianne, pieces from her grandmother that should have been passed along to her daughters. Shortly after their wedding, Marc had presented the box to Jill, gleeful at what he'd accomplished. Jill had been horrified and had never worn any of the pieces, but neither had she returned them.

She used the last of her monogrammed stationery, and though it took three attempts to write, she was satisfied with the result.

Dear Dianne,

I'm returning something that never should have been taken from you in the first place.

I'm sorry to have kept it this long. It's too much to forgive but please understand that I'm sorry.

Jill

She tucked the note inside and taped the box closed, then found Dianne's address in Marc's office and wrote it, in bold letters, across the box. She'd mail it on her way out of town and would pay for express delivery and insurance. It was the least she could do.

When she left the Summit house, closing the door firmly behind her, she knew she'd never return.

And that was okay.

Chapter 13

The rain that began as a late afternoon patter when Jill left the post office turned into a downpour on the Garden State Parkway, drumming on the roof of her car and spattering across her windshield. As a result, traffic backed up, and what should have been an easy trip of just over an hour turned into a hard three. Ahead of her was an endless line of taillights as cars merged from four lanes to two, so the State Patrol could manage a fender bender a few miles ahead.

This trip to Dewberry Beach was a business errand, nothing more. Her task was to list the house and price it low, aiming for a quick sale and a fast close. At least that's what Jill told herself as she jabbed the radio station buttons on her console. Accepting this house in trade for the fraudulent mortgage was a mistake, Jill could see that now. She should have insisted Marc pay off the loan or gone to the judge if he refused, but she hadn't. She'd let her emotions take over, she'd been so angry at what Marc and Cush and Nadia had done. Now, all she felt was vibrating anxiety. She should be at Ellie's, looking for a job, but instead she was wasting time driving down to the shore to sell a house she knew almost nothing about—except that Marc had cheated on her there.

She did her best to steady herself. Phyllis had said emotion was a trap and she was right. The Dewberry house was an anchor and would pull her under if she lost focus. This was a project, same as any other, and the key was to break the whole into smaller tasks. She'd done her research. She had her to-do list. Stick to both and she'd be fine.

The house was closed for the season and it would take some time to open it up again, but Jill had a plan for that too. She'd found an affordable motel on the edge of town and made a reservation. Maybe a motel wasn't the best way to spend her limited money, but the alternative was to sleep in the same house Marc had shared with his mistress and that was almost unthinkable. So she'd get a good night's sleep and in the morning, an early start to readying the house for the property agent the following day. It was a good plan, solid.

Now all she had to do was find the motel.

By the time Jill arrived at the exit for Dewberry Beach, dusk had fallen. The pounding rain from earlier had slowed to a dull patter, and the gathering mist made navigating difficult. The air inside the car felt close, heavy and thick. As she waited for the traffic light to change, Jill cracked her window, hoping the fresh air would clear her head.

When the light changed, Jill continued on her way, relying on her car's GPS to guide her to the motel. She might not have found her way otherwise, especially in the dark. She'd only been to the shore a few times and Marc had driven while she napped. She came to a narrow bridge and slowed the car to cross the inlet, hearing her tires hum against the metal grating. On the far side, fishing trawlers had docked for the night, and Jill could hear water slapping against the hulls. The air shifted as she drew closer to the ocean. It was thicker and threaded with the scents of the shore, a muddy low tide, salty air, woodsmoke and fall.

The website for the Dewberry Beach Motor Lodge described the property as secluded, which was fine with Jill. She hadn't planned to walk along the beach, and she didn't want anything from the shops in town. The pictures provided online looked basic, not even close to the luxury Jill had grown accustomed to, but even that didn't matter. She didn't plan to stay long.

"You have arrived at your destination."

Jill stopped the car and switched on her high beams, stunned. There had to be a mistake, a terrible mistake.

The property in front of her—the one her GPS insisted was the motel—had been abandoned, and from the look of it, for a long time. The asphalt in the parking lot was buckled, leaving potholes big enough to destroy the undercarriage of anyone stupid enough to drive through. The lawn was weedy and overgrown, probably a haven for vermin, and a rusty chain-link fence circled what Jill imagined had once been a pool deck. The pool itself had been drained, the last bit of water a stagnant green. In the corner was a stack of twisted lounge chairs, rusting into dust.

But the worst thing was the structure itself, the place Jill had assumed she'd be spending the night. The motel was not one building but three. Three small cabins that could be generously described as "chilling." On one, the front door was missing entirely, and Jill didn't want to imagine what lurked inside. Another seemed to have no roof at all, just a gaping hole covered loosely with a blue tarp that flapped in the wind. The third cabin seemed intact but not inhabitable. The front windows were cracked, and the moldy curtains hung in tatters.

Jill stared at the property in front of her, open-mouthed. The motel's website had taken her reservation, though not her payment, which was something at least. But she had a plan, a carefully constructed plan that included staying at this motel. Of course she wouldn't now. She'd seen motels in horror movies that were more welcoming. And because the Dewberry Beach Motor Lodge was the only motel in town, there was only one place left for her to stay.

She closed the windows and put her car in gear. It was late and this place was creepy so the last thing she wanted to do was linger. Before she drove away, she tapped in the address for the house into her GPS. It wouldn't be so bad, staying at that house, would it?

She could manage a night or two.

A five-minute drive put her back on the main road where she picked up Route 35 to Dewberry Beach. Closer to town, the road narrowed from four lanes to two. As she slowed, she noticed the scenery had changed, the feel more inviting—the cottages cedar-shingled with wide front porches set with chairs for neighbors and friends. The homes were decorated for Halloween too. Pumpkins lined the front steps, and cobwebs stretched across the shrubbery. One house had arranged a scarecrow, wearing fishing waders and a pirate hat, sitting in a chair with his arm extended as if he were waving to the neighbors.

It was unexpected, the idea that a shore town didn't shut down during the off-season. Jill has assumed it would. Most of the properties in the Hamptons did, and Jill couldn't think of one instance they'd visited this town outside of summer. And hadn't Marc routinely shuttered the Dewberry Beach house for the winter, even hiring a company that specialized in winterizing summer homes? They brought in the outdoor furniture and stored it, unplugged appliances and cleared the house of unwrapped food. It was a full weekend job, and when they were finished, they set the house alarms and locked the door behind them.

The road to the house wound through the little town, and Jill slowed even more. Old, sturdy trees lined the street, stretching their branches to meet overhead. The canopy above the street was striking, and Jill felt as if she were traveling through a tunnel, with the warm glow of streetlamps lighting her way. Jill slowed the car almost to a full stop just to take it in. The sight would be even better in the daylight, with the sun shining through a veil of fall color, and Jill made a mental note to notice it on her way out of town.

She continued to the house. As she got closer to the ocean, she smelled the sea air and the scenery changed once again. The road was dusted with gritty beach sand that crunched under Jill's tires. Here, front gardens were filled with plants that didn't mind a bit of ocean spray. Jill recognized stately clusters of beach grass, scrubs of sea lavender, and hardy climbing roses. All of it conjured memories of summer, reminding Jill of Aunt Sarah.

Jill didn't recall any of this from previous trips. With Marc, the trips to Dewberry had been perfunctory and filled with purpose—a quick party to host, clients to meet. She and Marc arrived together and left immediately afterward, so lingering wasn't part of the plan. She'd never seen the town up close, and she was surprised, now, at how idyllic it appeared.

But the town of Dewberry Beach was small and the drive through it was short.

"You have arrived at your destination."

Jill stared at the house in front of her, looming like a black monolith against the gray horizon, and her heart sank. It was by far the biggest house around, almost like an office building in a neighborhood. It wasn't at all charming and wasn't intended to be. With three floors, nine bedrooms and six bathrooms, it was meant to impress weekend guests. Worse was that it had a contrived nautical theme that Jill had always found off-putting. The exterior was painted a storm-cloud gray with crisp white trim because the designer has liked the color combination. And the shiny black shutters, meant to be protection against ocean storms, were purely decorative and didn't latch. The oversized entrance was flanked with a pair of huge gas lanterns that a designer in New York had decided fit the theme and so had ordered from a catalog. According to papers found in Marc's office, landscaping on the property was meant to look "beachy," but it didn't look that way to her. The plants brought in were tropical, not native, and the stones in the dry bed had been machine tumbled before being cemented in place. Around the back were two outdoor decks that faced the ocean, a rooftop patio, and a three-car garage.

Marc's designs had borrowed heavily from massive summer homes in the Hamptons. But what worked in East Hampton didn't work in Dewberry Beach, a fact that seemed to surprise everyone on Marc's staff.

Resigned, Jill pulled her car into the side driveway and slipped into the garage. She clicked the button to close the door behind her and listened as it sealed shut. This space, like the closets in the Summit house master bedroom, was massive and opulent. The storage racks overhead groaned with bundles of deck furniture and umbrellas, set out as decoration in the summer but now wrapped in plastic and stored for the winter. Alongside were surfboards no one had used, beach chairs with tags still attached, hammocks no one had napped in, and a volleyball net for games no one had played—all perfect accessories for a curated summer.

The garage air was sealed so tightly against the elements that it was impossible to smell or hear the ocean, just steps away. With a snort, Jill remembered that Uncle Barney's old garage had been so weathered, and the siding so warped, that even the lightest breeze whistled through and ruffled your hair. But his was a working garage, filled with a jumble of bicycles in line for repair and projects he always "meant to get to." It wasn't anything like this.

Jill unlocked the door and reset the alarm.

She found the main electrical breaker and switched it on with a satisfying crack, then listened as the house awakened. She remembered the last time she'd been here, at that awful party Brittney had arranged. That woman had positioned herself at the front entrance, greeting guests as if she were the one co-hosting with Marc instead of Jill. Which, given what Jill knew now, was closer to the truth.

That was the reason Jill had booked the motel, the memories. This house was a reminder of Marc's betrayal and the bruise was still healing. Most of the pictures Brittney sent had been taken here, and it was painful for Jill to be here. But it couldn't be helped, not yet at least. Tomorrow she would stage the house, and the day after, she'd meet the agents to sign the listing agreement. They had already assured her the closing could be handled remotely, and Jill planned to do just that.

The short hallway from the garage led to an oversized kitchen and on to the rest of the house. She paused briefly at the catering pantry for a bottle of mineral water and twisted the lid open. As she sipped, she viewed the house with a critical eye. The first floor was entirely open, designed to hold a hundred people in the summer. The windows, decks, and patio were arranged to allow a sweeping view of the ocean from every corner of the house. The furniture, upholstered in shades of beige, was supposed to present guests with an idea of beach sand. It all seemed utterly ridiculous to Jill, as far removed from an authentic beach house as one could get, especially the floating staircase leading guests to the decks on the second floor. No real beach house had a floating staircase.

However, a hidden panel beside it activated the only feature of the house Jill actually liked. She stepped forward and pressed the button. As the motor whirred to life, the floor-to-ceiling curtains on the back wall parted, revealing an unobstructed view of the beach. She'd always loved the view from these windows: the sandy shore, the tide line, the rising waves, and the horizon, all in one uninterrupted sweep. Now it seemed almost surreal with the full moon glimmering on the sea. Jill stood for a long time watching the waves crest, then tumble toward the shore in a spray of white.

Eventually, she returned to the kitchen. She assembled a simple meal from food left in the catering pantry: canned soup, fancy crackers, and a bit of dark chocolate. By the time she'd finished, it was late, but she felt better. The key to spending the next two days in this house, Jill reminded herself, was keeping busy.

Venturing upstairs, she checked the guest bedrooms, making a mental tally of the bare mattresses that needed linens and the empty bathrooms that needed fresh towels and flowers. Last on her list was the master bedroom at the far end of the hall. As she made her way there, she wondered whether that room should be staged differently. It had a private deck, after all, and she should highlight it. Maybe she should make the most of it with a bistro table and chairs from the garage. A coffee service from the kitchen might be a nice touch too.

She opened the door and froze.

The bed had been slept in, the sheets and blankets twisted and thrown on the floor. The quilt lay in a heap, the pillows cast aside. Near the door was a discarded pile of Marc's clothes—the sweater she'd gifted him for Christmas, the watch she'd had engraved for his birthday.

Closer to the bed was a scrap of crimson lace, carelessly removed on the way to something more urgent. And in the center of the bed, an unmistakable imprint.

Marc and Brittney had shared this bed.

It stood now as they'd left it. That was Brittney's crimson lace on the floor, Marc's new watch by the bed. Standing at the scene of her husband's betrayal, faced with evidence of what he'd done, felt very different than accepting a vague idea of it. Seeing it laid before her was a gut punch that no amount of steady breathing could soften. And this time Jill didn't try. She left the room and stumbled down the stairs toward the garage and the safety of her car—her own car. There, she allowed the tears to come unchecked, mourning a man she'd loved with her whole heart. Letting go of a life she'd thought was perfect.

After a long time, she made a place for herself in the back seat, using a sweater for a pillow and a jacket for a blanket, because she refused to sleep in that house.

Chapter 14

Jill woke the following morning, her head groggy and her body cramped from the night spent in the back of her car. But she woke with purpose—her only goal was a strong cup of coffee and a completed to-do list. If she'd learned anything from the lost weekends on the couch watching home shows with Ellie, it was that staged houses sold faster than empty ones. Most of the tasks ahead of her would be mindless—piling fluffy towels in the bathrooms or plumping pillows on the guest-room beds. And if she could find them, scented candles on the dining table and a bowl of green apples in the kitchen.

At some point, the master bedroom would need to be addressed, because she couldn't leave it that way, but she couldn't face it now. The main job she dreaded was hauling the outdoor furniture down from the storage racks and dragging it up to the deck. Everything was wrapped in plastic and stacked together like Tetris pieces so it would be difficult, physical work. But that was too much to even think about before coffee, so Jill headed back into the house.

She left the garage, entered the house, and froze. She'd forgotten to close the curtains the night before and was rewarded with a magnificent sunrise. A pallet of watercolor pinks and blues washed across the horizon, and soft morning light spilled into the living room. The ocean turned a deep purple-blue as the light changed and the waves calmly rolled toward the shore.

Jill stood rooted to the spot, gazing at the sea, completely captivated.

Someday she would have her own cottage by the ocean, and it would be a modest house like Aunt Sarah and Uncle Barney's. She'd spend her mornings puttering in the flower garden, with a sassy gray cat by her side. At the end of the day, she'd sit on an Adirondack chair angled toward the sea and watch the light fade. And she'd be happy.

But that dream was years away and might never happen at all if Jill didn't get to work. So she did. She vacuumed the rugs and mopped the floors, though neither seemed to need it. She made the beds, readied the bathrooms, but left the master for later. By noon, she'd finished folding the last towel and decided it was time for a break. The heavy teak furniture could stay where it was for now. She grabbed a baseball hat and sunglasses and headed for the beach.

At the bottom of the beach stairs, Jill slipped off her shoes and dug her toes into the sand, pushing past the soft surface to find the coolness underneath. She rolled the cuffs of her jeans to her knee and continued to the water, feeling the satisfying give of the sand under her feet. This was a perfect fall day, blue sky and clear sun, a bit colder than it had appeared from inside the house. Though the midday sun shone as brightly as it could, a chilly breeze swept in from the ocean.

Jill slipped on her sunglasses and turned toward the surf. On the off-season, especially this close to Halloween, Jill had expected the beach in this town to be deserted, but she was mistaken. It was true that it was different than it had been in August—the water wasn't packed with swimmers, and the beach wasn't strewn with towels or anchored with billowing umbrellas—but there was still activity. Near the water, two men walked along the tideline, one of them with a toddler perched happily on his shoulders. An older couple rested on a bench by the dunes, leaning into each other with a comfortable ease that comes from a long and happy marriage. Further ahead, a dog chased a driftwood stick into the waves, emerging a few minutes later with his prize, dripping and satisfied. And finally, in the tidepool near the jetty, a sandpiper played tag with the incoming tide.

Jill breathed in the heady scent of the ocean and watched the wind lift the water into white caps. She saw a trio of surfers in wetsuits straddle their boards beyond the breaking waves and idly wondered if they were cold.

It really was beautiful here. And while it was true that Jill didn't like Marc's house, she hoped that whoever bought it would appreciate the beauty of their surroundings.

She turned to look at the house he'd constructed. One of its features was its unobstructed view of the water from almost every room. It was definitely a selling point and one of the things she planned to highlight at the listing meeting. Staring at the house now, she noticed for the first time how close the structure was to the property line. It hugged the dunes while the houses on either side—and along the beach—remained a respectful distance behind. Startled, Jill saw what the placement of Marc's house meant for neighbors on either side: while he was rewarded with a sweeping ocean panorama, they were restricted to only a sliver of the ocean and a full view of Marc's house.

"What a horrible thing to do." Jill glared at what Marc had created. "What an *awful* house."

"I'll say it is." The voice came from beside Jill. "Everyone in town hates that house."

Jill turned to see a woman standing next to her with a glare that matched Jill's. An older woman, she had an apple-round face with pinked cheeks and was dressed for walking the beach. A brightly printed scarf, secured firmly under her chin, protected her hair from ocean gusts. The woman's windbreaker pockets were lumpy with beach finds and Jill smiled at a memory. When Jill was younger, she and her cousins had orbited Aunt Sarah on evening beach walks, darting away to gather fragments of shells, slivers of driftwood, or nuggets of sea glass, then running back to share their treasures. No matter what they found, Aunt Sarah would marvel, then fold it into a tissue for safekeeping and slip it into her pocket to bring home. Jill wondered if the woman before her was gathering things for her own grandchildren.

"Is that right?" Jill asked, almost afraid to hear the answer.

"You better believe it. You see that house over there? The little one?" She gestured to the house next door—a sweet little cottage overshadowed by Marc's. In the yard, a woman in a wide-brimmed hat stood before a spindly tree.

"Yes, sure I do."

"Nancy Pellish lives there. That's her with the pruning shears—again." The woman's lips formed a tight frown. "She's been trying for years to save that plum tree and it's not going well." She sighed as she shook her head. "Her grandfather brought that tree over from Italy and planted it in the yard to remind him of home. He tended it for years and it grew lush and tall. Every fall, he'd share the harvest with neighbors and friends—he even tried his hand at plum wine one year."

"That must have been fun," Jill offered.

"It wasn't." The woman grimaced. "The poor man didn't know the first thing about making wine—could have given us all brain damage. Anyway, my point is that it used to be a magnificent tree, substantial, you know? Now look at it." The woman tutted. "Nancy's tried every-thing—special fertilizer, pruning, staking—even hired a specialist to come out, but nothing helps. She's going to lose that tree."

"Is it sick?" Jill asked.

"It's not sick. It needs sun," the woman replied simply.

Jill looked again and understood what the woman meant. The neighbor's garden—the majority of her side yard, in fact—was cast in shade, overshadowed by the structure of Marc's house.

"Folks around here call that thing 'The Monstrosity,'" the woman continued. "And we've been complaining about it for years."

"Complaining about this house?" The news was surprising and not in a good way. "Complaining to who?"

"Anyone who'll listen. Not that it's made any difference, mind." The woman's frown deepened. "We even filed a petition once, with some state agency. Dick and Nancy Pellish were the ones who started it. Dick's an attorney, so he drew it up. Nancy was charged with gathering the signatures and she collected quite a few, I'm told. But in the end, nothing came of it."

Jill groaned. Petitions would surely influence a house sale and not in a good way.

The woman misunderstood Jill's groan as one of solidarity. Bolstered, she continued her story. "I was there the day the new foundation was poured, you know. Two houses stood on this lot, both destroyed by the hurricane. The man who built this house stole them both."

"That sounds terrible." Jill hoped the woman was exaggerating.

"Oh, it was. We were in such a state after the hurricane. You can't imagine the chaos."

"The hurricane? Do you mean Hurricane Sandy?" Jill had a vague memory of watching the news coverage. "That was so long ago."

"November of 2012." The woman's expression faded. "Years by the calendar maybe, but not so long ago in memory. Many of us residents are still recovering. The storm's destruction was physical and lasted less than a week, but what came after lasted much longer and ripped our hearts out." She narrowed her eyes and glared at what Marc had built. "That house right there is plunder. The man who built it was a pirate, all there is to it."

"You mean it was illegally built?" Jill held her breath, awaiting the answer.

"No, it was legal." The woman scoffed. "But legal and moral can be two very different things. That house would never have been allowed to go up if Hurricane Sandy hadn't come along. That man took advantage of a terrible situation. Of course the planning commission should have stopped it, but they didn't."

"Why not?" Jill asked. "Why didn't they stop it?"

"It's a long story and not a pleasant one." Abruptly, the woman shook off the memories and her mood lightened, like a sunbeam peaking from behind a storm cloud. "Oh, listen to me go on like we both have nothing better to do. The day's too nice to talk about all that." The corners of the woman's eyes crinkled as she smiled. "Here I am talking your head off, and we haven't even been introduced. My name is Betty Grable." She dropped her voice and her cheeks dimpled as she grinned. "No relation to the movie star, though I have been told the resemblance between us was remarkable, especially in my younger days."

"It's nice to meet you," Jill said, laughing. "I'm Jill G—" She stumbled a bit on her new name but recovered in time. "Jill DiFiore."

The woman tilted her head as she considered. "Don't believe I know a DiFiore. Are you new in town or are you visiting?"

"I'm visiting, just for a little while. I'm a photographer. The scenery here is beautiful."

"I believe you picked the best time of year to come. Dewberry Beach is at her best in the fall if I say so myself. Much less crowded. A person can breathe in the off-season." Betty nodded, good humor restored. "I'll let you get to it then. You don't want to waste a day as beautiful as this chattering with an old woman. Go—enjoy the scenery."

They said their goodbyes and the woman continued her walk.

Suddenly the idea of immersing herself in the sights of the shore was too compelling to put off. She'd done enough. Everything else could wait. This light would not. She paused a moment to make sure no one was watching. Then she ran up the beach stairs and slipped into the house to retrieve her camera.

Within a few minutes she was outside again. As the autumn breeze drifted up from the ocean, Jill closed her eyes to breathe in and she was transported to Aunt Sarah and Uncle Barney's house. The best summers of her life had been spent there, without a worry in the world. She could spend whole days on a lounge chair outside, lost in the pages of a book. Afternoons were spent on the screen porch with Uncle Barney listening to approaching thunderstorms and guessing how far off they were. At night there was camping in a backyard tent with cousins, and flashlights, and ghost stories. Jill remembered blankets of fireflies at night and itchy mosquito bites beneath sunburned skin.

The same briny scent laced the air in Dewberry Beach, but this time of year it was threaded with woodsmoke and the snap of fall. She zipped her jacket, shouldered her camera case, and made her way to the dunes. There, she found clusters of wild roses growing in a sheltered corner of the beach stairs. Jill readied her camera and started to work, experimenting first with texture and then with color, framing shots of crimson rose hips against sugary sand. She kneeled to capture the delicate petals of the last remaining rose flower against a backdrop of splintery wooden stairs, then wandered to the tidepools near the jetty. There, she photographed grumpy hermit crabs defending their shell homes with their tiny claws raised, and seagulls scavenging through clam shells. And when the angle of the sun changed, she switched to a telephoto lens to capture the curl of a perfect wave as it reached for shore.

She would have happily spent all day behind her camera. The sky was the bluest she'd ever seen it, and the rumble of the ocean filled her soul. There was so much to photograph—the wispy beach grass, the play of light against the ocean, the determined sandpiper by the jetty. But of course she couldn't—there was still work to do at the house before tomorrow's meeting and she had to get going. She gathered her things and packed them away, intending to return to work, but her stomach growled, reminding her that the only food in the house was unappetizing leftovers in the caterer's pantry. She'd had enough of that. It was time for real food. Jill turned away from the house and headed into town to find lunch.

The shops in Dewberry Beach were a few blocks from the beach, and all of them had been decorated for Halloween. There were bright orange pumpkins carved with triangle eyes and snaggle-toothed grins displayed at the entrances, bundles of dried cornstalks tied to the light poles, and a banner stretched across the street advertising an upcoming fall festival. The town itself was small, with less than a dozen shops, and only a handful of those were open. In the center of town was a bakery that seemed to be doing a brisk business. Next to that was a tiny newsstand with its door propped open. Across the street was a firehouse next to a wide grassy field.

About a block or so before the fire station was a sandwich shop that looked interesting. It was a small cedar building with a few tables set on a patio and a sturdy overhead sign that read "Dewberry Deli," and Jill was drawn in by the smell of fresh bread, oregano, and garlic. Her stomach rumbled again, as if it could barely believe its good fortune. When was the last time she'd allowed herself to eat a real New Jersey sub? Years, probably. There was always a dress to fit into or an event to attend. Not anymore.

Inside, the shop was a hum of activity as customers placed their orders and the man at the counter scribbled them on a tiny pad. He ripped the page from his order pad and passed it across the counter in one fluid movement, as if he'd performed the same action a million times before. On the back wall were wire baskets filled with crusty Italian bread, and above that was a three-panel chalkboard that served as a menu. Jill bit back a smile as she noticed the chalk had faded in places, making many of the selections almost unreadable. It seemed to Jill that customers either ordered from memory or they ignored the menu completely, ordering whatever they felt like.

As Jill waited for her number to be called, she turned her attention to the display case in the front of that shop. It was beautiful, with a gently curving glass front, soft wood trim, and white enameled shelves. Inside the case was food reminiscent of Jill's childhood summers—bowls of pesto and peas, marinated peppers and mushrooms, spiced olives, Caprese salad with fat chunks of fresh mozzarella. Toward the end, where one might expect dessert, there was a simple sign in black print that read "Go to Mueller's."

Ellie would love this place.

"Fifteen." The man's eyes were sharp, but there was humor behind them, as if he were on the edge of laughter and, if asked, he just might share the joke with you.

"That's me." Jill held up her slip of paper as proof.

"What can I get ya?"

It had been a very long time since Jill had ordered a deli sub and she was out of practice. "Um. Turkey, please. With provolone. Do you have provolone?"

"'Course we do."

"Okay, then provolone too—but not a lot. Just a slice or maybe half a slice."

His brow creased in confusion. "You want half a slice of cheese?"

"Yes." Jill nodded firmly. "I do."

He sighed as he scribbled on his pad. "Half or whole?"

"Half. I just said."

"Sub. Do you want a whole or half sub?"

"Half. Definitely half. With vinegar only—no mayo—lettuce, tomato, peppers, black pepper, and oregano. And a pickle on the side if you have them."

The man's brow arched as if he were waiting for something.

"Please," Jill offered.

He laughed at that, deep and rumbling, and she smiled in return.

"What do you want for your side?" He gestured to the case filled with salads. "Pesto ziti and peas is fresh this morning. Marinated tomatoes, peppers, and mozzarella just put out. Feta with fresh oregano's coming if you want to wait for it."

"Oh, no thank you. Just a green salad please. No dressing." The choice was automatic, from years of dieting.

He looked up, frowning in confusion. Jill assumed he hadn't heard so she repeated herself, louder this time. "Green sal—"

"Yeah, I got it." The man's green eyes danced with mischief. "What's the matter, you don't want to try my nonna's food?"

"What?"

"My nonna." He pointed his stubby pencil toward the display case. "She makes all the salads."

"I'm sure they're very—"

"So you want to at least try the pesto?"

"No, I do not," Jill spluttered. Who did this guy think he was?"

"Tell ya what." He shrugged as he ripped the page from the pad. "I'll throw in the pesto, gratis. You come back and tell me if it's not the best *piatto* you ever had." He shifted his focus to the man filling orders. They looked similar and Jill assumed they were brothers. They had the same dark wavy hair, the same muscular build, the same cheekbones.

"Fine," Jill said, annoyed. She'd accept it, but she didn't have to eat it.

The man smiled as he turned. "Petey! Order up."

As she waited for her order, Jill wandered around the small shop. She eyed the rack of chips and browsed the cooler of drinks. She passed a side table with a collection of shakers filled with red pepper flakes, oregano, parm, and bottles of vinegar. In the back, near the door, was a bulletin board, tacked with a haphazard collection of notices. Most were old, offering babysitting services or surf lessons. The ink on some of them was so faded, the cards so layered that Jill wondered how many summers they'd been posted.

Just as she was about to turn away, a simple notice tacked to the corner of the board caught Jill's attention. Written on a recipe card in neat script, the ad made her breath catch.

Photographer wanted for fundraising project.
Minimal experience required.

Jill's pulse quickened. Photographers for any job were never hired without experience. Even with references, the best she'd ever managed was an assistant's job, loading film or memory cards and changing lenses. To be the one in charge? That never happened, certainly not without formal training.

"Do you know anything about this notice?" Jill turned to a young woman wiping the tables. "The photographer job?"

She shook her head. "I think it's been there for a while. You can take it if you want."

Jill tucked the card in her pocket as she collected her order from the front counter. Then she made her way to a table outside to enjoy her lunch in the crisp autumn air. The sandwich was delicious, perfectly made and even better than she remembered. Afterward, she crumpled the papers and rose from her chair.

As Jill returned her tray to the table by the front door, a thought occurred to her and she felt a smile spread across her face. Despite her initial feeling, she'd tried Nonna's pesto. The man behind the counter was right: it was the best she'd ever eaten.

Jill chose a more indirect route back to the house because she was distracted by the colors of fall leaves against the blue sky. She meandered, turning down one side street and then another just because they looked interesting. Before long, she'd taken out her camera and tucked the lens cap into her pocket. The work she'd done earlier that morning at the beach was good and she was pleased with the photos.

But it was time to widen her scope.

The town of Dewberry Beach was so small that there didn't seem much chance of getting lost, so Jill let herself wander, following the pull of curiosity. It was a glorious afternoon, and as she got swept up in her work, she felt the weight of uncertainty and worry slip from her shoulders. She followed a path across a narrow footbridge and spied a man helping his daughter free a tangle of crabs from a net. They were happy for her to take pictures, so she did. Her first photo showed the pride in the little girl's face as she held up her catch. The second captured water dripping from the net and spattering on the wood below. The third was a picture of them together, with the man's arm around her shoulders, the love clear on his face as he looked down at his daughter.

As the afternoon waned, the air cooled and the sun began its descent. It was clear that the chores she'd been putting off couldn't wait any longer. The house agents would be arriving early the following morning and she needed to be ready. It was time to make her way back.

Tucking away her camera, she returned to the main street, knowing she could find her way from there. At the corner, she came upon a white clapboard church and she stopped, captivated by its charm. She followed an oyster-shell-lined path around the building to a tiny courtyard garden with a stone bench beneath a shady tree. The last of the summer sunflowers grew against a picket fence, their heads bending under the weight of the seeds. Jill watched a clump of seagrass fronds sway and a moment later felt a gentle breeze brush across her face. Everything about this church was understated, except the stained-glass window just below the spire. A puzzle of deep red and vibrant blue, it was an unexpected pop of color in the simple building. She stood for a moment, watching the sunlight work its magic. The colored glass panels absorbed the afternoon sun, then cast it back across the sidewalk in a wash of purple.

It was the perfect ending to her day in Dewberry Beach, unexpected and surprising.

It was dark by the time Jill returned to the house, and her mood shifted. The teak deck furniture was much too heavy to pull down from overhead storage, no matter how hard she tried. After a few attempts, she abandoned the project and left tomorrow's appointment to fate. She pulled a blanket from a trunk and settled herself into a loveseat in a hidden alcove, lifted the window to feel the breeze, and pulled out her camera to review the images she'd taken that day. After a moment, she put the camera down, satisfied with the work she'd done.

As she listened to the roar of the waves and the last of the summer crickets, she closed her eyes and let herself drift off to sleep.

Chapter 15

The real-estate agents arrived exactly on time, in a sleek black Mercedes they parked in the circular driveway in front of the house. Their website said they specialized in upscale vacation properties for affluent clients. Their client reviews were good, and the number of houses they'd sold was respectable. All that was encouraging. But the reason Jill had selected them was because of the three firms she'd emailed, they were the only ones willing to meet with her right away. She hoped that would be lucky.

Jill greeted them at the front door, eager to get to work.

"You must be Jill DiFiore." The man wore a conservative dark suit, a crisp white shirt, and a tasteful paisley tie. As he extended his hand, Jill noticed the gold watch on his wrist, heavy and circled with tiny diamonds. Hopefully bought with commissions. "I'm Seth Ackerman."

"Yes, thank you for coming." Jill shook his hand. His grip was warm and reassuring, a good sign.

Seth turned to the woman beside him, who was wearing a simple black dress and blazer. She had a briefcase slung over her shoulder and a tablet in her hand, ready to get started. "This is my associate, Sheri Kessler."

"Hello, Sheri." Jill smiled. "Please come in."

"Great house." Seth's gaze swept the dramatic front entry, the two-story window above the wide front doors, the blue-slate flooring, and the original Picone on the opposite wall.

"Thanks. Let me show you the rest." Jill led them through the foyer into the main part of the house. She'd opened the drapes on the far wall to showcase the view. Everything inside the house—the bleached hardwood floors, taupe area rugs, and low beige furnishings—was designed to fade into the background so all the focus would be the sweeping view of the ocean. And it worked—today especially, the view was undeniably magnificent. Nothing but sandy beach, dancing ocean, the endless horizon.

Seth stopped to take it all in. Even Sheri stopped tapping on her tablet long enough to look. It was a good decision, opening all the drapes to show that view. That view would sell this house. Hopefully soon.

"Wow," Seth said finally. "I did not expect that." His voice faded as he absorbed it, and Jill let him. The more he liked it, the harder he'd work to sell it. Finally, after clearing his throat, he said, "Your email said you wanted to sell quickly?"

"I do."

"I just might have a client in mind." Seth brushed his palm across his chin as he considered. "They're looking for something further north but might consider coming down this way, if only for this view."

"It's pretty spectacular," Sheri agreed.

"Do you mind if we start upstairs?" Seth asked as Sheri set down her briefcase. "A quick look around before we talk specifics."

"Of course. Go on up." Jill swept her hand through the air, happy that they hadn't asked her to join them. She'd been upstairs exactly twice since her arrival, both times to stage the bedrooms, and both times had been painful. Jill would not force herself to go up there again. "The door leading to the rooftop deck is at the end of the short hallway."

Forty-five minutes later, Seth and Sheri descended the stairs, Seth dictating notes and observations to Sheri, who scribbled on the tablet as she trailed behind.

Seth whistled. "This is some house, upstairs and down. And the rooftop deck is perfect for private parties. At least, that's what I told Marc anyway."

Jill startled, convinced she'd misheard. "I'm sorry, did you say, 'that's what I told Marc'?"

"Yes," Seth confirmed. "Your husband contacted me a couple of times to ask my opinion about selling this house. I'm surprised he didn't mention it."

"So am I."

"I offered to sell it for him, years ago, but he wanted to handle it in-house."

Jill assumed "in-house" meant Brittney.

"Well then, what's your opinion on why this house hasn't sold?" Jill asked.

Seth shrugged. "Could be anything from not finding the right buyer to financing not lining up. Marc didn't tell me *why* he was having trouble, just that he was, so I dropped it."

Sheri interrupted. "I've finished entering notes. Only thing left is the kitchen and garage."

"Coming." Seth headed into the kitchen as Sheri settled into a chair close by.

"Ready?" he asked Sheri.

Sheri nodded, her stylus poised above the screen.

"Professional grade appliances. Ten burners, gas." His fingers grazed the stove as he walked past. He gestured to the tile behind it. "Hand-painted tile backsplash. Pot filler attachment on the wall. Warming oven below."

"You forgot the induction microwave underneath the island. It's a built-in." Sheri pointed to an appliance Jill had never used or seen used.

"Good catch." Seth paused to take several pictures with his cell phone. "Two dishwashers, a commercial refrigerator deep enough to handle party platters. This is all really good." He lowered his phone and turned to Jill. "All the appliances stay?"

"Yes," Jill answered. She couldn't imagine what she'd do with any of them.

"Okay. We can get model numbers later."

Seth opened a door and flicked on the wall switch. "Walk-in pantry with room for storage."

"There's another storage room down that hallway," Jill offered. "Caterers use it to store platters, dishes, and party food."

"Excellent. Clients love extra storage." Seth glanced at Sheri. "Make a note of that please."

His voice rose as he continued down the hallway. He tapped on the door to the garage. "Attached garage. We saw it on the way in. Two-car?" He paused for confirmation.

"Three," Jill corrected. "One spot is tandem. And there's overhead storage across all three."

"Even better." Seth joined them and took a seat. "We should position this house as more than just a summer home..." His voice trailed off as he thought. "Are you planning to sell it furnished?"

"Yes." A designer in New York had selected everything in this house from websites. The contents were lovely, and expensive, but Jill had no use for or attachment to any of it. "They can have anything they want. Furniture, linens, towels, wine in the rack and food in the pantry—"

"I get it." Seth laughed as he held up his hand in mock surrender. "We'll get a full inventory later. Right now, a broad picture is fine. The client I have in mind is looking for move-in ready, so selling it furnished would definitely be a plus." He leaned back in his chair. "If you're ready to list with me, let's draw it up. I'll call my client from the car on the drive back and I'll let you know what he says."

Jill pretended to consider it, though there wasn't much choice. None of the other agents she'd contacted had even bothered to respond to her inquiry. So it was fortunate for her that Seth seemed like he knew what he was doing.

"What about pricing?" Seth folded his hands on the table. "Do you have a number in mind?"

Enough to clear the mortgage, Jill thought, but she didn't want to appear desperate. Instead, she said, "I'd like to know what you think."

"Okay." He pulled a report from his bag and showed it to Jill. "After you called, I did some preliminary research, pulling comparables from the area. This house is unusual for the location, more in line with inventory much further north, like the Hamptons."

She'd done her own research and Seth's report confirmed her findings: this house didn't belong in a sleepy town like Dewberry Beach. They studied Seth's report, arriving at a price that would attract a larger pool of buyers. Still, the number was high compared to neighborhood homes.

"Selling it quickly is more important to me than making a huge profit," Jill told him. "Should we go lower?"

"Believe it or not, if I list it any lower, buyers will think there's something wrong with it and they'll stay away," Seth said. "I've seen it before. So no, I don't think so."

Jill glanced at the listing price again. It was more money than she had ever seen before, but the mortgage would take up most of it. So Jill signed the listing.

A few hours after they'd arrived, their business was concluded, and Jill's house was listed.

"Your neighbors," Seth asked as he and Sheri rose to pack up their things. "What do they think about this house?"

"What do they think of it?" Jill echoed.

"Dewberry Beach is a small town," Seth pointed out as he shouldered his bag. "We both know this house is a bit… large for the neighborhood. I'm just wondering if you've heard anything or know their feelings toward it?"

"One disgruntled neighbor can destroy a closing, especially if they're well connected to local politicians," Sheri added. "Remember that property over in Sag Harbor? How hard it was to close? We had to get court approval for everything, even the inspection. Added months to the closing."

"I remember," Seth groaned. "That was awful. Just a few vocal neighbors can scare off buyers who don't want trouble. We almost lost that Sag Harbor sale entirely." He straightened as they headed for the door. "But let's not get ahead of ourselves. This is a great house and you've offered it at a bargain price. It should go quickly."

After they left, Jill let out a breath she hadn't realized she'd been holding. It was true that this house was wildly out of scale compared to those around it and probably shouldn't have been built at all. But the time to object was before it was built, not before it was sold. For whatever reason, the town had allowed Marc to build this house, and its residents had no right to complain about a change of ownership afterward.

Their dispute was with Marc, not with her.

Chapter 16

It was time to leave Dewberry Beach.

With the listing agreement signed and the house properly staged, there was nothing to keep her here. Jill blew out the scented candle, straightened the chairs, and gathered the green apples from the bowl. She made her way upstairs, closing the windows and drawing the shades as she went. She'd leave the quilts on the beds and the towels in the bathrooms, figuring the house would show better that way. Securing a listing with an agent was a huge step forward, and Seth's comments about having a buyer already in mind lifted much of the worry from her shoulders.

On impulse, she grabbed a towel and headed for one of the guest rooms. She would celebrate with a long, hot shower and a fresh change of clothes. Afterward, she felt more like herself. The next step was to find a job, so on her way out of town, she planned to telephone temp agencies from her car to follow up on leads. As Jill stuffed her dirty clothes back into her suitcase, she felt something in a jeans pocket and remembered the card she'd taken from the bulletin board at the deli. She dug it out and smoothed away the creases, reading the notice again.

It was probably nothing. Or, if it wasn't nothing, the job had probably been filled already.

But what if it hadn't? What if they were still looking for someone? What an opportunity that would be.

Jill stood and stared at the card, wondering if she should call—just to see. Her cell phone chirped to signal an incoming email. She pulled it from her pocket and unlocked the screen, uneasy to see two separate messages from the bank that serviced her mortgage.

Dear Customer,

This letter is to inform you that, per your request, we have made a change to your account. If you did not authorize this change, please contact us immediately.

That one was no big deal. The judge had helped Jill change her name from Goodman to DiFiore, and Phyllis had helped her file the paperwork with the bank.

She skimmed the second email with a renewed sense of dread.

Dear Ms. DiFiore,

This letter is to inform you that property taxes are due on October 30 for the property you hold in Dewberry Beach. Please be advised the tax amount may have changed from the previous year. If you have already paid, please forward a receipt to us showing payment. If you intend us to pay them as part of your mortgage, please contact us for instructions about depositing additional funds to cover the payment.

Jill dropped into a chair… property taxes. She hadn't considered property taxes. She hadn't realized she needed to, and the amount was substantial. After arbitration, Jill had pulled together every dollar she had, and the budget left no room for surprises. Property taxes were definitely a surprise. Jill's mind raced as she swapped one expense for another and still came up short. Selling her car or trading it in for something cheaper was a possibility; she'd look into it. One thing was clear: she had to find a job right away and that meant leaving Dewberry Beach.

So, as intriguing as it was, the photographer job was not meant to be. Disappointed, Jill stuffed the card back into her pocket and finished packing. She'd just zipped her suitcase shut when her cell phone rang. She flicked on the screen and smiled when she saw it was Ellie.

"Ellie, hey," Jill answered. "Is the wedding over already?"

"Nope. I'm on break. I'm calling because I needed to talk to someone normal, Jilly. Rich people are so weird—completely out of touch. You won't believe the things I've seen in only a couple of days." Ellie groaned. "But I can tell you all about it later. Right now, tell me about you. What's going on down there?"

"Well." Jill pushed her suitcase aside and sat on the edge of the guest bed. "The property agents just left so that's something."

"Oh yeah? How did that go?"

"I liked them. I signed the listing and the guy said he's already got a client in mind, so I'm hopeful."

"That's great." Ellie hesitated, clearly not buying Jill's forced enthusiasm. "So why don't you sound happier?"

"Oh, I am," Jill said quickly. "I really am. It's just that…" Jill pulled the index card from her pocket and stared at the print. She shouldn't even be considering this. She needed to find a job and quickly. The house, the mortgage, the property taxes—when she thought about the amounts involved, she could barely draw a full breath. But there was also a tug of possibility, a whisper that she didn't want to ignore. It reminded her of photography classes and workshops, and how much she loved her work.

So, yes, she had financial obligations, but didn't she owe herself something too? Something beyond money?

"This is crazy, but I found a help-wanted ad for a photographer tacked to a community bulletin board and I really want to call. I'm not even sure it's a real job but I can't leave without knowing. What do you think? Does that sound terrible?"

"Depends. What does it look like?"

"Well." Jill turned the grubby card over in her hand. "It's handwritten on an index card so it's probably not a scam. It was left in a deli down here."

"Down there? You mean in Dewberry Beach?" Ellie snorted. "Oh, please. The way you talked, I thought you might have found a notice at a rest-stop on I95. Dewberry Beach is like Cape May. What's the job?"

"They want a photographer to help with a fundraiser—a lead photographer, not an assistant, which is a really big deal. There's not a lot of detail—not any, really—just a phone number and that one sentence." Jill turned the card over again. "What's interesting is that it says 'minimal experience required.' I've never seen a job posting like that, not ever."

"Have you called the number?"

"I've been busy with house stuff," Jill began, but Ellie cut her off.

"Definitely call," she urged. "At least then you'll know. It might be nothing, or it might be great. You won't know until you call."

Jill knew that the responsible thing was to throw away the card and forget about the job. To drive back to Ellie's, sell her car, and pay the property taxes. And yet. Opportunities like this didn't come along every day. In fact, they didn't *ever* come along.

"You there?" Ellie's voice pulled Jill from her thoughts.

"Yes, sorry. I'm here."

"Call the number. See what they say. Maybe it's the real deal."

"You're right." Jill straightened. "Of course you're right. I'll call them now."

"If anything about the interview location sounds sketchy, text me before you interview. I'll watch the dot."

Jill laughed at the absurd idea of sharing her live location in a town like Dewberry. "I think I'll be okay."

"That's the spirit," Ellie replied. "I gotta get back to work. Lemme know what happens."

"Absolutely. I'll call you later."

After she hung up, Jill dialed the number printed on the card.

"Hello, Grable Inn."

"Hi. I'm calling about the help-wanted card you posted in the Dewberry Deli. About a photographer for a fundraiser?" Jill winced at how immature she sounded, so she cleared her throat and added, "I'm calling to see if the job is still available."

"Are you? That's wonderful." The woman muffled the phone as she called to someone else in the room, "I *told* you girls putting a card in Danny's place would work." Returning her attention to Jill, she said, "I'm so glad you've called. Your timing is perfect; we're meeting right now, in fact, to discuss the fundraiser. Are you free to come over?"

"Um, sure." Jill fumbled for a pen. "Where are you?"

"We're meeting here at the Grable Inn. Are you familiar with Dewberry Beach?"

"Um, a bit. If you give me the address, I can find it."

Jill scribbled down the address and said she would leave right away. The woman promised they'd hold the important parts of the meeting until she arrived, which Jill took as a good sign. On her way out, Jill grabbed her portfolio from the car. The last time she had opened this portfolio was to show her work at the Brockhurst mansion, a lifetime ago. The smudged bridal portrait had not been well received and Jill had briefly considered removing it altogether. But she was proud of the work she'd done in Brooklyn that day and proud of the grade she'd received on the project, so she'd left it in.

She slipped out the side door, careful again not to be seen, and followed her phone's directions to the Grable Inn.

Chapter 17

The Grable Inn was one of Dewberry Beach's older homes, built at the turn of the century far from the oppressive heat of the city. It was a grand Victorian that reminded Jill of a gingerbread house, with its rounded tower, intricate scrollwork, multi-paned windows, and a fat pelican weathervane firmly planted atop the pitched roof. Just inside the white picket fence, a sign welcomed guests, and a slider board below advertised a current vacancy. As Jill unlatched the gate, she noticed a thread of rose vines between the fence slats. The fall weather had taken the flowers, leaving behind only the rose hips, and the contrast between the crimson-colored berries and the white fence was striking, and Jill wondered about the woman who lived inside.

As she followed the path to the front door, she caught the scent of freshly turned earth and noticed a bed of deep orange chrysanthemums planted nearby. On the front porch was a scarecrow dressed in overalls and gardening boots, with a thatch of straw hair under a wide-brimmed hat. He was positioned on a chair, overseeing the garden as if he'd done the work himself, and Jill laughed. Surely someone who'd put together something like that wouldn't question why Jill hadn't graduated with an art degree, as Mrs. Brockhurst had.

Just as she was about to ring the doorbell, the front porch light flicked on. An older woman bustled to the screen door and pushed it open, her face wreathed in a smile. Jill's own smile faded when she recognized her as the woman she'd met the day before, on the beach. The one who'd called Marc's house The Monstrosity, said it never should have been built, and mentioned petitions. What would she do if she knew Jill owned that house?

"You must be the photographer who called?" The woman pushed the door open. "Welcome."

"I am." Jill steeled herself as she went inside. Despite the uneasy start, it felt good to be recognized as "the photographer" instead of "the assistant" or "the temp." She wanted this job, and how hard could it be to keep herself anonymous? She extended her hand, in a show of confidence. "I'm Jill DiFiore."

"I'm Betty Grable. It's lovely to meet you, dear." As the woman clasped both of Jill's hands in hers, her eyes narrowed. After a moment, she spoke again. "We've met before."

"We have. Yesterday on the beach."

"Oh, that awful house." She tutted. "I remember now." Then she frowned and lifted her shoulder in a gentle shrug, as if the house was her fault. "Of course, that thing has nothing to do with you, and since we agree on its awfulness, there's nothing more to be said. Let's not spoil a new friendship." She planted her hands firmly on her hips. "It's nice to meet you properly, Ms. DiFiore. May I take your coat?"

"Thank you. But please call me Jill."

As Betty turned away to hang her coat, Jill felt herself relax. The front room was warm and smelled faintly of lemon furniture polish and cinnamon. Two cozy chairs had been placed on either side of the hearth, with a well-loved couch and a sturdy coffee table in between.

A colorful crocheted afghan had been folded neatly and draped over the back, and a selection of magazines were carefully fanned on the coffee table. Looking closer, Jill saw that all the magazines were about gardening. The accompanying newspaper was a slim local one called the *Dewberry Beach Trumpet.*

"Are you a gardener?" Jill lifted her gaze from the coffee table to the woman. "I noticed your rose vines outside on the fence. The rose hips are beautiful, and the flowers must have been glorious in bloom."

"Oh, they were!" Betty clasped her hands together in delight as her smile widened. "That rose vine is very special to me. It was the first thing I planted when I bought this house forty years ago. Since then, the plant's been dug up and re-homed—oh, I don't know—half a dozen times. I think it prefers the trellis instead of the fence, truth be told, but the trellis is being repaired at the moment—our salty sea air gets to everything—so we trained it against the fence. The funniest thing is, it was Brad, Kaye's son—you'll meet Kaye in a minute—who suggested training the vine around the fence slats while he rebuilds the trellis. The boy's a wonder with gardens."

Gardeners universally share an enthusiasm for happy plants, and Betty's chatter made Jill smile. Aunt Sarah had been a gardener too, and Jill remembered how easily she and her garden club friends could while away an entire afternoon discussing the perfect plants for a summer bed. It made Jill happy to imagine how much Aunt Sarah would have liked Betty.

"But never mind that." Betty flapped her hands in the air as she realized she'd gotten off track. "As I said on the phone, your call was perfectly timed. We've kept everything warm for you. Well, the tea has gone cold, but the spice cake is still warm. Come back and meet the girls. We'll tell you all about the project we need help on."

Betty ushered Jill to a snug kitchen where a group of four older ladies sat around a chunky wooden table. In the center was a quaint tea service placed atop a white lace doily, and a tumble of plates and napkins and forks were piled next to a warm cake. The smell of nutmeg and molasses filled the room and Jill breathed it in, remembering Aunt Sarah's tiny blue kitchen. As they made room for Jill, in the hubbub of scooting chairs and bringing out an extra placemat, she had a moment to look at the women gathered at the table. They ranged in age, Jill estimated, from fifties to eighties, with an easy camaraderie that suggested their friendship was unwavering. They chose to meet at the kitchen table and welcomed Jill as if she were part of the group already, just what Aunt Sarah would have done—and that was a good sign.

Already the experience was very different from the Brockhurst interview.

"Ladies, this is Jill DiFiore, the photographer," Betty announced.

There was that title again. Jill felt a flicker of pride.

"Jill, this is Mrs. Ivey." Betty started her introduction with the most senior member of the group. Seated at the head of the table, Mrs. Ivey reminded Jill of her first-grade teacher, a woman who had the power to silence a noisy classroom with a frown and comfort a child with a kind word. She wore a cardigan over a printed dress, as Jill's teacher had, though Mrs. Ivey was quite a bit older.

"It's nice to meet you," Jill offered.

The woman's gaze sharpened, as if she may have recognized Jill. Which of course was impossible. Marc had discouraged her from mixing with the locals at Dewberry, so she never did. She was confident that nobody in Dewberry Beach would know who she was.

"Mrs. Ivey works with the town to get us what we need for the festival. Securing permits, blocking off the streets, setting up first aid stations: all of it," Betty continued. "There's no one better placed to navigate the bureaucracy of local government, even in a town as small as Dewberry."

"I was a middle school English teacher for many years and that comes with certain privileges." Mrs. Ivey's voice sounded haughty, but her blue eyes twinkled with unmistakable mischief.

"Most of the town council were students of yours. I hear they're still afraid of you," one of the women teased as she reached for a plate. Tall and thin, she wore a sensible knit cardigan, and her short brown hair was swept off her face and held back with tortoiseshell clips. "Remember that council meeting you busted in on last year? It was supposed to be closed-door, but no one dared to bar you from it."

"And this is Kaye," Betty interrupted with a laugh. "Kaye will always tell you what she thinks, and we love her for it."

"Nonsense," Mrs. Ivey addressed Kaye, as if Betty hadn't spoken. "The only students who had reason to be concerned were the ones who neglected their work." Mrs. Ivey's expression suggested suppressed laughter, as if she were in on the joke.

The woman seated next to Kaye spoke up. "The fact that everyone in town—*without exception*—still calls you 'Mrs. Ivey' says something, don't you think?" The woman turned her attention to Jill. "I'm Brenda, by the way. It's nice to meet you."

Jill liked Brenda immediately. She radiated an easy confidence, as if she were happy with the world and content with her place in it. She wore a black turtleneck sweater over baggy jeans, and her long dark hair was swept into a bright scarf knotted behind her ear. But it was her necklace that utterly captivated Jill, an intricate mix of turquoise nuggets and silver balls, threaded on delicate silver wire and woven loosely together. The pattern of blue and silver absorbed and reflected the light as she moved, an effect that proved all the more striking against her black sweater.

Betty must have noticed Jill's gaze. "Brenda is our resident artist."

A kettle whistled on the stove and Betty rose from her chair to see to it. "More hot tea in a moment, ladies," she called over her shoulder.

"Brenda's in charge of artist submissions for the auction on Friday," Kaye said, picking up the introduction. "She was the one who pushed us to start an amateur show too, and that's been very successful." Kaye stifled a smile. "And her most recent contribution was the open call for a crafts table."

"Don't remind me." Brenda rolled her eyes and groaned. "The painted-shell people."

"Who are the shell people?" Jill asked as she noticed Mrs. Ivey shudder good-naturedly.

Kaye reached for Brenda's arm and squeezed. "Year before last, we all had the idea to expand the festival. We wanted to make the art gallery more accessible to emerging artists in the area, the ones who had no other place to show their work. Sounds like a good idea, right?"

Jill nodded.

"What we wanted was a mix of fine art and handmade crafts."

Brenda sighed as she sagged against her chair. "That's not what we got."

"What we *actually* got," Kaye snorted, "was an avalanche of bleached shells—glittered, painted, and hot-glued to everything from beer can airplanes to wicker picture frames."

Betty called from the sink as she filled the kettle, "Wasn't that the year Mrs. Ivey arranged for local news coverage to promote the festival?"

"Now, now," Mrs. Ivey cut in. "The idea of a place for local artists to show their work is very good. I hope we haven't given up on that."

"We haven't. I still think it's a good idea." Brenda leaned toward Kaye and bumped her with her shoulder, her expression affectionate. "Next time we'll ask them what they plan to sell. You can be in charge of that."

As they chatted and got to know each other, the conversation flowed along with the tea. The sound of laughter filled Betty's small kitchen. Jill leaned into the warmth of their group and wondered what it would be like to count these women as friends.

Betty added, "Don't forget that it was your idea, Kaye, to put the art auction online so people outside Dewberry Beach can participate. That decision alone doubled our profits, three years running." Betty turned to Jill. "Kaye's son-in-law, Ryan, does all the technical stuff. He's a wizard—he sets up the website and does live updates during festival weekend." Then her voice softened as she flicked her gaze to Kaye. "And Kaye's daughter, Stacy, just had another baby girl."

The tea made, Betty brought a tray to the table. On it was a fresh teapot with a matching mug for Jill. Both were so unusual in shape and color that they had to be handcrafted. The round base of the mug was designed to nestle into the palm of your hand, and the wide handle could be lifted easily, even with gloved or mittened fingers. Perfect for fall evenings beside a fire pit.

"Those are beautiful," Jill commented.

"Our Brenda is very talented," Betty said, as pleased as if she'd made them herself. "She made the entire set. I only bring it out for very special occasions."

"Enough about *my* work." Brenda swished her hand through the air, pressing for a change of topic. "Did you happen to bring examples of yours?" Her gaze flicked to Jill's portfolio. "I know we said no experience necessary, but I'd be interested in seeing whatever you brought."

"Yes, of course." Jill retrieved her case and passed it to Brenda.

Jill watched Brenda unzip her portfolio and leaf through her photographs, holding her breath when Brenda slowed. Once or twice, Brenda paused to look at an image then murmur softly before turning the page. When she came to the final page, the bridal portrait taken in the Brooklyn warehouse, she stopped altogether. Lifting her gaze to meet Jill's, her expression changed, to one that looked very much like surprise.

"Tell me about this one." Brenda's fingertips tapped the brickwork behind the bridal veil. "Have you ever shown it?"

"Shown it?"

"Formally." Brenda passed the portfolio to Kaye, who also examined it. "I'm guessing from your reaction that the answer is no."

"N-No, of course not," Jill stuttered, unsure of what to say. "I… No."

"Ladies, as far as I'm concerned, Ms. DiFiore has my vote for the job," Betty interjected. "I was sure even before seeing these lovely photographs. This young lady dislikes The Monstrosity as much as we do."

Mrs. Ivey looked up from Jill's portfolio with a peculiar expression. "You don't say."

Jill hesitated, remembering what the real-estate agent had said about neighborhood goodwill. She wanted this job but *needed* to sell the house.

"It seems a bit out of proportion," Jill said firmly, "so, no. I don't like the house."

"The Goodman palace? Nobody likes that thing." Kaye frowned as she picked up the conversation. "Chase and I were invited to a party there this past August and we went, even though I *knew* we shouldn't have." Her frown deepened. "I'd made the mistake of hoping the invitation was a sign that the Goodmans had finally decided to mix with the rest of us—those who actually live here—but it wasn't. I didn't even meet the wife."

"Mix with us? Fat chance," Betty scoffed. "They've owned that house for years and I've never seen either of them in town. Not once. I hear they bring everything down from New York, even their weekly lawn maintenance crew. Pretty sure that's what drove Gerta's landscaping company out of business."

"Anyway," Kaye continued, clearly still annoyed about the party two months before. "No one from town was there, not even the Pellishes or the Murphys. Can you *imagine* throwing a party without inviting your next-door neighbors?"

Jill flinched as she realized that Kaye was Kaye *Bennett*, married to Chase Bennett, the man Marc had been hounding for years.

Chase had been a titan in the world of New York finance for almost thirty years. He'd founded a private consulting firm that was said to be the only honest voice in a maelstrom of opportunists. Presidents consulted him, newspapers cited his opinion as expert, and if a CEO was lucky enough to persuade Chase to sit on their board, the company was almost guaranteed success. His firm had a lengthy waiting list, and Marc had been trying to get on it for at least as long as he and Jill had been married, without success. Three years ago Chase had suffered a serious heart attack at his office and the doctors weren't sure he would ever fully recover. Eight months ago, newspapers reported that Mr. Bennett had sold his company and retired to his family's summer home in Dewberry Beach. Marc had been overjoyed at what he called a "perfect opportunity." The clambake party was planned soon afterward and somehow Marc had arranged for Chase to be there. But the Bennetts had left the party early and honestly, Jill didn't blame them. Marc could be relentless.

The good news was that Jill had never been formally introduced to either Kaye or Chase Bennett, so neither would be able to connect her to Marc's house. Still, it was better to be careful.

"Maybe we should save that discussion for another time?" Brenda proposed gently.

"You're right." Kaye shuddered, as if physically shedding an unpleasant memory. "Sorry. I guess it's still a sore subject."

The tension in the air dissolved and Jill lifted her gaze. She happened to glance at Mrs. Ivey and noticed the woman staring at her with the same quizzical look. As if she'd made the connection and knew exactly who Jill was. But of course, that was ridiculous—Jill had never met Mrs. Ivey before tonight.

"Ladies, shall we continue?" Brenda directed the conversation back to the festival. "The online art auction will be held on Friday evening. It draws a substantial crowd and is our biggest fundraiser. We need photographs of Dewberry Beach that will make you feel as if you're part of the community."

"Maybe something like this?" Jill reached for her camera. She pulled up the images she'd taken that day and showed them to Brenda.

Brenda nodded, her smile widening as she flicked through. "Yes. These are exactly what we need. We have more than enough summer pictures but nothing from fall or winter. Nothing from the off-season." She looked up, puzzled. "These are very good. Are they recent?"

"Yes. I've been in town for a bit and there's a lot to see," Jill explained. "I can transfer these pictures to an SD card if you want to use them."

Kaye set her mug on the placemat with a gentle thump. "We might be getting ahead of ourselves. Maybe now would be a good time to explain about the job, what we need, and what it pays. You might find that you don't want it."

"Good idea," Mrs. Ivey calmly announced, her gaze resting on Jill. "You should have all the facts before you make any big decisions."

Jill couldn't imagine being offered a lead photography job and not accepting, but she didn't want to appear overeager, so she agreed. "Yes, that's a good idea."

"The festival is called Light Up the Bay and it started years—no, decades—ago. To benefit the school…" Betty turned to Kaye. "It was Kaye's idea originally, so maybe she should explain."

"The idea may have started with me," Kaye objected gently, "but the execution was definitely a group effort. Years and years ago, the *Dewberry Beach Trumpet* ran a story about a public school not far from here that refused to serve meals to children who carried a negative balance on their account. Lower income children in that school system were served breakfast in the morning as well as lunch, so denying them both meals meant they were forced to go all day without eating. It was barbaric and completely unfair." Kaye frowned. "Between us, we collected enough to pay off many of the balances. But the following year it happened again. So we decided we needed a longer-term solution."

"We incorporated," Betty announced confidently.

"Not quite," Kaye corrected, reaching across the table to squeeze Betty's hand. "We're a non-profit. Chase helped with the filing and the financials. Then we all worked together to organize the fundraisers. For a long time we did a little of everything: raffles, bake sales, rummage sales. We auctioned off babysitting or dog-walking services—whatever we could think of—but our needs were always bigger than our proceeds."

She nudged Brenda with her shoulder. "And then this one here suggested an art auction." Kaye's smile widened. "We have quite a few local artists and Brenda is one of the best."

Brenda frowned, clearly uncomfortable with the praise, but Kaye reached for her arm. "I know for a fact that the pottery you donated was headed for the Tungsten Gallery in Manhattan. That made the news—local and regional."

Brenda laughed then. "Mrs. Ivey made sure it did."

Mrs. Ivey's eyes sparkled over the rim of her teacup. "One of my former students is a features producer at WABC in New York. She was delighted to help."

"That first year we raised enough money to pay off the children's overdue accounts," Kaye continued. "The next, we raised enough to pay for *all* meals for every kid in that school for the whole year."

"That's incredible," Jill said.

"It was, so we kept it going." Betty glanced at Kaye. "We have a few smaller fundraisers during the summer, but the biggest of the year by far is Light Up the Bay."

"When does it start?" Jill had seen the banner stretched across the street but couldn't recall the dates.

"This weekend," Brenda said. "The live auction happens on Friday. We already have photographs of the pieces up for sale. The artists provided them, and Ryan—Kaye's son-in-law—put them on the website, ready to go. But the page needs something more. Right now, it looks as if the auction could be held anywhere. We want a more local feel, photographs of the shore, the town, the community setting up the festival venues. We realized we need a full-time photographer to make that happen, and that's why we tacked the card on Danny's board."

"Danny's board?" Jill was momentarily confused.

"The Dewberry Deli," Mrs. Ivey offered. "If you've been here for any length of time, you must have eaten there. It's one of the only restaurants in town open during the off-season."

"Oh, I have. I didn't recognize the name 'Danny.'"

"Danny Esposito and his brothers own the shop now. They bought it from their mother, Mary Ann. She still works there sometimes, as does her mother. Nonna's salads are legendary in Dewberry Beach."

Jill remembered the pesto and bit back a smile.

"The art auction is what will generate the most money," Kaye continued, lifting a slice of spice cake from the plate. "But the Light Up the Bay Festival spans the entire weekend. It's evolved to what we hope is a family event. A banquet and the art auction are held on Friday at the Yacht Club. Saturday morning is the Pumpkin Run, followed by a pancake breakfast at the fire station. Saturday afternoon is the Halloween carnival, with the community cook-off and then lanterns across the bay at night. Sunday is the boat parade and milk carton race. I think that's everything." Kaye's brows knit together. "We want pictures to show the mood, to draw in online bidders. Make them remember how wonderful Dewberry Beach is."

"Something to give summer residents a chance to reconnect," Jill offered.

"Exactly," Brenda said with a smile. "What's tricky is that there's a lot going on this weekend, in a lot of different places." She glanced at Betty. "Betty, do you have any extra flyers?"

"I think so." Betty rose from the table and rummaged through a box of auction material until she found what she wanted. "This is the last of them." She laid the flyer on the table, then settled back into her chair. "The rest are up. The banner's been strung across the road near Mueller's Bakery too. The firefighters brought out their ladder truck and hung it the week before last."

"Can I keep this?" The schedule of events would be useful. Jill studied the page.

"Ideally, we'd like a variety of photographs from every venue—or as many as you can get to. We realize you can't be everywhere at once," Brenda explained. "You do the best you can, and we'll make it work."

"I think Jill is just what we need," Mrs. Ivey put in, with that same knowing smile. "She knows what's important. She'll do the right thing."

"Right." Kaye reached for a spiral-bound notebook and flipped through it. "We haven't told you what the job pays yet."

"It doesn't matter. I'll do it anyway," Jill said, and Kaye glanced up, confused. Jill explained, "It's for a good cause—a great cause actually. The money you save from not paying me can be put toward school lunch accounts."

Jill had known hunger when she was a kid. It was frustrating not to be able to focus in school and humiliating to have to ask for food. Jill wanted better than what she'd had for the children in that school. She'd figure out the money later; maybe lower the house price even more, or work two jobs instead of just one, to make up the difference.

"Nonsense," Brenda said sharply, though her expression was soft. "We can afford to pay you. In fact, we insist on it."

They spent the next several minutes discussing the logistics of getting Jill's pictures to Ryan. She'd been given free rein to photograph anything in Dewberry Beach that looked interesting, so long as the images were natural. The work paid surprisingly well, better than anything Jill would have gotten from a temp job, and the best part was that she'd be allowed to keep copies of her work for her portfolio.

For the rest of the meeting, Jill positively glowed, feeling her luck had finally changed.

With their business concluded, the meeting adjourned. Brenda rose to clear the table while Betty filled the sink. Kaye and Mrs. Ivey walked Jill out and paused at the front door.

"Starting tomorrow won't be a problem?" Kaye asked. "I realize this is short notice, so we'll try to make it easier for you. Parking at the Yacht Club is limited, I'm afraid, and the building itself can be difficult to find. We'd be happy to pick you up if you tell us where you're staying."

"Oh—I'm staying with a friend." Jill waved a breezy hand through the air. "I'm sure she knows where it is." She hated lying to these women, especially after they'd taken a chance on her, but she didn't feel as if she had a choice. They'd made their feelings about The Monstrosity very clear and might not have offered her the job if they knew she owned it. And she really wanted the job.

"How nice." Betty commented, out of interest. "Is your friend anyone we know?"

Mrs. Ivey laid her hand gently on Betty's arm.

"Alright then," Kaye continued. "We'll be there early. See you tomorrow."

"I'm looking forward to it." Jill shrugged on her jacket as Kaye returned to the kitchen and was surprised when Mrs. Ivey saw her out.

"A great many people are counting on you, Jillian." The older lady reached out to gently grasp Jill's arm. "Please don't let us down."

Jill shook off Mrs. Ivey's strange comment as she made her way back to the house, focusing instead on everything the women had said about her photographs, committing each compliment to memory. Brenda had remarked on Jill's instinct for capturing texture and light. That was something she'd been working on, so to have that encouragement from someone as accomplished as Brenda? Well, that was everything.

Marc had called her passion a hobby for so long that Jill had almost begun to believe it. But not anymore.

And although she still entered the house through the garage, so as not to be seen by the neighbors, she would not spend the night in her car again.

Those days were over.

Chapter 18

The chirp of an incoming text woke Jill before her alarm did. Bleary-eyed, she pushed herself upright, squinting against the screen's light as she skimmed the message.

Client I mentioned is interested. Wants to see the house as soon as possible. Hoping for this morning?

Now fully awake, Jill composed a quick reply and sent it off.

This morning is fine. I'll be out all day.

Heart thumping, she stared at the three pulsing dots on the bottom of her screen, waiting for a reply. Could it really be this easy?

Great! We'll be there around nine. Shouldn't take long.

Excited, Jill pushed away the blankets and headed for the shower. It seemed that her luck had changed after all.

Before leaving the house, she gave it a quick once-over, plumping pillows and running the vacuum once more. Satisfied the house was show-ready, she stocked her camera bag and let the excitement of the day propel her forward.

She was ready with her camera when a gust of autumn breeze swirled a handful of crimson leaves across the sandy beach steps. And when the wind spun the leaves into a vortex, Jill slowed the shutter speed to blur the image. The result was a wash of fall color against a canvas of sandy beach. On the dunes, she found another scatter of wild roses and photographed the jagged green leaves, edged with lacy frost and dotted with frozen dewdrops. Then, her attention drawn to activity on the beach, she switched to a telephoto lens and captured the foamy churn of seawater as a black Lab frolicked in the surf. Further out, she saw a lone surfer on a faded green surfboard, waiting for the perfect wave.

As she made her way from the beach into town, she saw again that everything had been decorated for the festival and paused to look closer. Every shop had something out, even tourist shops closed for the season. A rusty wheelbarrow overflowing with lumpy gourds was parked outside the T-shirt shop, a tier of haybales stacked beside the ice cream stand. Even a web of fake cobwebs had been stretched across the doorway of the beach-pass office. She took several pictures for the festival website then continued into town.

Even from two blocks away, she could see a flurry of festival activity in front of the fire station. Work crews unloaded long tables from a flatbed truck, delivering them to the lawn, where another crew were busy erecting tents for the cook-off. Hurrying forward, Jill pulled out her camera and went to work. She found a group of bleary-eyed volunteers awaiting the morning's instruction, and captured expressions of excitement and exhaustion. Moving to the green, she watched a man set up his grill for the cook-off, noting his expression as he scooped wood chip from the bowl of water. The man reminded her of Uncle Barney, who would not even consider starting the grill unless he had a packet of soaked mesquite chips ready. Jill lowered her camera and watched the man tuck the wood into his foil packet, feeling a thread of warmth expand in her chest as she remembered Uncle Barney doing the same. He would have loved this place; they both would have.

Eventually, Jill crossed the street to the bakery, drawn by the need for freshly brewed coffee with cream. A rustic scarecrow reclined on an Adirondack chair near the entrance, casually dressed in a neon-pink Dewberry Beach sweatshirt, faded jeans, and dingy white sneakers. Someone had laid a copy of the *Dewberry Beach Trumpet* on the scarecrow's lap and opened it to the weekend schedule for the festival. Jill snorted in appreciation; Uncle Barney would have laughed at that.

Inside, the shop was loud and busy as numbers were called out and customers placed orders. Jill pulled a paper number from the dispenser and waited for it to appear on the neon board behind the counter. There were a few customers ahead of her but no one Jill recognized. As she waited, she peered into the glass case at the platters of Danishes, Italian cookies, and cupcakes. Behind the counter were trays of golden-brown muffins the size of softballs. And over by the wall were baskets of crusty, fresh bread. How long had it been since she'd had a real corn muffin? Or had allowed herself to have any kind of muffin at all?

"Number forty-five?"

Jill raised her paper, and the woman pulled the cord to advance the number, then pushed the sleeves of her gray cardigan up to her elbows and offered Jill a weary smile, as if it had already been a long day. "What can I get for ya?"

"She'll have a plain green salad, Irene—dressing on the side," a deep voice behind Jill rumbled with laughter.

Jill turned to see the man from the deli, the one who'd taken her order. His dark blue volunteer fireman T-shirt fit him quite well, Jill noticed, as she searched for a retort.

It turned out that Jill didn't need one because the woman's eyes widened in delight the moment she spied him. She reached across the glass case to grab his hand in both of hers and her tone lifted. "Danny, honey. How are ya? How's your mom?"

"She's better. Dad's taking her up to Foxwoods this weekend so she's pretty happy."

"Good. Good." A smile wreathed her face as she dropped her voice to a conspiratorial whisper. "Can I grab you something? We have the cream-filled donuts you like, just made. On the house."

"Nah, not for me, thanks. I'm good." As he shook his head, he shifted his weight and Jill noticed a faint scent of cologne that wasn't entirely unpleasant. "I'm just here to pick up our coffee order."

"For the guys across the street?"

"Yeah. Roy said he called it in."

"Lemme check to see if it's put together." She heaved a long-suffering sigh. "Festival weekend is always a madhouse."

Jill waited for him to apologize—or at least acknowledge that he'd pushed ahead of her in line—but he didn't. He just stood, patiently waiting for his order as if Jill wasn't even there.

"I was going to order a muffin, you know," she said finally. If only to break the silence.

Danny turned toward her, nodding thoughtfully. "Good choice. The muffins are really good here. Blueberry's the best."

As he started to turn away, Jill blurted, "You were right about your nonna's pesto. I liked it," then immediately felt stupid for continuing a conversation he clearly had no interest in. "It was good," she finished weakly.

"Here ya go." Irene bustled from the back room loaded with an armful of flat pink boxes. "I got coffee coming too." She jerked her chin behind her. "Darby's making a fresh pot. You boys got enough cream and sugar over there? I know how you like your coffee sweet."

"Yeah, I think we're good." Danny took the boxes, then offered a magnificent smile as he lifted his chin toward Jill. "Give the coffee to Green Salad over here. She can help me carry it over."

"Is that right?" Irene's eyes narrowed with sudden interest.

"No, that's *not* right," Jill snapped, annoyed at the assumption. She'd just left a terrible marriage and had absolutely no desire to date, or flirt, or meet anyone. Her life was her own now and she had no intention of sharing it. She lifted her chin and continued, "I happen to be working."

"Oh sure, of course." Danny nodded, though the smile remained stubbornly in place. "G'head with your order. What did you come for?"

"Coffee and a muffin please. A *corn* muffin," Jill added defiantly. She'd entered the bakery with the intention of ordering a fat blueberry muffin, but not anymore. She wouldn't give him the satisfaction.

"I'm sorry but Danny got the last of the corn muffins," Irene said.

Jill pointed to the stacked metal trays behind the counter. "I see them right there."

"Nah." Irene frowned. "Sorry. Those ones are reserved for someone else… a big order at the Yacht Club."

Danny lifted the boxes of pastry in his arms. "Got plenty of corn right here. In fact, they're still warm. All you have to do is help me carry this stuff over."

"That was a good batch, and fresh out of the oven too," Irene mused. "Awful that you missed it, but you got Danny right there."

"That's fine," Jill replied firmly. "I'll have a blueberry instead."

"Ooooh, sorry." Irene's wince seemed manufactured. "We're out of those too." She stepped to the side to block Jill's view of the baking trays in the kitchen. "Sorry, honey."

"Cranberry then," Jill continued. Surely they had cranberry left? No one liked cranberry muffins.

Irene lifted her shoulder in a gentle shrug, but Jill didn't believe her.

Danny lifted his boxes one more time. "There's a couple of cranberry in here, if you want them. All you have to do is help me carry the coffee across the street."

"Fine." Jill slung her camera bag over her shoulder.

"You good with everything else?" Irene asked Danny as she produced an enormous urn of coffee and handed it to Jill. The urn was heavy, but it was warm, and the smell of fresh, hot coffee was heaven. Jill's stomach growled, reminding her that she hadn't eaten a proper meal in a while.

"Come to think of it," Danny answered. "I think we might be low on cups—"

"Say no more." Irene rounded the counter and tucked a fat tube of insulated cups under Jill's arm. When she was finished, she patted Jill's arm. "There ya go, honey. All set."

Jill said nothing.

"Thanks, Aunt Irene." Danny's tone fizzled with suppressed laughter.

"You got it, sweetie," she replied. "See ya for Sunday dinner. Don't f'get to bring your brothers."

Jill and Danny crossed the street to the firehouse where the crew waited eagerly for their morning break. Danny was swarmed almost immediately, which was fine with her because in the frenzy were interesting pictures. Coffee and muffin forgotten for the moment, Jill pulled out her camera and started work.

The shiny fire engine parked in the bay of the open fire station attracted waves of excited children, and it wasn't long before the driveway and the green space beside it were filled with kids and their parents. And because firefighters are proud of the work they do, they soon abandoned their break to show people around.

Jill was ready with her camera. Slipping into the background, she captured some of the best images of the day. The excitement on a little girl's face as she was lifted into the driver's seat of the truck. The wonder in another child's eyes as he listened to radio chatter on an oversized headset. Jill widened her range to include firefighters and photographed them restocking supplies and checking equipment. One shot she was particularly proud to have captured was a pair of women pulling the hoses from the rig to check them for wear. Their concentration reflected the seriousness of their work because a missed rip or hole would be disastrous at the scene of an emergency.

Jill might have stayed longer, but she had to get going. Just as she zipped her camera case shut, she noticed Danny walking up beside her.

"Leaving already?" He offered her a cup of hot coffee, which she accepted.

"They're expecting me at the Yacht Club." She cradled the cup in her palms and felt the warmth spread to her fingers. "So yeah, I gotta go." She noticed for the first time that she'd slipped into her old South Jersey accent and that Danny didn't seem to mind. Marc would have.

"Thanks for helping me carry the stuff from the bakery," he said easily as he handed her a blueberry muffin folded into a napkin. "Not sure the guys would have forgiven me if I had brought them cold coffee. Hey, listen…" His tone changed so abruptly that Jill turned her attention back to him. He gestured toward the bakery. "That thing back there with Aunt Irene and the muffins? That wasn't anything. She's always like that—she likes to kid."

"Oh yeah, sure." Jill shifted her gaze back to her camera, feeling a bloom of embarrassment rise from her chest. "I knew she was kidding. Anyway, I should get going. I don't want to be late." She turned and called over her shoulder, "Thanks for the coffee."

Jill walked away, relieved. Danny was handsome, no doubt about it, but the ink on her divorce papers was barely dry and Jill had no interest in dating again.

Not that he'd asked, she reminded herself.

Chapter 19

On her way to the Yacht Club, Jill planned to stop by the Bennett house to drop off the SD card. Kaye's son-in-law Ryan needed the photographs Jill had taken already, and Kaye had texted Jill to ask that she bring them by. It seemed an easy enough thing to do.

The Bennett home was a modest house on a quiet street, not at all what Jill would have expected from such an affluent family. Just two stories, shingled with gently weathered cedar, and three windows on the second floor framed with slim black shutters. Pots of yellow chrysanthemums dotted the front steps, leading up to a welcoming front porch set with Adirondack chairs and carved pumpkins.

The front door was open to the crisp autumn air, so Jill knocked on the frame.

A young woman's voice called from inside the house, "C'min. It's open."

Jill pulled open the screen door and stepped inside but didn't venture further than the small foyer. Surely the woman hadn't intended to let anyone all the way in. "Hello?"

A woman about Jill's age emerged from the kitchen, wiping her hands on a tea towel. Her shoulder-length dark hair was pulled back into a low ponytail and she was dressed in yoga pants and loose T-shirt. She seemed approachable and nice, and Jill liked her immediately. Under different circumstances, they may even have been friends.

"Oh, sorry." She tucked the towel into her waistband as she walked toward Jill. "I was expecting someone else."

"I'm Jill, the photographer that's helping with the festival." Jill withdrew the SD card from her camera case. "I was told that Ryan might need these pictures? For the website."

"That's right—now I remember. Mom texted that you might drop by. I'm Stacy. Ryan's upstairs with the baby right now but he should be down soon. Do you have time for a cup of coffee?"

Jill wasn't sure she should spend any time in the Bennett home. Even though she was certain they didn't know who she was, the town was small, and people liked to talk. It was better to keep her distance. "I'm afraid I can't stay. They want me to photograph the gallery set-up and I'm afraid I may already be late."

"I get it," Stacy answered easily. "Festival weekend is a busy time for everyone. Lemme just grab a new SD card to replace the one you're giving Ryan, and you can be on your way. It's back here."

Stacy led the way to the kitchen and Jill followed, reluctantly.

As they entered the kitchen, Jill was surprised at how much the room reminded her of Aunt Sarah's cozy kitchen at the Cape. The warm yellow walls, the lace curtains in the windows, even the sponge in the holder on the side of the sink. There were a trio of labeled canisters—flour, sugar, and tea—tucked into a corner beside a wooden bread box. On the refrigerator, a scatter of plastic fruit magnets anchored wrinkled finger paintings and snapshots of friends and vacations. The atmosphere was light, casual. If the kitchen was the heart of the home, then the Bennett home was genuinely welcoming.

"Here it is." Stacy held up a small plastic case. "Ryan loves the pictures you've taken already. He said they're just what he needs for the website and wants to know if he can get a copy of whatever you shoot today." She held up a second case. "Do you need an extra card? We have millions of them."

"No, that's okay. I have a few myself." Jill laughed, patting her camera bag. "I'll make sure Ryan gets a copy of everything."

"Great. And you said you're on your way to the Yacht Club now?"

"I am," Jill replied as she tucked the card in her case.

"Do you mind if I walk with you? I haven't been out of the house since the baby was born and I'm dying for some fresh air. It's not far." Her expression turned mischievous. "And I can show you a secret shortcut."

"How can I possibly refuse that?" Jill smiled, and it occurred to her that Ellie would have liked Stacy too.

"Let me just get my sneakers and we'll go. They're upstairs." Stacy bounded up the stairs, leaving Jill alone.

Unexpectedly, an older man rounded the corner into the kitchen. They locked eyes, and Jill tensed as she recognized him. While Marc had been busy doing everything he could to orchestrate a meeting with the elusive Chase Bennett at the party, Jill had kept to herself. But in a quiet corner of the second-floor deck, she'd happened to run into a nice older man and struck up a conversation. They'd chatted about nothing in particular, and Jill had shared a memory of her summers spent at the Cape. The man had said that Uncle Barney seemed like an honorable man, an observation that had warmed Jill's heart. The conversation had been brief, and she hadn't gotten the man's name then, but now, of course, she knew exactly who he was: Chase Bennett. The same Chase Bennett who knew Marc and had actively avoided doing business with him, for reasons Jill could only guess at.

One thing was for sure: Chase knew about Marc's house and was aware that Marc had been trying to sell it. Now he knew that Jill was here it was only a matter of time before he put the pieces together.

Jill stared at him, her mind racing with all the ways this could fail.

The estate agents were showing the property to a potential buyer this very morning and the man standing before her had the power to stop everything.

Before either of them had a chance to speak, Stacy pounded down the stairs, sneakers in hand.

She glanced at her father and smiled. "Oh, Dad, you're back. This is Jill DiFiore, the photographer helping Mom with the fall festival."

"DiFiore, is it?" Chase's gaze sharpened as he considered.

Jill swallowed. "Yes. It is now. I'm divorced."

"Are you? How long have you been divorced?"

"Dad!" Stacy admonished. "Really?"

"No, it's okay," Jill rushed. "It only happened recently. I found out my husband isn't who I thought he was, and I couldn't be a part of it."

"Is that so?"

I'm nothing like him, Jill wanted to say, but of course she couldn't. Instead, she settled for, "He wasn't honorable, like my Uncle Barney."

Stacy blinked, confused. But the message wasn't for Stacy.

"I see. Interesting." He scrutinized Jill for another moment, then turned his attention to his daughter. "Stacy, I can't seem to find the bag of mesquite chips. Do you know where it is?"

Unexpectedly, Jill felt a flare of annoyance—both at Chase's casual dismissal of her and of the power he held over her. The power she'd given him to decide her fate. As owner of The Monstro—correction: the beach house, she could do whatever she wanted with it. Sell it. Live in it. Give it away if she wanted to. She knew neighbors objected to it—and she understood why—but the time to protest was over. Permits had been issued, construction completed. The house was legally hers and if anyone tried to stop that sale, Jill would fight back. Somehow.

"Brad used the last of it on the ribs the other day," Stacy answered as she bent to tie her laces. "The new bag is on the shelf—red label this time, instead of blue."

"Thanks. I'll look again." His expression changed. "Are you going somewhere?"

"Finally getting out of the house." Stacy pushed herself to a standing position. "Just a short walk to the Yacht Club with Jill. I'll be right back."

"Do you mind swinging by Applegate's Hardware on your way back? I need a new grill brush for the cook-off, and I need to start the marinade before your mother comes home. Oh, and get another bag of mesquite, will you? I can't afford to run out this year."

"Sure, Dad," Stacy replied. "Don't overdo it though. I'm not sure Mom would be happy with all this activity of yours."

"I could say the same to you, young lady." Chase arched a brow, revealing a glimpse of the stern businessman underneath. "You should be upstairs resting."

Stacy's answer was to kiss her father on the cheek. "This is your third grandchild, Dad. I think I know what I'm doing. I'll be back later."

"Okay. I'll see you later," Chase answered. Then, because good manners dictated that Chase say goodbye to Jill, he turned to her, but his expression changed. It became more guarded. "It was nice to meet you, Ms. DiFiore."

"And you too, Mr. Bennett." Jill replied. He'd given nothing away and she couldn't tell what he planned to do, if anything.

Stacy pushed open the back door. "We'll go out this way. Shortcut's through the back."

Outside, Jill stopped.

"Oh my gosh," she breathed as she took it all in. "This view…"

"Isn't it great?" Stacy smiled at Jill's reaction. "I never get tired of it."

The backyard of the Bennett home bordered a salt pond with a bank of cattails growing from the muddy shore to frame the view. A mix of sturdy trees shaded the water from overhead sun, and delicate weeping willow branches provided a home for wildlife. In the shallows, fallen tree branches were left undisturbed, providing shelter for mallards and rest for turtles. The air was still this time of day, nothing but an occasional duck quacking or a fish splashing to break the silence. On the ground, water broke in gentle waves.

"This is magnificent," Jill said finally. The front of the Bennett house was so unassuming. It gave no hint that this sanctuary lay behind it. What a treasure.

"I think the deck is the best part of the house, to be honest. My grandfather carved it by hand, as a gift for my grandmother because she loved to sit and watch the ducks on the pond." Stacy touched the finished wood as they walked closer to the pond. "It took him an entire year of weekends to build it. I always remember that when I come out here, how patient and meticulous a man he was."

Jill pointed to the nautical rope that served as a handrail, knotted at intervals and threaded through brass fittings. "The craftsmanship is unusual. These details…"

"My grandpa was a craftsman, a woodworker. He specialized in dock construction, and he loved being near the water."

Chase pushed open the back door and called to his daughter. "Stacy, I can't seem to find the molasses. Would you mind getting some on the way back?"

"Sure, Dad."

"Great. Just charge everything to the house account. I need a few more things for this weekend, do you mind getting them? I have a list."

As Stacy crossed the deck to retrieve the list from her father, Jill realized that what she liked most about this house was its simplicity. Nothing was "curated for effect." It was a simple house meant for family. And a family lived here.

"This deck is in such good condition," Jill said when Stacy returned, "it's hard to believe it was built so long ago."

Stacy laughed. "Tell that to my brother—he's the one who's in charge of taking care of it. My grandfather was very exacting; he left detailed instructions on its upkeep." She pointed to a small shed in the far corner. "That used to be his workshop. My brother Brad works there now; he runs his landscaping business from there."

They continued across the yard and through a grassy lot that bordered the property. Overhead, ocean breezes had swept the sky clear of early morning clouds, leaving only a brilliant crisp blue. The air was fresh, touched with salt and filled with possibility.

"Do you live in Dewberry Beach full-time?" Jill started the conversation as they traveled a narrow footpath along the creek.

"Thinking about it," Stacy replied as they fell into step together. "We're staying with my parents until we decide. The kids are enrolled in school here and they seem to like it. It'll be a big change from what we're used to, but I think it'll be good for us."

"You all live with your parents?"

Stacy laughed. "We do. You know, if anyone had suggested that at the beginning of the summer, I'd have called them crazy. But yes, all of us—my brother's here too—live with my parents at the moment. It's tight, seven people and a newborn living in a small house with two bathrooms. Parts of it can get dicey, but it has benefits too. Mom and

Dad are getting to know their grandchildren in a way they couldn't have before, and I think it's good for all of us. Ryan and I had been going in a million different directions where we lived before and we've slowed down. It's nice. We've looking for a place in town, but I think my mom likes us all together in one house."

"It seems like a sweet little town."

"It is. My brother and I have spent every summer in Dewberry Beach since we were born. My parents met here as kids, in fact. They bought the house from my grandparents after they married, and we'll probably buy it from them if they ever want to sell it. Well," Stacy amended with a swish of her hand, "either my brother or I will. We haven't decided, but the house will definitely stay in the family."

"What a great legacy."

"It really is. Growing up, I had a dozen mothers in this town, watching out for me, ready with a Band-Aid for a scrape or a popsicle on a hot day."

"It sounds perfect," Jill said, because it did. Her own childhood had been tumultuous, and it had been wonderful to spend summers with Aunt Sarah and Uncle Barney on the Cape.

To Jill's surprise, Stacy laughed. "Not always. The same women who offered up comfort and reassurance did not hesitate to tell my mother if they saw me riding my bike too fast or crossing the street against the light." She side-eyed Jill. "I don't know if you've noticed but we don't have a lot of traffic down here, but to this day, I still can't bring myself to cross the street if the light is red."

The path opened up to a residential street, another road lined with shady trees. The morning sun filtered through a tangle of bright autumn leaves clinging stubbornly to their branches, and the result washed the sandy street in shades of yellow and orange. The houses here seemed more like cottages, with shady porches and colorful front gardens. Almost every home had displayed carved pumpkins, and a few had taped crayoned drawings of cats and ghosts to the windows. But there was one homeowner who had opted to go all-out for the holiday. There, a pair of bony skeletons peeked out from behind the porch columns, a witch's broom hung from the tree branches on the sidewalk, and orange string lights laced the front shrubbery.

Jill slowed to marvel, and Stacy snorted.

"We take Halloween very seriously here," she explained as she waited for Jill.

They took Halloween very seriously in the upscale neighborhood Jill had shared with Marc too, but they celebrated very differently. Every year, landscaping trucks descended on the first of October, with work crews, ladders, and miles of tiny white string lights. Decorators from fancy nurseries arrived next, arranging wheelbarrows, straw bedding, and trendy fall gourds that looked nothing like the bright orange pumpkins Jill had known as a child. In all the time she'd lived with Marc, Jill had never once been allowed to put up so much as a wreath on the door. The job fell to professional decorators and the result had been lovely but cold.

Jill preferred the Dewberry Beach version.

"It's not all homey like this," Stacy said, as if reading Jill's thoughts. "This is one of the few original streets, untouched by developers."

"What do you mean?"

"This is what Dewberry Beach *used* to look like when I was a kid, but it's changed, especially near the ocean."

"You mean because of the hurricane?"

"Yes, but not only that. People buy houses here then decide they want something bigger or different, so they expand the first floor or add a third. The remodels change the look and feel of the town, and it's divided the town into before and after. But that's a gripe for another time." Stacy shivered as if to shake off the mood. "Anyway, that's more than enough about me. What about you? What brings you to Dewberry Beach in October?"

"I came with my camera," Jill answered truthfully. "When I stopped for lunch in the deli, I happened to see the notice for a photographer. That led to an interview and the festival job."

"How lucky for the committee that you found the notice," Stacy commented as they strolled. "Is it interesting, taking pictures? Do you like it?"

"I love it. It's a hard industry to break into, especially if you want to do artistic work instead of commercial, which I do." Jill shifted the weight of her bag across her shoulder. "What's particularly nice is that your mom's group is giving me artist credit on the website, *and* they're letting me use the images for my portfolio."

"Is that unusual?"

"It really is. And I'm grateful."

"Brenda's on the committee this year too, isn't she?"

"Yes. I saw some of her work—she's incredibly talented."

"We have quite a few artists around here, believe it or not. If not in Dewberry Beach proper, then scattered around the area. The auction gives them a chance to show locally, because the closest gallery is miles from here."

They rounded the corner of a dead-end street and came to the gates of the Yacht Club. The sight of it was jarring. An unexpectedly imposing structure in such a quiet neighborhood, it clearly did not belong. A formal entrance was marked with a pair of iron gates that opened to the wide circular driveway of meticulously raked white gravel. A patch of grass in the center of the courtyard was so artificially green that it looked like carpet. And if that wasn't enough to stake their claim, the Yacht Club's burgee stood tall, the fabric snapping smartly in the bay breeze. It didn't seem right that a building like this could exist in Dewberry Beach. It felt pretentious and gawdy.

The attendant at the guard station waved them through and Jill glanced at Stacy, puzzled.

"I know." Stacy rolled her eyes. "I can't even stand to come here anymore, it's changed so much. When locals lost control of the board, developers took over and everything went sideways." She pointed to a structure built on pilings that jutted out over the water. "Look at that mess over there. They built a *swimming pool* over the water." She scoffed. "When I was a kid and we wanted to go swimming, we ran to the end of the dock and jumped off—right into the bay. Back then, the entire building was only meant to store lifejackets, boat line, bumpers. Boat stuff. Now look at it." She shook her head. "They even put a ballroom on the second floor."

"So why use it for the festival?"

"Because as much as I've come to loathe this place, it's the only space in town big enough to hold the auction." She frowned. "They charge us a fortune to rent the space for our fundraiser. A *school* fundraiser." She grimaced. "This club is built on town land and they were even granted a waiver to enlarge the building after the hurricane, but the new board has a short memory and no sense of obligation. And you know what's worse?"

"What?"

"Just last summer I was one of them. I brought the kids here. To the pool deck." Stacy opened the oversized front door. "Thankfully, I've changed since then."

Jill stepped into the foyer and hesitated, a bit unnerved by the grandeur. The reception area reminded her of a wedding she and Marc had attended a few years before. They too had had an ornate flower arrangement on a marble-topped side table, a guest book and silver pen near the entrance, and a coat-check off to the side.

Jill glanced at Stacy. The setting seemed so out of place.

"I know." Stacy rolled her eyes again. "Horrible, isn't it? And it gets worse. C'mere, lemme show you." She led Jill to a series of old photographs documenting the club's history. The first showed a group of men in overalls framing a wooden shack on the edge of the bay, a pile of cast-off cedar planks nearby. "Dockworkers built this place back in 1930-something as a place to store boat equipment. A lot of them fished on the weekends. See right there?" Stacy tapped a blurry figure smiling for the camera. "That's my great grandfather."

"Your family's lived here that long?"

"They have," Stacy replied. "My great-grandfather built the house originally and my grandfather added the deck."

The remaining photographs revealed a gradual change to the building. It grew in size—one year adding docks; in another an outdoor deck. And scattered among the building pictures were snapshots of men dressed in overalls and absolutely beaming.

"They look pleased," Jill remarked.

"They are—and they should be," Stacy answered. "Most of the original building was constructed by hand, using the same crew. But it was small, so they could. Still, look at how proud they are."

What a time that must have been. As Jill glanced at the photographs, she almost wished she was there.

"What's this?" Jill stopped at the first color photograph in the line-up. The men were gone. The boathouse was gone. Both had been replaced by heavy machinery and blueprints. "What happened here?"

"The hurricane happened." Stacy's frown was deep. "C'mon, we should get going."

They climbed the sweeping staircase to the ballroom on the second floor. On the walls overhead, a patchwork quilt of regatta flags dating back to 1931 hung from the exposed beams. Ironic that they'd kept the awards but changed the personality of the club that had earned them.

When they reached the top of the stairs, Stacy turned. "The ballroom is right through those double doors. I should go see about Billy Jacob's table, make sure he's got everything he needs for the signing." She gestured to an author signing table that had been set up in a bright alcove just outside the ballroom. On the floor, peeking out from under the tablecloth was a small box. Stacy bit her lip, considering. "That doesn't look like enough books."

"Billy? The signing is for *the* Billy Jacob?" Jill asked. *A Winter to Remember* was one of her favorite books.

"Yes."

"Billy Jacob lives in Dewberry Beach?"

Stacy laughed. "Not exactly. He's an interesting character. He owns a brownstone in New York—Brooklyn I think—but he comes here to write. It's a long story, but the gist of it is that last summer he grew very fond of our little town. He was convinced the air was 'pulsing with creative energy' or something just as weird. He finished his latest book here and even talked about staying. Anyway, he was here when he learned that developers were interested in land on the edge of town. But he snapped it up before they had a chance to buy it."

"I get it." Jill nodded, a bit disappointed. Marc had built his entire business on speculation, buying land then leveling it to make room for houses. She wanted Billy to be better than that.

Stacy hesitated. "No, I'm not sure you do. Billy bought the property, an old motel, so developers *couldn't* build on it. He wanted to preserve it." She shrugged. "He has no idea what to do with it now, of course, but he saved this town from another Monstrosity and that counts for a lot."

Jill felt a flush on her cheeks. It seemed that everyone in town hated Marc's house.

Chapter 20

The Yacht Club ballroom spanned the length of the second floor and had finishes that reminded Jill of an old-world luxury liner. The walls had been paneled in dark mahogany and lined with gold-framed portraits of past commodores, regattas, and award ceremonies. Overhead was a flutter of burgees from area sail clubs, and Jill hoped they were displayed in the spirit of camaraderie and not to embarrass an opposing team who'd lost a race. But as the whole place oozed with one-upmanship, Jill was afraid the display wasn't kindly meant.

She shook off that feeling, focusing instead on the sweeping view of Barnegat Bay from oversized windows on the far wall. Today, the scene was especially breathtaking. The late October sky had deepened into a brilliant deep blue, and the mid-morning sun sparkled against the gentle waves in the bay. On the horizon, a flotilla of daysailers tacked into the breeze. Jill slipped her camera from the case and eagerly got to work. The ballroom was a hive of comings and goings, and Jill captured as much as she could. Ryan had asked for background shots, so she made sure to include the displays and volunteers setting up, anything he might find useful for the website.

It was around lunchtime when she finished. As she packed up, her mind turned toward food and she wondered, idly, if the Dewberry Deli was open. And if Nonna had made anything new.

Just as she clipped her camera bag shut, Brenda called her over.

"I noticed when you came in, but I didn't want to disturb you," she said, as she brushed a strand of hair from her face with the back of her hand. "Did you get some good pictures?"

"I think so." Honestly, this was the best job she'd ever had. Freedom to take any picture that looked interesting was exhilarating, and she'd done some of her best work since she'd arrived. She could happily make photography her life's work.

The items Brenda was unwrapping and setting up for display was a tea set, a hand-crafted pot, and two sturdy mugs. The craftsmanship was flawless, but it was the colors that captivated her, a gradient of blues and grays blended in the glaze that made Jill think of the sky just before a summer thunderstorm.

She wanted to run her fingertip along the glaze, just to be a part of it. She raised her gaze to Brenda. "May I?"

Brenda's smile widened as she nodded. "Of course. Pick it up. This set is meant to be used and I hope it will be."

The mug was heavier than it looked, and Jill traced the glaze with her fingertip, turning it over in her hands as she marveled at the swirl of color. It was when she looked closer that she noticed the delicate gold seams that threaded the piece. The effect was stunning.

"Is it Kintsugi?" Jill had heard of the technique, fusing gold to broken shards of pottery, but she'd never seen an example up close.

"It is. Do you know it?"

"Not very well unfortunately, though I'd like to."

"The technique comes from the Japanese idea of flaws and imperfections," Brenda explained. "The potter creates a piece of pottery, perfect and whole, then breaks it intentionally. The shards are gathered and mended with melted gold in such a way that highlight the breaks. The idea is that a Kintsugi piece is unique and more beautiful for having once been broken. I believe it speaks to resiliency. And strength."

"It's exquisite," Jill decided as she placed the cup back in the display.

"I'm so glad you like it, but that's not why I called you over," Brenda said. "We've had a last-minute cancellation in our emerging artists gallery, and I think you should take the spot. For one of your photographs. The work in that gallery won't be included in the judging, but it's good exposure if you're interested."

"Are you kidding?" Jill straightened, excitement surging through her. "I'd love to. What do you need me to do?"

"Well, for starters select the image that best represents your work. We only have room for one, so whatever you choose should be the very best you've got. Then you need to have it printed, framed, and delivered here by Friday morning."

Jill could feel herself deflating. She could never manage to get all that accomplished in such a short time. Getting a photograph show-ready in two days was next to impossible. Framing alone would take almost a week.

But Brenda was unfazed. She tore a corner from a slip of paper and scribbled down a phone number. "I know it seems like a lot, but I have a guy. He does gallery work for us and I've already talked to him about you. He said that if you can deliver to him by tomorrow morning, he'll mat and frame it. Bring it here first thing Friday and we'll have a space for it."

"Are you kidding? That's wonderful, thank you," Jill said, taking care not to gush.

"One more thing. The guidelines say that the piece needs to be related to Dewberry Beach in some way so choose something you've recently done. The final choice is yours, of course, so bring him whatever speaks to you."

The opportunity made Jill brave and she dared ask a question that she might not have otherwise.

"Do you *like* my work?" she asked. "The photographs in my portfolio from yesterday at Betty's house, did you like them?"

Brenda's gaze lingered on Jill. "The truth?"

"Yes."

"I think you have potential, but you need to learn to trust your instincts. I liked the photographs I saw at Betty's house, and your recent work is even better. It looks as if you've found your voice and that's always important." Brenda pursed her lips as she thought. "You know, my favorite image is still the bridal portrait. The composition is unexpected and that's good, but the magic, for me, is the expression on the bride's face. She'd clearly forgotten you were there and that's when the magic happens—when your subject stops posing. Anyway, there's something about that photograph that has stayed with me."

Jill blushed. Someone as accomplished as Brenda had complimented her work—work that Marc had dismissed as a hobby. Surely, she'd misheard.

"Oh, the look on your face." Brenda laughed good-naturedly as she reached for Jill's arm. "I felt the same way when a potter I admire told me he liked my stuff."

Their conversation was interrupted by a clatter at the entrance to the ballroom. A pair of delivery men laden with cardboard boxes entered the room and the energy changed noticeably. Volunteers gleefully abandoned their work and went to meet them.

"Oh, good! Lunch is here." Brenda glanced toward the commotion. "And not a moment too soon—I'm starving. Let's go see what Danny and his brothers packed up for us."

"Danny?"

"Danny Esposito from the Dewberry Deli. That man has a heart of gold, I tell ya. He donates lunch for all the volunteers—every volunteer at every site in town—on festival set-up day. We can afford to pay but he won't let us, insists that we think of it as his contribution. He's a good man." She dropped her voice to a whisper. "*And* you should taste his Nonna's salads. They're amazing."

Lunch was served on a long table in a sunny corner of the ballroom. Someone had spread a patchwork of tablecloths across the surface, adding a splay of colorful cloth napkins and bowls of deep red apples for a homey and inviting effect. They'd arranged a bounty of food in the center—platters of fat sandwiches, serving bowls of salads, and plates of vegetables. Nearby was a coffee and dessert table groaning with pastry donated by the bakery. Volunteers filled their plates and returned to the table to catch up after the morning's activities. Jill leaned into the hum of conversation, remembering meals around Aunt Sarah's dinner table and the chatter of cousins.

They were interrupted by a woman, harried and red-faced, bursting into the room.

"You will *never guess* what just happened!" She rushed to the head of the table to make her announcement. Planting her hands on her hips, she leaned forward. "They're *selling* The Monstrosity."

Conversation halted.

Finally, someone ventured, "Nancy, are you sure? How do you know?"

"There's a For Sale sign in front—I saw it myself—*and* I think they're showing it right now. A bunch of people got out of a Mercedes. I saw them on my way over here." She clasped her hands together in a desperate plea. "Now's our chance. We need to *do* something."

"Nancy," one woman nearby said gently, "we all hate that house as much as you do, but what do you imagine we can achieve at this point?"

"Have you forgotten what that man did? Taking advantage of Marva. Stealing her home. Have you forgotten what that man did to Pete? Destroyed his career, that's what he did. Don't you remember how humiliating it was for Pete to be called in front of the town council to explain what he did—after what *that devil* did, more like. Pete thought he was doing Dianne a favor and look what happened to him."

"You're right. I'm in, whatever you want to do," a woman further down the table spoke up. "Marva was one of my best friends. I'll never—ever—forget the lies that man spun to get her property."

"And let's remember what he did to the families over in Mantoloking," Nancy pressed as her cheeks flushed. "We can get a bit of justice for them too, while we're at it. I still have the petitions; they're still valid. We can show him—" She drew breath and her voice broke. "We'll show him…"

Another woman rose from her place and went to Nancy. She circled her arm around Nancy's shoulders and led her from the table. Though Nancy no longer held everyone's attention, her announcement had changed the energy of the room. As Jill listened to the table's hissed conversation, she felt their outrage grow and fill the room and decided she couldn't stay. She pushed her chair back from the table.

"I need to get going," she lied to Brenda, then stood. "Ryan's waiting for the gallery pictures." Her impulse was to run from the room, but she held back because she didn't want to attract attention. Before this moment she hadn't understood the depth of rage this town held for Marc and what he'd done. What did Nancy mean when she said he'd stolen the land? And had he really destroyed a man's career?

Outside, the crisp air touched her skin and cooled her burning face. Jill paused at the bottom of the stairs, drawing in deep breaths to steady her pounding heart. If she were completely honest—and there seemed no better time to be—she should admit, at least to herself, that Marc's business dealings were not always above board. One time a subcontractor had come to their house, trying to collect for a job he'd finished, payment he insisted was overdue. He'd brought receipts for materials he'd bought himself and a paper to show his work had passed inspection. He'd said money was tight and that he had a family to feed, but instead of working things out, Marc had threatened to call the police and the man had left. When she questioned Marc later, he'd insisted the man had been paid but it didn't look that way to Jill. That man had been desperate.

If Marc had treated this town the way he'd treated that subcontractor, it would explain why they loathed him so. If there was something dishonest here, Jill couldn't be a part of it. She needed the truth and there was one person in town who would know it. One person who understood business and the ways her husband might have twisted things to his advantage.

Jill steeled herself and headed back to the Bennett house; she was going to see Chase.

Chapter 21

Jill found her way back to the Bennett house and followed the path from the sidewalk to the front door. She lifted the brass knocker and let it go, listening to the sound reverberate in the quiet street. Jill realized she was probably the last person Chase wanted to see but she had questions that only he could answer. Nervously, she flicked a bit of sand from her jeans and waited for him to answer the door. She told herself that because she'd had no part in whatever Marc did, she wasn't culpable now, and she almost made herself believe it.

Through a side window, Jill spied Chase moving toward her, though he didn't see her. Her heart thumped as he twisted the knob and opened the wooden door. At first his expression was benign and vaguely welcoming, as if he'd expected a neighbor dropping by, but the moment he recognized her, his expression hardened.

They spoke through the screen door. "If you're looking for Kaye, she's still at the Yacht Club, setting up the art gallery." He hesitated for just a moment, and when he spoke again his tone was cool. "But you already knew that, didn't you? So why are you here?"

"I know that you know who I am, Mr. Bennett, and by now you've guessed that I've come to Dewberry to sell the house." His expression hardened and she rushed to finish. "But I have questions—"

He cut her off. "I'm not interested."

So Jill tried again. "I divorced Marc because he's not a good man."

"So you said."

Jill straightened; she didn't know how much time she had before he shut the door and her chance was gone. "I found out that Marc stole from me," she said. "A woman pretended to be me, signed documents for a mortgage, and left with a fat check. I never saw a dime of it. I took the house because Marc refused to pay the loan. I have no interest in it, beyond selling it."

Chase's expression was unchanged. "If all you want is to sell that house, I can't help you."

"That's not all I want," Jill blurted, stretching out her hand to prevent Chase from closing the door. "I don't know what Marc did to this town, but I have a feeling it was terrible. If it's in my power to fix it, I will."

"Let the girl in, Chase." Mrs. Ivey suddenly appeared in the background, surprising Jill. "At least let's hear what she has to say. No harm in that."

Chase hesitated but finally pushed the screen door open and allowed Jill to enter. "We'll go to my office."

Jill followed them down the hall to a small room that overlooked the front garden. As they settled in, she couldn't help but compare Chase's office to Marc's. Both were intended for work, but that's where the similarities ended. Marc's office was massive, with shelves of reference books bought and forgotten, and glossy pictures of his newest projects lining the walls. It was cold and sterile, designed to gain the upper hand in business. By contrast, Chase Bennett seemed confident of his place in the world and had no need to stake a claim or impress anyone. His office was cluttered with well-thumbed newspapers and business journals stacked on the floor, and the desk was scattered with charts and graphs. Chase may have retired from his work in the city, but his interest in business clearly hadn't diminished.

"I wonder if I should record this?" Chase posed and Jill flushed, knowing it was Marc who had made these people so cautious that the mistrust he'd sowed now extended to her.

"You can if you want to," Jill replied evenly. "I have nothing to hide."

"Let's not start off as adversaries," Mrs. Ivey said gently. "We should remember that Ms. DiFiore has come to us willingly and that her ex-husband preferred the shadows."

"Fair enough," Chase agreed, albeit reluctantly. He regarded Jill for a moment before continuing. "Before we answer your questions, I want you to tell us everything you know about that house."

"Okay." Jill nodded as she dropped her gaze. It was a reasonable question, but the answer made her look foolish. But she wanted Chase's cooperation, so she raised her gaze and began to speak. "I didn't know about the house until well into our second year of marriage, and only then because we hosted a client party there. Marc preferred to keep his business separate from our personal life." She paused because he'd done more than that. From the beginning, he'd said that the best way for her to help his company was to "look pretty." So she did, and for a while that was enough.

Mrs. Ivey shifted in her chair and the movement brought Jill back to the present.

"Sorry." Jill cleared her throat. "During the few times we visited Dewberry Beach to host parties, Marc insisted that I was not to venture into town or speak with anyone other than the clients. He said my job as hostess was here, with him, entertaining his guests." She sighed. "That was just a couple of years ago but it seems so much longer. There were many things in my marriage that I overlooked, Mr. Bennett, and

I'm not proud of it. I lost myself trying to be what Marc wanted, but it turned out that it wasn't me he wanted. He didn't even know me."

Outside, Jill saw a tangle of kids riding their bikes down the street. It seemed that school had let out for the day and they were on their way home.

She returned her attention to the room and finished her explanation. "One of the reasons Marc gave for keeping his work separate was his ex-wife, Dianne. He told me that her interference almost cost him his entire business. That she was unbalanced, mentally ill, and abusive to their daughters—"

Mrs. Ivey gasped.

"What's wrong?" Jill glanced at Chase. "What did I say?"

"Nothing I hadn't expected," he replied. "Please continue."

"I'm sure she's not like that. I didn't question it, though I should have. The truth is that I didn't question *anything* Marc told me because I was stupid enough to believe I had to earn his love and that obedience would do it." She held Chase's gaze, hoping he would see that she spoke the truth, even though it made her look childish. "I don't know anything about the house or what Marc did to get it, but I want you to know that I wasn't part of it. All I want to do is sell it and move on."

"But you *are* part of it," Chase declared, even as Mrs. Ivey reached for his arm. "If your only goal is to sell the house, without caring how it came to be, how is that any different from what Marc did?"

Jill sat, too stunned to speak. After everything she'd told him, he was still comparing her to Marc. They weren't the same at all.

"Did you hear a word I said?" Jill's voice rose in disbelief. "I'm a victim here too. Can't you see that? I can think of a million places I'd rather be than here, owning a house everyone hates. I hear you guys have a petition and someone named Nancy is already talking about using it to block the sale," she accused, her anger propelling her forward. "But you seem to have forgotten: the building permits on that house were approved, which means the construction is legal. The *house* is legal. The time for you guys to get all up in arms about how much you hate it was back then. Not now."

Jill's chest heaved and her outburst was met with silence. She looked away, embarrassed for having lost her temper but justified with her point. She had come here to try to make things better and they were refusing to see her side.

This was the last time she'd try.

As she collected her things, she heard the heat register click on and felt a soft whoosh of warm air on her face.

Outside, a car drove past the house and Jill noticed that the afternoon light had faded. She felt her chance to make things right slipping away too.

She rose from her chair. "I apologize for losing my temper. My aunt Sarah would have been horrified to hear me speak that way to you. Before I go, I want you to know that the reason I left Marc is because he had an affair. The house you call The Monstrosity is where he lived with his mistress. That's why I hate it."

She moved toward the door, but Mrs. Ivey stopped her. "Just one moment please."

Mrs. Ivey turned to Chase and squeezed his arm. "We need to tell her. She needs to know."

"I had no idea you wouldn't know." Chase lifted his gaze to meet Jill. "And for that I apologize. Please sit."

As Jill reluctantly reclaimed her chair, Chase crossed the room to switch on a lamp, bathing the room in a warm yellow. On his way back, he drew the front curtains closed and Jill wondered if that was purposeful. So the neighbors wouldn't see this meeting, see Chase consorting with the enemy.

"Eight years ago this town faced the worst natural disaster any of us could imagine." Chase settled behind his desk with some difficulty. "Hurricane Sandy wasn't supposed to be a hurricane at all, did you know that? It was a 'tropical depression' and was located so far out to sea that it hardly bore mention on weather reports. Storms like that spring up by the dozen as the weather changes in the fall. But when it began to gather strength, people in its path paid attention. The winds picked up and the sky darkened, even as weathermen reported that Sandy had indeed changed course, but still there was no need for concern—it was still miles from shore. They said that even if the edge of the storm grazed the coast, the most that shore towns could expect would be a few days of heavy rain, nothing more. And we believed them."

Chase drew a ragged breath. When he continued, his tone had changed. He seemed detached, as if the only way he could tell this story was to remove himself from it. "As the storm gathered strength, it was upgraded twice. Even when meteorologists finally classified it as a hurricane and named it Sandy, they told us not to worry. They said it would continue up the coast, safely offshore. But they were wrong. When the storm made landfall, just above Atlantic City, no one was ready. By the time they issued the order to evacuate, it was too late. And the winds were relentless. Hurricane Sandy pounded the coast of New Jersey for almost four days, and when it was over, the landscape of the entire shore had changed."

Chase paused. The silence was thick, broken only by the hallway clock chiming the hour.

After a moment, Mrs. Ivey picked up the thread, her voice soft. "We were in shock, many of us, watching live coverage on the news.

We witnessed our town and landmarks that had been part of the fabric of our lives for decades destroyed in the time it takes to draw breath. For a long time, we weren't allowed back, and only then for an hour at a time. Some people didn't come back at all. The destruction was too much for them."

"We can't blame them," Chase added, his expression grim. "The damage was unimaginable. The pictures on television were horrific but it was worse in person." He paused to rub his face with his palms. "Houses that had been part of this town's landscape for more than a hundred years were reduced to rubble. People lost homes and businesses in the most horrific way. Things they'd spent a lifetime on, they left one day and returned to nothing."

"That was when Dianne came down," Mrs. Ivey added.

"Dianne?" Jill asked. "Do you mean Marc's first wife? Why would she come here?"

"She came to help of course." Mrs. Ivey looked momentarily startled that Jill would ask. "Dianne had lived in Dewberry Beach her whole life. She was one of my favorite students, in fact. Loved reading. Loved to write. Her father, Peter Muscadine, had been elected to the planning commission just a few months before the storm."

"Wait," Jill interrupted. "Peter Muscadine is Dianne's father? Isn't the planning commissioner the one who would have issued Marc's permits?"

In all the years she'd been married to Marc, Jill hadn't known that his connection to Dewberry Beach had been through Dianne. He'd never mentioned it. Jill had assumed he'd selected this town by chance, because land was available and developing it made good business sense. It seemed there was quite a bit about Marc that she didn't know.

"That's right, he was." Mrs. Ivey's expression was fierce. "But it gets worse. After the hurricane, Dianne had lost contact with her father.

She was frantic, but the State Patrol wouldn't let her into town to look for him, wouldn't allow her past the roadblock. She'd married by then, you see, and had moved away so the address on her driver's license wasn't local. She couldn't get within forty miles of here, no matter how hard she tried."

"What do you mean, 'reach her father'?" Jill asked. "Even if he wasn't evacuated right away, he must have reported to a shelter sometime later? Or at the very least had a cell phone? Couldn't he have telephoned Dianne to let her know he was safe?"

"You can't imagine what it was like." Mrs. Ivey shook her head. "Cell towers were down. Electricity grids were blown. Even the water was off because the pumping stations were flooded with sea water. Nothing worked."

Jill dropped her gaze. She'd heard about Hurricane Sandy of course; everyone on the East Coast had. But she hadn't lived through it and couldn't grasp how horrific it really was.

It occurred to her that a hurricane didn't explain the town's anger toward Marc, or their hatred of the house he'd built. He had nothing to do with the storm. She returned her attention to them and found Mrs. Ivey looking at her expectantly, as if she were waiting for Jill to draw some sort of conclusion. But Jill didn't understand.

"What did Marc do?" she asked finally. "How is he a part of this?"

Chase went on, his expression hard. "When Dianne was finally allowed in, Marc drove in with her. I found that strange because he'd never expressed the slightest interest in Dewberry Beach before, but I was willing to give him a chance. At the time, Marc had just taken over his father's company and he was eager to make a name for himself, show the world that he was just as good as Frank Goodman."

Jill shifted uneasily in her chair.

"But while Dianne shoveled muck and sifted through debris left by the hurricane, Marc tracked down property owners," Chase said. "He introduced himself as Dianne's husband and told everyone how much he and Dianne had always loved Dewberry Beach—"

"A town he'd never been to before the hurricane," Mrs. Ivey interrupted. "Dianne had always come without him."

Chase nodded. "Marc told everyone that his new company was flush with cash and what better use for it than rebuilding an iconic New Jersey shore town?" He twisted in his chair, his movements jerky and edged with anger. "I should have known then, should have stopped him."

"I won't hear it." Mrs. Ivey reached for his arm and squeezed. "Don't you dare blame yourself. Dianne believed him—we all did. Everyone was taken in." She glanced at Jill. "Before we knew what was happening, two of this town's oldest residents sold their property to him for a fraction of what it was worth."

"Sell? Why would they sell?" Jill asked. "He was a contractor. If he wanted to help, why didn't he offer to rebuild their homes?"

"Because there wasn't anything to rebuild. Nothing on either of those lots except splintered wood," Mrs. Ivey explained. "Everything—a family's entire life—had been sucked into the sea in the receding tide."

"I don't understand," Jill said.

Chase leaned forward. "He took advantage of them, don't you see? When Marc went to see them, he leaned heavily on Dianne's reputation as a lifelong resident. They believed his offer was fair, and when he promised to build a cottage on their property, they believed that too. Even if they couldn't live in it themselves, they wanted that for Dewberry Beach."

"But he lied," Jill breathed, suddenly understanding how Marc could afford not one but two oceanfront properties in one of New Jersey's most affluent shore towns.

"He lied." Chase's voice was a sigh.

"Marva was my best friend. Kaye's too," Mrs. Ivey added. "I've known her for fifty years and I'll never forget the look on her face when she was told her life had been dragged back to the sea. Everything she owned, all her memories were gone—her grandmother's clock, her wedding china, all her photographs. Even her grandchildren's plastic beach toys from the shed in the backyard. The hurricane stripped everything from her, and it was heartbreaking. But what that man did to her was far worse because he did it on purpose."

"I'm sorry but I still don't understand. For Marc to build anything on that land, it would have to be permitted. And it was," Jill said as she ran her fingers through her hair. "He filed blueprints. Surely anyone who looked could see that he was lying to them."

"Remember that Dianne's father, Peter Muscadine, was the planning commissioner?" Chase said. "In a town as small as Dewberry, Peter wasn't just on the planning commission, he *was* the planning commission. As you've guessed, he approved the permits without seeing them."

"He was part of this?"

"No, no. Absolutely not." Mrs. Ivey shook her head firmly. "Peter Muscadine was one of the best men I've ever known. He didn't have it in him to lie, and he loved this town. He was a simple man, truth be told. He would give you the shirt off his back if he thought it would help you, and that's where Marc saw his opening."

"You have to understand that in Dewberry, we take people at their word, trust what they say. It's a bit old-fashioned, I agree, but it's one of the things that makes this place great. So when Marc lied, all Peter saw was his daughter's husband, giving his word."

Jill sagged against the back of her chair. Peter Muscadine's trust would have been just the opportunity Marc needed.

Chase rose to snap on a little space heater by the door. "But Peter was just the first step. In normal times, Marc's deception would have been noticed. But these weren't normal times." The space heater whirred to life. "The bureaucracy that followed the hurricane was almost as bad as the storm. Insurance adjusters came to town, noted the damage, and refused to pay. Policies meant to protect from flood damage suddenly didn't apply, even with six feet of water lapping at the foundation. And the effort just to clear the roads, restore power and water was staggering. It was easy to hide in the shadows of that, and he did."

Jill felt a lump twist in her stomach. This was exactly the type of "advantage" Marc lived for.

"After he filed the plans, Marc amended them. And Peter approved the changes without reviewing the paperwork."

"Peter had other things on his mind," Mrs. Ivey added. "We all did."

Even as Chase nodded, Jill could tell that he'd always blame himself for what Marc did. For not seeing it.

Chase fell silent and Mrs. Ivey continued. "Even after we suspected what Marc was planning, there was little we could do to stop him. We tried talking to him, but it was useless. He is a greedy man," Mrs. Ivey sighed. "In the end, Peter accepted the blame for everything because that's the kind of man he was. He was summoned in front of the town council for a formal investigation—it was humiliating. He resigned that very afternoon. Within a week he'd sold his house and left the town he'd lived in all his life. A town he loved with all his heart."

"I had no idea." Jill closed her eyes. Suddenly, an idea took shape. Did Marc approach you or anyone else in town?"

"He wouldn't dare," Mrs. Ivey answered for Chase. "Why do you ask?"

"Because he never builds just one house. That's not how he works. He builds developments and puts a model home on site to show buyers. He didn't do that here," Jill explained. It was one piece that didn't quite fit.

As soon as she gave voice to it, Jill regretted her question. The story had gone beyond what she intended and seemed to be taking a toll on both of them. And her question was callous.

"I'm sorry," she said. "I was just thinking out loud. Please continue."

"There's not much more to tell," Chase replied, though his expression had shifted. He seemed wary now. "Marc filed papers to have the state clear debris from the waterfront lots he bought—for free, I might add. That process alone took the better part of a year. There was a petition at first and a few half-hearted protests, but it didn't matter. The lot was vacant for so long that we thought he might have reconsidered, but he hadn't. Later, he brought a crew down from New York and built what stands there today."

Jill sagged against the back of the chair. "I wish I'd known."

"We all wish that," Mrs. Ivey said. "For a long time, Dianne blamed herself, and it was heartbreaking to see. Even after the divorce, she was afraid to visit, and she'd lived here for most of her life. Marc took that from her."

"What about her father?"

"He lives near her, up in Rhode Island," Mrs. Ivey answered. "But he's not the same man he was."

Outside, dusk had turned to darkness. A patter of fall rain tapped on the windowpanes. Chase reached for a blanket and laid it across Mrs. Ivey's lap. She didn't seem to notice that she'd shivered.

"That man told us he'd come to help, but he didn't." Mrs. Ivey's voice shook with emotion. "He came to plunder."

The thought from earlier tugged at her. She needed to ask again, but she chose her words carefully this time. "During our divorce arbitration, Marc said his company hadn't earned a profit in all the time we were married, but I don't believe that's true. To prove it, he submitted a financial packet. Inside was a document from the state. I saw the seal." At the time, Jill had disagreed with what Marc had said but she hadn't looked closely at the financials. A mistake she regretted. "Then earlier today Nancy Pellish said 'after what he did in Mantoloking.' Do you know what she meant?"

"I don't," Chase said. "But Mantoloking's not far from here."

"Marc told the judge a property he owned had been declared a total loss. But the only properties I know of are the development in Summit, which he just completed, and the land in the Berkshires, which he just bought. Could the property he mentioned be the same one Nancy Pellish was talking about?"

"It's possible," Chase said slowly. "There are parts of Mantoloking that are still underwater, even today. The hurricane carved an inlet through a residential neighborhood over by the bridge. I think that town was hit the hardest."

Marc had testified that his business hadn't turned a profit in years, yet they'd both spent money freely. His watch alone had cost almost fifty thousand dollars, her shopping trips had been frequent and pricey. In addition, there had been country club dues, gym memberships, personal trainers, dinner parties, vacations—the list was endless. And that was only personal spending.

Chase interrupted her thoughts. "You said you came for answers. What did you want to ask?"

"I know that Marc arranged for you, specifically, to be at the party in August. Do you know why? Do you know what he wanted to talk to you about?"

"I assumed it was about investing." Chase shrugged. "Marc *always* asked me about investing."

But Chase's reply only stirred up more questions.

If Marc's company was losing money, he had nothing to invest. Why bother Chase? But Jill wouldn't press. Reliving the hurricane had clearly cost them something and Jill couldn't bring herself to ask for more. It was time to leave. She reached into her bag for her camera and removed the memory card.

"Would you mind giving this to Ryan? He needs it for the website." Then she rose from the chair. "Thank you for your time."

Pausing at the front door, she added, "I'm sorry for what Marc did. You can see now that I didn't have any part in it."

"I'm not sure that matters," Chase answered. "The fact remains: if you're selling that house, then you're part of it."

Chapter 22

Jill hurried back to the beach house.

After leaving the Bennett home, Jill cut down a side street to avoid the festival activity in town, though she didn't want to. In the few days she'd been here, she'd come to like Dewberry Beach—the people, the town, the shore. Avoiding them now felt wrong, like she was accepting blame for a scheme she'd had no part in. It bothered her that Chase believed that selling the house made complicit. This was Marc's doing, not hers. Why couldn't Chase see that? She kicked a stone in her path and it skittered across the street, smacking the opposite curb with a satisfying crack. Marc's lies had affected her as well; she was a victim too. But the worst part was that Marc was free to live his life while those he'd deceived struggled to find theirs.

Back at her own house and utterly exhausted, Jill let herself inside, locking the door and drawing the shades, hiding from the neighbors. But she already knew they were watching. She kicked off her shoes and settled into an alcove away from the windows, thinking that she should follow up with the real-estate agent, but she didn't have the energy.

After all she'd heard, several things still nagged at her: one of them was the idea that Marc had built a single house instead of a development.

He never did that, ever. How many times had she overheard him tell his associates, at parties or dinners, that profit came from developments, not singles. "Single builds lose money"—she could hear his voice as clearly as if he were standing in this room.

And the other was that Marc's whole business was losing money. That wasn't true either.

She'd been ordered to leave the Summit house because it had sold—the last house in a successful development. And if the development *wasn't* successful, how could Marc afford to move ahead with the Berkshire development? The money from the mortgage that Cush had stolen was significant, but not nearly enough to pay for the land Marc needed. So where did he get the rest?

It didn't make sense. None of this made sense.

Maybe she should start with the financial packet Marc had submitted to the judge.

Jill closed her eyes and tried to recall every detail about that day. There was a document in the packet, official correspondence from the state of New Jersey, that Marc had said proved his company had failed to turn a profit. She remembered the letterhead and the foil seal at the bottom. At the time, Jill had been furious but more concerned with losing her temper so she hadn't questioned it.

Maybe she should have.

Jill rose from her chair and went to get her laptop. Retreating to a guest bedroom in the back of the house, she drew the shades and began her search. With only a vague idea of what she was doing, Jill looked for the document Marc had given the judge. Her first thought was that, as a court document, it might be part of the public record, but Jill couldn't find it.

Several hours later, a bigger picture began to form, but it was murky. Jill printed documents and pictures that seemed like what she needed, even though she wasn't sure. Everything she discovered seemed to offer some clue, and yet nothing came together.

The chirp of her cell phone startled her. Straightening, she winced at the crick in her neck. As she reached for her phone, she noticed the room wasn't as dark as it had been when she'd started.

"Hello?" Jill's eyes felt grainy and dry.

"Hello, Ms. DiFiore. This is Sheri, Seth's assistant?" a chipper voice began immediately. "He asked me to call you. I hope it's not too early."

Jill cleared her throat. "No, not too early at all."

"I'm calling with good news: the client Seth toured the house with yesterday is very interested. He's requested another showing and wants to bring his team down this morning, if that's okay with you?"

"He has a team?" Jill echoed, her head fuzzy from lack of sleep.

"Yes. He's hired an architect and an engineer to look into expanding the widow's walk on the roof. It's got such a great view, there's really no reason not to." Her voice was much too cheery for this early in the morning and it made Jill's head ache. "They were delighted to discover that the property has almost no restriction on building or expanding. Such an advantage, don't you think?"

"Yes, it is," Jill agreed, without enthusiasm. Of course there would be few restrictions. Peter Muscadine had trusted his son-in-law.

"So do you mind if we come down and measure? Maybe take some photographs? If things go well, Seth might have an offer for you very soon."

"Sure. Of course. Come whenever you like."

"Great!" Sheri gushed. "We hoped you'd agree. Seth and the client are on their way to you now. This showing will be a long one. But, with luck, it will be the last."

"That's fine. Take as long as you like. I'll be out all day."

After the conversation ended, Jill rose and threw some things in her bag. On her way out the door, she grabbed the pages she'd printed, along with her camera case. She needed to talk to someone she trusted.

Chapter 23

Ellie was still away when Jill arrived back at the apartment. Dropping her bags, she made her way to the spare bedroom, pushing away all thought of Dewberry Beach and the festival as she shrugged off her coat. Right now she was supposed to be delivering her photograph to Brenda's framers. More than anything she wished she could. It hurt to lose this opportunity.

And what would Brenda think of her when she found out who she was?

What would they all think?

The obvious answer was that they'd think she was no better than Marc. And that judgment wasn't fair.

Sometime later, Jill woke to the sound of the front door opening. The light outside was dim, and her head felt fuzzy from the oddly timed sleep.

"Hello?" Ellie called.

"I'm in here," Jill croaked as she sat up.

Ellie appeared at the guest-room door, looking contrite. "I'm sorry, I didn't know you were sleeping."

"It's okay. I need to get up anyway." Jill pushed the blanket from her legs. "How was the wedding?"

"Fine. The Brockhursts paid well, but I didn't like it. I'm not sure organizing posh weddings in the Hamptons is the best career path for me." She reached for the door. "You want to go back to sleep?"

"Uh-uh." Jill shook her head as she stood. "I'm hungry. Have you eaten?"

"They gave us a boxed lunch, but honestly, I could seriously go for a Mama G's pizza."

Jill smiled. It felt good to be with her best friend again. So why did her thoughts pull her toward Dewberry Beach?

They ordered a pizza and set the box on the coffee table when it arrived. Ellie grabbed two beers from the refrigerator and settled on the floor, just like they used to, and as they ate, she told Jill about the Brockhurst wedding—the luxury and the guests. She described the woman who'd brought her twins to an adults-only reception and had been furious that on-site childcare hadn't been provided. And the teens who'd crept into the wine cellar for a bottle of their own, setting off the alarm in the process. It almost felt like old times—almost.

When the pizza was reduced to just a few crusts tossed into the box, Ellie's attitude became more serious. Her gaze sharpened as if she were trying to solve a puzzle.

"Something happened at the shore, didn't it?" she asked as she pushed herself up from the floor. "Something you haven't told me."

"Well, the sales agent may have found a buyer already, so that's good news... great, in fact," Jill offered, deliberately stalling. Ellie looked tired and Jill wasn't sure this was the right time to present her findings. "And they're measuring today. Or maybe they already have. The days are starting to blend."

Ellie paused, her eyes narrowing as she considered. Finally, she shook her head. "Nope. That's not it." She took two more beers from the refrigerator and handed one to Jill.

Jill twisted the top and tossed it into the pizza box. She thought of the mortgage she wouldn't have to pay and felt better. This was a good ending for a house she never should have taken in the first place. Maybe what happened next wasn't up to her.

"Jilly," Ellie prodded. "Out with it."

Jill set the bottle down with a sigh. "I don't know. There might be something, but it's complicated."

She rose to get the printouts from her bag. When she returned, they pushed the pizza box aside and spread everything across the coffee table. Jill explained the things she'd uncovered, fitting together what she'd learned about the house Marc had built, what Chase had told her, and what she'd overheard at the Yacht Club, but there were still gaping holes in the story. Holes that clouded the truth.

"It didn't make sense to me that Marc would be content with a single house in Dewberry Beach. He doesn't work that way," Jill finished as she sifted through the pages. "I may have found something but I'm not entirely sure."

She slid a page to Ellie, who set her beer down and frowned. "What am I looking at?"

"It's a plat map of four adjoining properties Marc owned in Mantoloking. I think it's where he wanted to put a development. I think Dewberry was part of a larger plan."

"Why would he spread out like that?"

"For one thing, oceanfront property at the shore is wildly expensive, especially at Dewberry Beach, so maybe he couldn't afford it. But—and this is more likely—I think they wouldn't sell him what he needed."

Jill told Ellie what she'd learned, about Dianne's connections to Dewberry Beach and how Marc had used them to swindle property from hurricane victims. That after getting zoning approval from Dianne's father, Marc had traveled to Trenton to modify the permits, then brought in his own crew to put the house up.

"That's messed up." Ellie leaned back, stunned. "How can anyone be that terrible?"

"I should have listened to you, El." Jill scrubbed her face with her palm. "You're my best friend and you never liked him. I should have listened."

"I never liked him because he didn't treat you well. The business stuff… I had no idea. You couldn't have known either, so don't blame yourself."

"It gets worse." Jill pointed at the plat maps. "This whole area was underwater after the hurricane." She passed Ellie a picture showing the new inlet in Mantoloking. "This is what the neighborhood looked like before."

"Holy mackerel," Ellie whispered. "Is this right?" She touched the photographs with her fingertips. "Those poor people."

Jill took a breath. "This is where things get sticky, and I'm not sure if what I *think* happened really happened."

"Let's hear it." Ellie laid the picture gently on the coffee table.

"The dates suggest Marc bought this land *after* the hurricane, not before. Which is weird because by then it was completely underwater, unbuildable and worthless."

"Why would he do that?"

"Before the hurricane, it was waterfront. See?" Jill pointed to the map again. "That's Barnegat Bay right there. Waterfront."

"I don't get it, Jilly."

"Okay." Jill sat in the chair across from her friend. "Because this was waterfront before the hurricane, it was reasonable to expect it would be after. Officials expected floodwaters to recede and the coastline to return to normal eventually. But it didn't, and it never will. The force of the hurricane changed the coastline, so the land Marc bought is still underwater and worthless—or it *was*." She took a breath to organize her thoughts. She was about to accuse her husband of something so horrible that it made her careful. "I found this deed in the County Tax Assessor's digital archive." She lifted a page from the pile. "Marc's company bought a block of the most severely damaged properties along the new inlet. That was in 2013, right after the hurricane."

"Okay." Ellie took the page. "So what does it say?"

Jill pointed to the deed she'd printed. "He told the judge at arbitration that he didn't have any personal assets, but this says he did. He lied, El. To a judge."

Ellie squinted at the page. "Who's Cushman Lawrence the third?"

Jill rolled her eyes. "Technically, he's the staff attorney for Marc's company—he and his wife are the ones who took out the mortgage in my name."

Ellie's expression hardened but she didn't interrupt.

"This is where it gets tricky because the rest of it is so technical." She went back to her papers. "I found a buy-out program that provides money to homeowners who'd needed it, who'd lost everything. There were a million programs after the hurricane: programs, subprograms, charities and loans, state and federal and private. One of them—"

"I get it, Jilly. Can you narrow it down?"

Jill shot Ellie a look. "Do you have any idea how long it took me to sift through all of this?"

"And I'm glad you did. But can you summarize?"

"Fine. In the financial packet that Marc submitted was a document from the state declaring the Mantoloking property worthless."

"That's when he lied?"

"Not yet. His lie comes later."

"Okay, then. Keep going."

"After the hurricane, programs were set up to help residents whose homes had been destroyed and were funded without a proper plan for distribution." Jill rose from her seat and began to pace. "And all that money attracted the wrong kind of people, so the state added restrictions. One of the biggest was that commercial property wasn't eligible. So if you *did* submit commercial property, your claim would be rejected right away and you'd get a letter like this one." Jill scooped a page from the table. "I think *this* is the document Marc showed the judge."

"A rejection?"

"Yes, but the thing is, Marc wouldn't have accepted a rejection, especially with that much money involved. He would have appealed the decision—he appealed decisions all the time. So I kept looking."

"And?"

"Two years ago, the property classification changed again. And just like that, Marc's commercial property became residential and was now eligible for state money." She lifted another paper from the pile and offered it to Ellie. "Marc submitted a claim and this time, the state paid."

"So the financial packet is wrong?" Ellie scanned the page then looked up. "That seems like a pretty big deal. What're you going to do?"

"That part I don't know." Jill sat on the floor opposite Ellie. "Honestly, I'm not surprised, and I *should* be, you know?" She told Ellie about the subcontractor Marc had refused to pay and how the incident still bothered her. "That man had a family to support." She couldn't look at Ellie, so she found a crease on her jeans and smoothed it away.

"Why didn't you tell me?"

"I was embarrassed to, I guess. Marc seemed so perfect in the beginning—made me feel special, you know? He took me to places I never could have afforded to go on my own, opened a world I never imagined. But the most important thing was that he *chose me*. Marc could have had anyone, and I was the one he picked. Later, when things started to change, I thought I was the problem, so I tried harder to make him happy."

"Oh, Jilly." Ellie's voice was unbearably gentle.

Jill could feel the pinprick of tears but shook them off. She sniffed and swiped her sleeve roughly across her face. "It's fine. It's over now, Marc and me." She cleared her throat as she straightened. "But what he did to those people in Dewberry Beach is unforgivable. They don't get another chance." She finally raised her gaze to meet Ellie's. "That house stands as a reminder of what he did. I didn't understand before, but I do now. I have to do something."

"Like what?"

"I have an idea."

"Tell me." Ellie brightened. "Whatever it is, I'm in."

"You're lucky you caught me," Marc said when Jill called him on Friday morning. "I'm on my way back up to the new site. In fact, I'm leaving this afternoon."

"Then let me buy you lunch today." Jill softened her voice, though it made her skin crawl to do so. She and Ellie had come up with a great plan, but it depended on Marc meeting Jill for lunch. She sighed, manufacturing regret. "I just want to talk to you, Marc. It won't take long."

Marc hesitated and Jill held her breath.

"Sure, why not." She could almost see him shrug. "How about Woodblock? One o'clock?"

"Perfect. I'll make the reservations. It'll be good to see you again," she added, through gritted teeth.

She could feel Ellie tense beside her and for a moment thought she'd gone too far.

"You too, Jilly," Marc answered, his voice a deep rumble.

She disconnected and scrubbed the goosebumps from her skin. Then she glanced at Ellie, a slow smile curling her lips. "He said yes."

"Let's do it."

Chapter 24

By 12.30 p.m., Jill was dressed and ready to meet Marc.

She stood before the bathroom mirror in Ellie's empty apartment and drew a breath to steady her nerves. Appearance was everything to Marc, and she worried that her new haircut and clothes would be too much of a change for him. Even so, she refused to go back to the woman she was with him, even for this, so in the end, Jill decided to dress like herself. She paired a slouchy white T-shirt with a borrowed black pencil skirt, then added a low-slung black belt around her hips and zipped up Ellie's ankle boots. On her way out the door, she slipped on a black vintage leather jacket and added a swipe of bright red lipstick.

When she arrived at the restaurant, she walked to the hostess station.

"I'm Jill DiFiore. I'm supposed to be meeting someone?"

The hostess glanced at her book. "Yes. He's already seated. This way please."

They crossed the dining room toward the table Jill had reserved. As they got closer, she saw Marc sitting comfortably, his arm resting across the chair next to him, and her stomach lurched at the sight of him. After everything they'd been through, she'd expected him to—wanted him to—look haggard and stressed, but he didn't. Instead he looked much as he always had—confident and handsome, as if he hadn't a care in the world. Looking closer, Jill recognized the cashmere sport coat she'd bought him for Christmas the year before.

All at once, Jill faltered as the past slammed into her. She wasn't sure she could go through with this, wasn't sure she was strong enough. In business, Marc always came out ahead. What did she have? Nothing but a desire to right an injustice. That might not be enough, especially against someone like him.

"Are you okay?" The hostess's smile was etched with concern, and Jill realized that she'd stopped right in the middle of the dining room.

"Yes, thank you. I'm fine." Jill shook her head. "I thought I might have left my phone in the car. But I didn't. I have it."

She followed the hostess to the table, projecting a confidence she didn't possess. In reality, her dread grew with every step as she moved closer to Marc. She managed to smile at him before taking her seat and accepted a menu from the hostess, then pretended to scan the list of specials clipped to the front as she gathered her nerve.

"Your waiter will be right with you."

Jill nodded, not trusting her voice.

"Wow," Marc leered, as soon as they were alone. "You've changed. You look good."

Jill suppressed a shudder.

When she was ten years old, Jill had wanted to be an actress. That summer at Aunt Sarah's, Jill had written and directed a play that was so horrible she'd had to bribe her cousins with candy to participate. The costumes had been scavenged from trunks in the attic and the backdrops were mostly crayoned pictures. The play was awful and only kindness kept the audience in their seats, but that didn't matter. Jill had loved the idea of slipping into an entirely new personality.

She did that now.

"Thanks, I had it cut." Actress-Jill flicked her fingers through her hair, beaming at the man she'd come to loathe. "I thought it was time."

"New clothes too. I like it." His glance lingered a little too long.

She shrugged. Had she ever been attracted to that tone of voice? She certainly wasn't now.

Because she wasn't sure how to begin, she stalled a little. Settling into her chair, she opened her napkin and smoothed it across her lap. "How's Brittney?"

It was the first thing she could think of and clearly the wrong choice.

Marc's expression snapped shut and his eyes turned cold. "Why do you ask?"

"No reason." Jill reached for her water and sipped to clear her dry throat. Actress-Jill needed to get it together.

"What are you up to?" Marc's voice was wary. The moment Marc considered Jill an opponent, it was over.

"Up to?" Jill shrugged again, this time coquettishly. "I'm not up to anything."

"Jillian," Marc warned, his voice softer. "I know you. I know your tricks."

She tilted her head as if debating whether to let him in on the secret. She added a delicate sigh, the kind he used to find attractive. "Fine." She smiled as if he'd never had an affair. Or broken her heart. Or tried to ruin her life. "I guess I should know better than to try to fool you."

"That's better…"

"The truth is, I wanted to meet with you today because I'm thinking about starting a company, like you did."

"Oh, really?" He leaned back, amused. Jill pressed her palms together on her lap to keep from slapping the smugness from his face. "The Princess of South Jersey is going into business now?"

They were interrupted by the server who'd arrived to take their drink orders. From their very first date, Marc had insisted on ordering for her, and she'd never liked it. This was one thing, however small, that she could take back.

She saw him open his mouth to speak and shifted her gaze to the server. "I'd like an iced tea, lots of ice please." Then she kicked herself for choosing this moment to assert her independence. She should have let him order for her, same as always. What good did it do to antagonize him now?

She flashed an apologetic smile and hoped it was enough.

Marc ordered a Scotch for himself, a drink he only ordered with friends. This was encouraging.

After the server left, Actress-Jill picked up the thread of the conversation. She forced a breezy tone, laced with just a hint of flirtation, and hoped it wasn't too much. Actress-Jill could be a little over the top. "You did me a favor, you know, with the house in Dewberry Beach, though I have to admit, I didn't realize it at the time." She adjusted the stack of bracelets on her wrist in a casual way, as if their conversation was small talk charged with something more. It was part of the game.

"Oh? How so?"

"The place is a gold mine, Marc." She leaned toward him and lowered her voice to a whisper. "What you did down there was genius. I found the deeds for the properties in Mantoloking," she breathed. "It took me days to find them and even longer to put it all together."

"What were you doing digging around in the records office?"

The waiter arrived with their drinks and she reached for her iced tea and sipped, hoping to slow the pace. Marc was greedy but he wasn't stupid, and she needed to tread carefully. This plan wouldn't work if she pushed, so she'd make him come to her. As she set her glass down, she lifted her shoulder in a gentle shrug. "The agent wanted information for the closing. I had to find it."

That got him.

"Wait…" Marc stiffened. "You *sold* the Dewberry Beach house?"

"I did," she pouted. "I was disappointed to let it go, to be honest. But what's important is what I found…" She reached across the table for his arm, though she had to force herself to do it. "Marc. The Green Acres program is still accepting claims. It's still paying out." She bit her bottom lip, remembering how he liked that. "What you did with the Mantoloking properties was inspired. I want you to show me how to do it."

He shifted back. "I don't know what you're talking about."

"Fine." Jill shrugged. "Have it your way, but you should know there are other opportunities down there, a few you've missed. A couple of federal programs are still paying out too. But the claim needs to be perfect. And you've done it before…"

"What do you mean?" Marc's eyes brightened and she knew he was hooked. He was never one to leave money on the table.

"We should partner. I'll give you…" She pretended to consider. "Thirty percent?"

Jill rested her chin on her hand and waited. The emotions flickering across Marc's face were very telling. First there was disbelief at being discovered, then petulance at being called out, and finally greed. When she saw the others fade and greed remain, she knew she had him.

"Seventy-five," Marc countered.

Jill tilted her head and frowned. "Forty-five."

"Sixty-five."

"Deal." She reached across the table to shake his hand. "Now you have to tell me how you did it. I'm curious: were you the one who found the relief programs or was that Cush? Because I'm not sure he would have known how."

"It was me." Marc puffed up. "Cush does only what I tell him to do, nothing more."

"Okay then. Tell me how you did it." He retreated a little, so Jill tugged the hook. "Unless you don't need the money? The Berkshire project is going well?"

That did it.

Marc told Jill everything. How he'd tracked the hurricane's path—not out of concern for the victims but to identify the hardest hit areas as opportunities for later. Pushing the permitting through was easy because his father-in-law was a simple man and easily overwhelmed. After that, he went to Trenton and lied there too.

And then word had got out.

He'd had a feeling Chase Bennett was watching, but he couldn't be sure. So he'd moved south to Mantoloking, calling upon distressed owners and buying their ravaged homes for pennies on the dollar. He'd had no intention of rebuilding, he said. By then he knew the state would make property owners whole and all he needed to do was wait.

"My only mistake was having Cush change the zoning from residential to commercial."

"Because of the hearings?"

"No," Marc scoffed as he lifted his drink. "There were no hearings. It was a free-for-all back then and we submitted false papers. That part was easy."

"So why was zoning your only mistake?"

"It was a good idea at first." Marc sipped, mistaking her scrutiny for admiration. "There's no valuation for commercial properties so the claim I filed could be for whatever amount I chose, and it was." He chuckled. "We inflated the crap out of that property value. But then they changed the rules."

There was some hope the restrictions would be lifted eventually so Marc had waited. But he'd needed money to buy land for the Berkshire development and he didn't have it. He'd known he couldn't wait any longer, so he'd submitted the claim. When the payment had come through, he'd had Cush travel to Freeport to deposit the money in a special account.

"But it wasn't enough," Marc concluded. "We were short a couple hundred thousand."

"And that's why you took out a mortgage on the Dewberry house?" Jill asked, careful to keep the resentment from her voice.

To her surprise, Marc looked shocked. "You're not still mad about that, are you, babe? It was business, that's all. You were never supposed to find out."

"Sure. I understand." Though it was difficult, Jill flashed an appreciative smile. "But I interrupted. Please go on."

"Since you're at the shore now, you can set up a base. Scout out damaged properties and buy them for almost nothing. Send me pictures and I'll have them declared uninhabitable, even if they're not. We can fix that paperwork to say anything we want. Then we'll have Cush submit the claim—"

"Because he's done it before," Jill added. "Submitted a false claim?"

"Yeah. Some of those federal programs are so big they can't possibly review every claim—they just pay out." He leaned back, clearly pleased with himself. "It's the easiest money we'll ever make."

"You did all that?" Jill squeezed her hands together on her lap to keep them from shaking. "On the Mantoloking properties? You filed a fake claim, and it paid?"

Marc preened. "I did. And I would have submitted a claim for the Dewberry Beach house too, but I would have been caught. But you don't have to worry—federal programs will pay out forever. All they care about is the right documents."

Jill beamed, and this time it was genuine. She'd gotten what she needed. She gathered her things and stood. "Great. I think we're finished here."

"Where are you going?" Marc's brow creased with confusion.

Jill ignored him. Instead, she gestured to Ellie, who had been seated at the table behind them, at the second table Jill had reserved. "Did you get it?"

"I did indeed." Ellie's smile was triumphant as she rose. "Every bit."

"Then let's get out of here." Jill grabbed her coat and turned to leave.

"Wait," Marc commanded. Other diners had turned toward them, so he lowered his voice. "What is this? What's going on?"

Jill paused then, to savor the expression on his face, the indignation and confusion. It was glorious.

"Since you asked so nicely," she said as she slipped her coat on, "couple of things. First, you admitted to defrauding the federal government, which is bad."

"So bad." Ellie shook her head sadly.

"*Then* you told me you intended to do it again, which is worse." Jill shrugged. "But I'm just a Jersey Girl so I can't be sure. So I guess I'll have to send the video Ellie took on her phone to Chase Bennett's office and have him look at it. You remember Chase? Turns out he knows a lot about financial fraud *and* he still has federal connections."

Marc's face turned a shade of purple that she'd never seen before. And it was delightful.

"Jilly…" he croaked.

She laughed and it felt wonderful. "You are in soooo much trouble."

She walked through the restaurant with Ellie at her side.

"Next time can I wear a wire?" Ellie asked. "I've always wanted to."

"F'get it." Jill leaned into her friend. "That's all I can take."

Chapter 25

After returning from the restaurant, Jill headed for the bathroom and turned on the shower. Lunch with Marc had been tense and now she was exhausted. It wasn't only what he'd done—it was the person she'd become when she was with him. It was unnerving how quickly she'd changed for him, how ready she'd been to abandon who she was to become what he'd wanted her to be.

Jill stood in the shower for a long time, feeling the hot water warm her skin and trying to wash away the chill.

When she emerged from the bathroom sometime later, wrapped in a bathrobe, Ellie was ready. She had her laptop open and a look of deep concentration on her face.

"What's all this?" Jill asked.

"I've been busy. I uploaded the video to someplace safe." Ellie gestured to a flash drive. "I made a physical copy too, just in case."

"Thanks, Ellie." Jill made her way to the couch and collapsed.

"Can you believe he admitted to everything?" Ellie swept her hair back, her voice filled with excitement. "He's not *nearly* as smart as he thinks, which makes me wonder what else he's done. I wonder if we should look into it?"

Jill closed her eyes. "Sure."

"You okay?"

"Yeah, sure. I'm just tired." Jill straightened. They weren't finished yet. "I typed up an explanation and I think we should attach the video and mail it to someone important, but I'm not sure who. What do you think?"

"The judge, maybe? The one who mediated your divorce?"

Jill took a minute to consider, then shook her head. "I don't think so. What Marc did seems bigger than that."

"So what do you want to do?" Ellie rested her back against the couch. "Somebody needs to see this."

"I was kidding before, when I mentioned Chase Bennett, because it was fun to see Marc scared. But now I don't think the idea is so crazy. Chase was a big deal before he retired, so chances are good that he'll know what to do with it." And even if the video wasn't enough to trigger an investigation, Jill wanted Chase to know she'd tried. "If he doesn't, he might know someone who does."

"On it. Do you have an email for him?"

Jill rose to fetch a slip of paper from her camera bag: Ryan's contact information. "Not directly, but if you use this one, I'm pretty sure Chase'll get it."

"Okay. I'll send it right now." Ellie turned her attention back to the screen.

As she returned to the couch, Jill's cell phone rang with an incoming phone call. It was the real-estate office. "This is Jill."

"Hello, Jillian, this is Sheri from the Manhattan Group."

"Sheri, hi. How are you?"

"I'm well, thank you. And you will be too, in a minute." Sheri's voice was bright. "Seth asked me to call you with the good news. The client and his team finished their work sooner than they thought. He *loves* the house and wants to submit a formal offer. In fact, he and Seth are in the office writing it up now. Seth wants to present it to you tomorrow morning and asks if 8 a.m. at the house is convenient. Said he knows you're an early bird," she added with a chuckle.

She wasn't, but that was okay. The important thing was the offer. Could this really be the end?

"Yes, of course," Jill said. "I'll be there."

"Great. He'll see you then."

Jill disconnected the call and glanced at Ellie. "The house sold," she said, stunned. "I'm supposed to meet the agent at the house tomorrow morning."

"I'm totally going with you."

Chapter 26

Because traffic on the Garden State Parkway was unpredictable and the agent appointment was early in the morning, they decided to drive down right away and spend one final night in Dewberry Beach. The idea of staying at The Monstrosity didn't bother Jill as much as the thought that this would be the last time she'd ever visit the town. Once the rest of its residents found out who she was, she wouldn't be welcome.

They stopped for gas at a rest-stop on I95 and Ellie ran in for two coffees from The Dunk. As the rich scent filled the car, Jill's thoughts turned to the morning she'd ordered coffee and muffins at Dewberry Beach, but she pushed them away. It was time for her to move on, and her new life wouldn't include Dewberry Beach. It couldn't. She paid the attendant for the gas and they continued on their way, the traffic unexpectedly light for a Friday afternoon.

"So this is it, huh?" Ellie asked as she pried the plastic lid from her coffee. "You get the offer tomorrow and you're done? Do you know how much it is?"

"No, but it doesn't matter. I'll take anything that pays the mortgage and covers closing costs."

"Jillian." Ellie lowered her coffee cup and side-eyed Jill. "That house is worth a fortune. A huge house on two lots of oceanfront? I've seen the listing. The money you get from that could be a whole new start—you could *literally* do anything you want—and don't you deserve that? After what Marc did to you?"

Jill flicked her blinker and passed the sturdy Volvo in front of her. How could she explain to Ellie what she couldn't understand herself? That she'd come to appreciate Dewberry Beach and liked the people in it. That she understood why they hated Marc's house so much, that it was a symbol of greed built by a man who'd swindled them. And she hated it too.

"No, I don't want to profit from the sale."

"So what's left? Keeping it? I thought you couldn't afford that?"

"Absolutely not. I can't keep it," Jill said quickly. "I can't even afford the water bill in a house that big."

"Okay, so if you had a choice…" Ellie waved her hand dramatically in the air, caught up in the game of "what-if." "If you could magically make *anything* happen, what would you do with that house?"

"I'd raze it," Jill said simply, and the truth of it surprised her. She told Ellie what Chase had told her that night at his house, and the things she'd overheard at the Yacht Club. Personal accounts of how horrific the hurricane had been and how Marc had made it so much worse. "That house will always be a reminder of how Marc cheated them and it's painful for them to see it every day. Wouldn't it be great to give them a do-over? After everything they've been through?"

"Yeah, I guess it would," Ellie agreed. "It sounds as if you really like Dewberry Beach, Jilly."

"I guess I do," Jill replied. "The town, the people, they remind me of summers at Aunt Sarah's."

They drove in silence for a while, each of them lost in their own thoughts. Jill wondered about the art auction and if Brenda had found someone to fill her spot in the gallery. She remembered how carefully the volunteers had decorated the Yacht Club ballroom, the strings of white lights threaded through the tree branches outside, and she imagined their soft glow against the evening sky. It was a party and the whole town was invited. And then she wondered if Danny would be there.

"Isn't that house of yours furnished? With high-end stuff? And appliances too?" Ellie asked abruptly. "What if you sold all of it to pay for bulldozers and dump trucks or whatever? You could demolish the house. Wouldn't that work?"

Jill finished the last sip of coffee then returned her cup to the console. "Funny you should ask. I've thought of it myself, even went so far as to search resale markets to see how much the kitchen appliances are worth. In fact, I still have the list somewhere—on Marc's desk at the Dewberry house, I think. Anyway, selling everything in that house, right down to the towels in the bathrooms and the platters in the butler pantry, would only be enough to pay off the mortgage. That still leaves the demolition, and I imagine bulldozers and dump trucks are expensive."

"Well, that's it then. With all those bills to pay, there's only so much you can do." Ellie sagged against the door. "Razing that house was a good idea though."

Jill shrugged because there didn't seem to be anything more to say. What she *wanted* to do and what she was *able* to do were two vastly different things.

Chapter 27

By the time they pulled the car into the garage at Dewberry Beach, the afternoon light had faded. Even before Jill switched off the ignition, she made sure the garage door was closed firmly behind them. This was the family weekend of the Light Up the Bay Festival, and activities would be scattered all over town. Besides the art auction she was hiding from, there were activities on the beach, and it was important that they didn't draw any attention to this house. Jill needed the sale.

They climbed out of the car and gathered their stuff.

As they entered the house, Jill flicked on a kitchen light that couldn't be seen from the street or the shore. Even after just a couple of days away, it was jarring to enter The Monstrosity. The interior space was meant to be lavish, but Jill still found it overwhelming and ostentatious. She much preferred the coziness of Ellie's apartment. They dropped their bags and Ellie asked for directions to Marc's office, which seemed an odd request but Jill let it go.

"Down the hallway, second on the left." Jill moved to the windows, pulling the drapes firmly closed.

Ellie returned, stuffing a paper in her back pocket. "How 'bout if I go pick up food for us? I can go into town—no one will know who I am. You think anything's open?"

"The deli should be." Jill drew a map on the back of an envelope. "If you go there, be sure to bring back sides. The salads are really good."

"Sides? Sure." Ellie looked at her quizzically. "You okay?"

"Yeah, sure. Just tired." On second thought, Jill switched off the kitchen light. "Go get the food. I'll be here when you get back."

"Okay. I'll be back soon." Ellie made her way to the front door, then turned. "I'm curious about something. That man you told me about—the one who didn't like Marc? Chase something? What did you say his last name is again?"

"Bennett." Jill pulled a blanket from a wicker basket and wrapped it around her shoulders. "Yeah, he didn't like Marc at all. Why do you ask?"

"No reason."

After Ellie left, Jill made her way upstairs, intending to take a hot shower, but when she couldn't summon the energy to stand, even for a few minutes, she drew a bath instead. She added the lavender bath salt that was meant for show and watched the ocean waves on the horizon. And when finally she wasn't able to hold them back a minute longer, she let her thoughts drift to the art show at the Yacht Club. To the auction that was happening right this minute, and to the empty spot that should have been hers. She wondered if anyone would have liked the bridal portrait she'd planned to show, and then because it was too painful to think about, she decided it didn't matter.

She stayed in the tub until the water grew cold, then toweled off and wrapped herself in a thick robe.

The real-estate agents were due to arrive early the following morning. They'd present the buyer's offer and Jill would accept it, whatever it was. This time tomorrow, she and Ellie would be far away from Dewberry Beach. They might even be celebrating the start of Jill's new life.

That's what she wanted, wasn't it? A fresh start?

So why wasn't she happier?

Ellie returned with food a while later, her hair and clothes windswept and her face pink from the cold. She nudged the door open with her hip, her arms filled with bags. As she entered the house, a gust of wind pushed past her, bringing with it the scent of woodsmoke and ocean air.

"You won't believe what's going on in town—the place is packed." She set the bags on the table and peeled off her coat, tossing it on a chair. "I thought you said town would be deserted tonight."

"I thought it would be. The art show is at the Yacht Club and that's over by the bay."

"That might be true, but there's also some kind of street fair going on." Ellie began unpacking the food: fat sandwiches and soda and tubs of salads. "Kids are running everywhere. Every shop door is propped wide open, and there are pumpkin string lights draped across the street."

Jill had been there when the volunteers had strung the pumpkin lights and she remembered wondering what they would look like at night. She hadn't been to a street fair since she was a kid. It sounded wonderful, and more than anything, Jill wished they could walk back into town to be part of it. But that wasn't possible of course. Ellie could, but Jill wouldn't be welcome there and the realization stung.

"Is that why you were gone so long?" Jill pasted on a smile she didn't feel. "I thought you'd gotten lost."

"What? Oh, yeah. I guess I did." Ellie's hand hovered over the light switch. "On or off?"

"Off," Jill blurted with more force than necessary. "Definitely off. I'm sorry, do you mind?"

"Of course not, but it seems unfair." Ellie sighed, resigned. Suddenly, she gathered everything up. "No. Forget this. You didn't do this. You didn't build this house. You're just selling it because you can't afford not to. There's a deck up top of this palace, isn't there? Let's go there. No one can possibly see us up there."

They carried their dinner and a couple of blankets up to the rooftop deck. In the waning light, they watched a trio of seagulls glide across the horizon as the waves rolled gently to shore. They tracked the surfer with the faded green board riding one final wave to shore. Absurdly, Jill felt an odd sense of pride at how hard the surfer had worked in the few days she'd been in town, how dedicated he was to his craft. She would have liked to have met whoever it was. Further up the beach, a man who had been throwing a driftwood stick for his dog decided to call it a day. He whistled and his dog came running. Jill would have liked to have met him too.

She and Ellie spent their last night at the shore outside, watching the moon rise over the sea. They stayed on the rooftop deck even when they could no longer see the ocean. They listened to the waves roar and the murmur of families on the beach calling out to each other as they walked along the shore. It would have been wonderful to have become part of this community. The idea was unexpected. She hadn't anticipated becoming so attached in such a short time.

When the chill of the late October evening became too much for even the blankets they'd brought outside, they decided to call it a day.

As Jill helped pack everything up, she felt a painful tug of regret. Dewberry Beach was a sweet little town and it had come to occupy a special place in her heart.

She would be sorry to leave it.

Chapter 28

The following morning found Jill at the dining table with Ellie on her left, the real-estate agents on her right, and a daunting amount of paperwork in front of her. Neither she nor Ellie had ever bought or sold real estate before, and it wasn't as easy as they thought it would be.

"This is a solid offer, Jill." Seth tapped the balance sheet for the second time, pleased with himself. "It's even better than I'd hoped. They want to start construction immediately so they're willing to pay a premium for a fast close."

Jill lifted the spreadsheet from the pile and looked at the numbers again. Seth was right—the offer was substantially over list price. If she accepted, she'd walk away with more money than she'd ever seen—enough to last for years. She could go back to school, get that art degree Mrs. Brockhurst had insisted she needed. She could afford to buy all new camera equipment—anything she wanted. All she had to do was sign the papers to accept the offer. Yet, she couldn't bring herself to pick up a pen, and her hesitancy was frustrating everyone at the table.

"Tell me again who these people are?" she asked, though she knew the answer because she'd asked twice before.

To his credit, Seth offered a patient smile. "It's not a person, Jill. It's a company—Shore Parties Unlimited." Seth slid their brochure across the table. "They specialize in corporate events and retreats. Off-site executive experiences are the next big thing, and this company wants to be ahead of the curve."

"They want this house to be a 'venue'? You mean, for parties?" Jill glanced at their brochure, though she didn't need to.

"Their only shore venue, as a matter of fact. This house was built for entertaining, so why not put the space to work?" Seth shrugged. "It's a solid business plan."

"I haven't heard of this company before. Are they new?" Ellie asked, and Jill was grateful for the extra time to think.

Seth's expression flickered with annoyance and Jill couldn't blame him. They'd been at the table far longer than they should have been and the questions she posed were ridiculous, even to her. What did it matter who the buyer was? She wasn't rehoming a puppy—she was selling a house.

Seth recovered and answered. "Shore Parties may be small, but they have money to spend. They're funded out of Atlantic City—one of the casinos, as I've said—and their parties are legendary. They set up lights, speakers, DJ equipment—and this location is perfect for pyrotechnics. The house itself has no restrictions and they plan to expand their events to use the beach as much as they can. Luckily, the front driveway is big enough to accommodate their party bus."

"Party bus?" That was new. Jill glanced at the circular driveway in front of the house.

"They liked the house quite a bit, but what *really* sold it was the lack of restrictions attached to the deed—that almost never happens." When Jill didn't respond, Seth continued. "They've drawn up plans to expand the house. I can show them to you if you'd like."

"Expand?" Jill parroted. "You mean beyond just the widow's walk?"

"Oh yeah," Seth said. "You should see. They plan to build right up to the property line. There's no reason not to, right?"

Jill frowned. Was that really the legacy she wanted to leave—that she had made Marc's Monstrosity even worse?

Seth misunderstood her hesitation and pressed forward. "This offer is good, Jill. Really good." He found the closing statement and slid it toward her again. "All-cash offer, twenty percent over your asking price, and we close in two weeks."

"To give them time to expand before next summer, I bet," Jill muttered. "They probably even have their own work crew, just like Marc did."

Seth pressed his back against his chair, exasperated. "I'm sorry, Ms. DiFiore, but I don't understand why you're not happier about this offer. It's exactly what you asked for. You wanted a quick sale; we have one. You wanted the furnishings to go with the house; they will. In fact, they want everything in this house—right down to the forks in the kitchen and the food in the pantry; something about feeding the contractors when they come."

"Can we get someone else?" Jill asked suddenly. "A family who'll fit in, with kids who'll like the beach and maybe bring their friends to visit?" It was what Dewberry needed, a family who'd appreciate the town. Not a company who'd take advantage of the building code.

"You want me to find a family to buy this house?" Seth echoed.

"Yes." Jill spoke quickly. "What if we lowered the price? I don't care about profit. I just want the right people living here. Someone the neighbors will like."

Seth blinked, clearly stunned. Jill squeezed her hands together as she waited. Maybe it could work.

"If you lowered the price that much and put the house back on the market," Seth said eventually, "an investor would snap it up before a family ever had a chance to see it. Then, a smart investor would put the house back on the market. He might even hire me to list it. In that case, I'd contact the buyer you turned down and we'd would sell to them anyway."

Jill shot Ellie a look of desperation.

Ellie understood. She rose from the table. "I, for one, could use a five-minute break. Would anyone like a bit more coffee? Won't take more than a minute to start a fresh pot."

Sheri glanced at Seth, then went to join Ellie. "I'll help you."

"Ms. DiFiore," Seth began, when they were alone. "Is it your intention to sell this house? Because I thought that's what you wanted when you hired me to list it."

"Yes, of course. You're right. I do need to sell this house," Jill said quickly.

Seth's phone buzzed with an incoming text and he glanced at the screen. "It's the buyers. They want to know if you've accepted their offer." He stood up. "I'll give them a call and tell them we're just finishing up."

Jill left the table as well. She made her way to the far wall, to the bank of windows overlooking the ocean. A wisp of fog floated across water and a pale orange sun lit it from behind. Even this early in the morning, there was activity on the beach. On the shoreline, a trio of young women walked together barefoot, their pant legs rolled to the knee. An unexpected wave reached them, and they jumped, howling with laughter as the cold water splashed their legs. Further up the beach, a man and his daughter kneeled on the wet sand, pointing to something in the tidepool. He grabbed her suddenly, breaking her concentration and making her giggle. A moment later, he wrapped his arms around her, enveloping her toddler body in a bear hug, both their faces alight with joy. Jill felt herself smile.

Then she imagined that same little patch of shore strewn with beer bottles and garbage from a party hosted in this very house. The noise and the traffic would change Dewberry Beach, and not for the better. The image made her recoil. She couldn't do it, couldn't take advantage of them as Marc had.

But she didn't seem to have a choice.

As much as she wanted to protect Dewberry Beach from Shore Parties Unlimited, she couldn't afford to. This was a solid offer and she couldn't afford to wait for another. And Seth was right—an offer this good would not come again.

She returned to the table, decision made. Even if it wasn't the one she wanted.

"I'm sorry, Seth, you're right. This offer is extraordinary, and you sold the house faster than I'd imagined." As she reached for the pen, a movement outside the window next to her caught Jill's attention. It was her neighbor, Nancy Pellish, in her wide-brimmed sun hat and gardening gloves, circling the plum tree her grandfather had brought over from Italy.

Jill glanced toward the front of the house, at the road in front of the Pellish home. The street was still in the quiet of the morning, the black asphalt road dusted with beach sand. She imagined a street lined with cars, littered with broken bottles and trash. The inside of this house thumping with music and noise.

The idea was heartbreaking, and Jill couldn't be a part of it.

"I'm sorry. I can't do it." She put down the pen and hoped Seth would understand. "I can't sell to Shore Parties. The people here don't deserve what's about to happen to them."

After delivering the news, Jill looked away. There would be repercussions, of course. Seth would refuse to continue the listing and the bank would foreclose. But after everything Dewberry Beach had been through, Jill couldn't bring herself to add to their pain.

"Looks like we've come just in time."

Jill's gaze flew to the foyer. Chase and Mrs. Ivey stood there, windswept and pink from the morning's chill, with Ellie right behind them. After the last conversation she'd had with Chase, she was surprised to see him here, suited up and determined, with a briefcase in his hand. Well, if he'd come to make her feel bad, he had another think coming.

As Ellie guided Mrs. Ivey to the table, Jill rose and went to meet Chase.

"Hello, Jill."

"Mr. Bennett."

"I've come to apologize. I like to believe I'm a good judge of character, but in your case, I was wrong. I know Marc's feelings about this house, and I imagined you felt the same way. When you came to town to sell it, I was convinced, but I was wrong. I've misjudged your attachment to this house as badly as I've misjudged you, and I'm sorry. I was so swept up in telling you our side of the story that I didn't listen to yours."

"What changed your mind?"

"Ryan showed me the video you sent him, from your lunch meeting with Marc." Chase glanced at Ellie and his expression changed. Jill thought she saw a flash of admiration. "Then Ellie came to see me yesterday afternoon."

"Ellie? As in my best friend Ellie?"

"Oh, yes. She had quite a bit to say to me and she can be refreshingly blunt." He smiled over at Ellie. "Among other things, she insisted that you didn't want to sell this house at all—that given the choice, you'd raze it to the ground. Is that still true?"

Jill glanced across the room to the side window, where Mrs. Pellish was cutting back her plum tree in a losing battle to keep it alive.

"Yes," Jill said simply. "It is."

Chase beamed. "Wonderful. Then the problem becomes one of finance and those are easy to solve." He gestured to the agents at the table. "Would you mind if I interrupted your meeting? I have an idea that will benefit both of us."

"Sure." She had nothing to lose now.

When they got to the table, Chase offered each agent a firm handshake before settling into a chair opposite them. "You must be Seth. And Sheri. I'm Chase Bennett, and I'm pleased to meet you both. Please excuse our interruption, but we have a proposal that you'll find interesting."

Confused, Seth glanced at Jill, who nodded for him to listen. She had no idea where this was headed, but if Ellie was involved, then she'd trust it.

Chase withdrew a folder from his briefcase and set it on the table. Then he directed his attention to the agents. "A friend of ours, Billy Jacob, owns a large brownstone in Brooklyn and he wants to sell it. We'd like you to list it and handle the sale." Chase slid several pages of photographs across the table. "Mr. Jacob owns this entire building."

Seth accepted the packet and flipped the pages. "The building's been restored. Original transom windows and fixtures, right down to the glass doorknobs." He glanced up, a smile on his face. "Pre-war brownstones are almost non-existent these days. Most of them have been divided into apartments but this one is whole. This one... this is a treasure."

"I'd hoped you'd think so," Chase replied. "We'd like to offer you Mr. Jacob's listing in exchange for dropping this listing."

Jill tensed. "Dropping this listing" wasn't what she wanted at all.

Seth looked to Jill. "Are you sure that's what you want to do? I know you're not crazy about these buyers, but you don't have to be. Their offer is solid, and if you turn them down, you'll be walking away from quite a bit of money."

Jill drew a breath. She felt Ellie beside her, and she trusted her friend. "I think we should listen to them, at least."

Mrs. Ivey rose from her chair. "Why don't we all go into the kitchen and chat a bit? I have some basic information to get you started and a few extra pictures of the renovation in case you want them."

Jill watched as Seth, Sheri, and Mrs. Ivey left the table and made their way across the room. Then she turned to Chase. "I hope you know what you're doing."

He withdrew a second folder from his briefcase and placed it in front of her. "Billy owns what is generously called a motel on the edge of town. Do you know it?"

Jill remembered Stacy mentioning it and nodded. It was the same motel she'd tried to check into when she first came to town. The place was ghastly.

"The property was beautiful in its time. A few cabins on mostly green space with a copse of shady trees and winding paths." Chase waved his hand through the air. "The details aren't important, except to say that now the property is terribly run-down and Billy doesn't have the interest or the time to revive it. Brenda has always wanted to transform the property into an artists' retreat, but we couldn't figure out a way to do that, until now."

Jill leaned back in her chair. "I don't understand."

"One solution fed the other, and it was brilliant. Brenda needs building material for her retreat, and you have a house that needs to be razed. Our idea is to buy everything we need for the artists' retreat from you—everything that can be salvaged, from furnishings and linens to, well, as I said, everything that can be salvaged." Chase reached into his briefcase for a stapled printout and offered it to her. "This list is a good start, but I think we can do better. We'd also like to buy fixtures, drywall, cabinets: everything."

"Where did you get this?" Jill glanced at the list. It was the inventory she'd put together back when she thought selling the contents might pay for the demolition.

"I got it from Marc's office," Ellie replied. "Last night, when I said I needed to borrow a pen? I found your list, then went to find Mr. Bennett."

"You did indeed," Chase answered. "Gave me an earful too."

Jill looked at the list again. "Will that work? I mean, Billy can have whatever he wants, and he's welcome to it, but it won't pay for bulldozers and haul-away. And what am I supposed to do with a vacant lot? I can sell it, but what if the buyer is another Marc?"

"I think we have everything we need, Mr. Bennett." Seth and Sheri returned to the table. He offered his hand and shook Chase's. "We'll be in touch and thank you." He turned to Jill and smiled. "I'll contact the buyers and tell them the house is off the market. I wish you the best, Ms. DiFiore. I really do."

Jill showed them out and returned to the table.

"They were nice," Mrs. Ivey decided. "So what did I miss?"

"Jill had just pointed out that clearing the land might attract another developer with Marc's lack of scruples," Chase explained. "Then we'd have the same problem."

"You didn't tell her?"

Chase shook his head. "Not yet."

"Oh, honey, that's the best part," Mrs. Ivey supplied, happily turning her attention back to Jill. "Collectively, all of us have lived in Dewberry Beach for what, five decades?" She glanced at Chase for confirmation. "Maybe longer," she amended. "Feels like longer. Anyway, our roots are deep and our reach is wide. We have connections to do this and to do it quickly. After the land is cleared, we restore the deed. Usually that would require a hearing, but the county clerk was one of my students. She'll help if I ask. And I will."

"Then we persuade the township to buy the smaller lot next to the Pellish home. We'll need that for an art gallery," Chase continued. "Dewberry Beach doesn't have one."

"What about the other lot?" Jill asked.

"I have banking contacts," Chase said. "We'll secure a construction loan to build a small cottage and pay it off when it sells. Shouldn't be a problem at all."

"It sounds like you've thought of everything." Jill blew out a breath, relieved.

It seemed that Dewberry Beach would survive Marc's greed after all. The town would get an oceanfront art gallery, where local artists could show their work. And beside it, Jill imagined a cozy, light-filled cottage in place of The Monstrosity with a family and children living inside. Nancy Pellish's plum tree would flourish in the sunlight and the neighbors' view of the ocean would be restored.

It really was the best outcome, even if Jill couldn't be a part of it. It was enough that she'd made things right.

"Good, so if we're agreed, we should get to work." Chase gathered the pages and tapped them against the table. "We'll start by contacting your bank on Monday. I'll speak to them and arrange things. The architect for the cottage is local and he can meet with us later in the week, if you're free?"

"Um, sure." Jill imagined the drive from Ellie's apartment, where she would be living while she looked for work, to Dewberry Beach. "I need to find a job," she admitted. "But I'll look for one with flexible hours so I can come down and meet you whenever I need to."

"You didn't tell her!" Mrs. Ivey frowned gently at Chase. "Honestly, Chase." She smiled at Jill. "The *Dewberry Beach Trumpet*, our local newspaper, is in need of a staff photographer, and Brenda has recommended you for the job. It's part-time in the off-season but you can supplement your income with freelance work that we can direct your way, or you can use the extra time to focus on your own photography."

"But…" Jill glanced at Ellie. The plan was for them to be roommates and she didn't want to abandon her friend.

"Oh, I'll be fine, Jilly." Ellie straightened, proudly. "You're looking at bestselling author Billy Jacobs's new personal assistant. Mrs. Ivey reminded Billy that this project will take the better part of a year and he lost his mind. He wants no part of the process, but I do! Can you imagine? Tear the structures down, rebuild, then organize the retreats, start advertising… it's a huge thing." Ellie's eyes glittered with happiness. No one loved a project more than she did. She locked arms with Jill and leaned in to whisper, "We should find an apartment down here, don't you think?"

"So, what do you say?" Chase smiled. "Are you in?"

"Yes, absolutely," Jill agreed.

"Then I guess we should get going." Chase helped Mrs. Ivey with her coat. "If Simon Paulson thinks he's going to win the cook-off tonight with that nasty sausage roll of his, he's got another think coming."

"Chase Bennett!" Mrs. Ivey's expression dripped with reproach, but even Jill could see that it was fake. Her eyes twinkled with laughter.

"It's true." Chase scowled. "That man makes the same thing every year and the wins are starting to go to his head. It's past time for him to face a real challenger. I've had chicken marinating for two days now, and this is the year that man's knocked off the podium. I can feel it."

With everything that had happened in the last few days, it took Jill a moment to realize Chase was talking about the festival. Of course they'd want to get back to it.

Jill watched while they gathered their things.

"Aren't you coming?" Chase asked.

"Really?"

"Really. You girls are officially part of the community now."

"Um, sure. Let me just get my jacket." Jill turned to hide her expression. Dewberry Beach felt like home. Aunt Sarah would have been pleased.

"Now be sure to visit the dessert tent and vote for my lemon pound cake," Mrs. Ivey said as Jill pulled the front door shut behind them. "Chase isn't the only one facing a challenger. Betty Grable makes a mean apple spice cake—you've tasted it, so I need all the votes I can get to win this year." She squeezed Jill's hand. "But I might. It feels like a lucky year, doesn't it?"

"It does," Jill agreed as they headed for the festival. "It really does."

The four of them walked into town, Ellie and Mrs. Ivey up front, Jill and Chase strolling behind. The air was crisp and fresh. Overhead, the canopy of fall leaves made brilliant pops of orange and yellow against the deep blue sky. As they got closer to town, there was the smell of charcoal fires and delicious things grilling. The festival flyers said the cook-off went on all afternoon, and judged categories included everything from appetizers to desserts. Tents and grills had been set up on the lawn near the firehouse for days, and as Jill watched people darting back and forth, adding the finishing touches to their tables, she wondered if any firefighters had entered.

Chase's cell phone pinged with an incoming call. As he found his phone and answered it, Jill waited with him.

Aunt Sarah would have loved this town. She would have found gardening friends here, and Uncle Barney would have found men to fish with, friends who hadn't yet heard all his stories.

Best of all, The Monstrosity would be demolished, and all traces of Marc would be gone.

Jill hoped to settle here someday, in an apartment or maybe even a cottage. If she found something affordable, she would fix it up and stay forever. This was the life that fit her—this was what she wanted. And staff photographer for the *Dewberry Beach Trumpet* was a perfect job. She hoped that lasted too.

Beside her, Chase ended his call. Sliding his phone back into his pocket, he chuckled.

"What's funny?" Jill asked.

"Not funny, satisfying," he corrected as they continued on. "When things look especially grim, I am reminded that the wheels of justice may turn slowly but the grind is exceedingly fine." They paused at a crosswalk to wait for the light. "That was my friend at the justice department. I forwarded him your research and the recording from the restaurant, along with a few thoughts of my own."

"Really?"

"Yes, really. He was calling to thank me. Apparently the recording and the attachments you included were enough to open a federal investigation into Marc's activities in Mantoloking. In fact, I wouldn't be surprised if the FBI executed a search warrant tonight. Won't that be a surprise?" Chase chuckled.

"The FBI? Why would they be involved?"

"The program Marc defrauded receives federal funding." The light changed and they crossed the street. When they reached the other side, Chase stopped to give Jill his full attention. "Defrauding it is a federal offense. But that's not the best part. Because it was your tip that started the investigation, you are what's known as a 'whistleblower.'"

"I don't understand what that means."

"We shouldn't get ahead of ourselves, but the amount Marc stole was significant. When the case against him is settled, you will receive a percentage. You may be coming into quite a bit of money."

"Enough to pay for a house? Maybe a small one?" Jill held her breath.

"I believe so, yes. With a bit left over."

"I want to buy the cottage," Jill blurted. "The one next to the art gallery, on the smaller lot."

"I thought you might." Chase smiled. "Remember that a reward is just a possibility, but we'll look at the numbers and see where we stand. In the meantime, we'll find you and Ellie an apartment and get you settled into Dewberry Beach if that's where you want to stay."

"I do," Jill said. "I absolutely do."

Epilogue

A rainy day at the shore can be a gift, especially in the off-season.

The pace of the day slows, offering a morning spent lingering over coffee and an afternoon watching old movies, still in pajamas. It was one of the best things about rainy days at the beach: a whole day lazing about, doing nothing in particular.

But today, Jillian DiFiore didn't have the time to be lazy.

She yawned and stretched under the blankets, surprised at how well she'd slept. From her bed she could see through the lace-curtained window out to the ocean. A veil of fog obscured the horizon, but it was early yet, and Jill was optimistic. The weather people had promised a perfect fall day and it felt like she'd get one. A train whistled in the distance, and the excitement of the day propelled her forward, so Jill pushed back the covers, grabbed her bathrobe from the peg, and ventured to the kitchen to find coffee.

"I knew you'd be up early." Ellie pulled a mug from the cabinet and filled it with fresh coffee. Then added a generous pour of cream and handed it to Jill.

"Thanks."

Jill and Ellie had been roommates for the better part of a year. At first, they'd found a garage apartment and stayed there, but once the work was completed, it had just seemed natural that they'd move into this newly built cottage.

Over the last year, The Monstrosity, Marc's monument to himself, had been demolished. In its place was this tiny cottage that Jill had designed herself. Three airy bedrooms instead of nine, a bright kitchen with a tiny center island made from refinished driftwood and lace bistro curtains to frame every window. Outside was a little wooden deck that faced the sea. Made from reclaimed wood, it overlooked the seagrass on the dunes and the ocean waves beyond, and it had become a favorite gathering place, no matter the weather: everyone's favorite place to sit.

Before demolition started, Billy Jacob had bought the contents of The Monstrosity—all of it—and Ellie had arranged for it to be stored. Jill was glad to be rid of it. She wanted a fresh start and that included furniture from flea markets and yard sales. She refinished everything herself, and the end result was a cottage filled with an eclectic mix of textures and colors, beach finds and craft-fair treasures. It was a gathering place for friends and exactly what she'd dreamed of.

Jill made her way to the deck and settled into a chair beside Ellie, glancing toward the horizon to watch the surfer weave a path on his green board across a rolling wave.

"That guy's become really good," Jill remarked.

"It's a woman," Ellie corrected. "She works in the cheese shop on the weekend. I'm kind of seeing her."

"El!" Jill exclaimed. "Why didn't you tell me?"

"It's early yet," Ellie said, but her smile was wide. "Nothing to tell."

The watched the ocean for a while, content.

"Marc's attorney called again. Third time this week." Ellie broke the silence, then arched her eyebrow in query. "You're not gonna call him back, are you?"

Jill snorted. "Nope. Not in a million years. But think about it: how desperate can they be if they want me to be a character witness?"

Ellie laughed, then raised her coffee mug in a toast. "I can't imagine."

Chase had forwarded Jill news of the indictments filed against her ex-husband. Marc had been charged with so many counts of state and federal fraud that he'd been forced to sell the Berkshire land just to pay the attorney fees. Rumor was that Brittney had left him and he was now living in one of Cush's guest rooms.

It turned out that the most damning piece of evidence was Marc's admission of past fraud and his intent to repeat it, on the video Ellie had recorded at the restaurant that day. When the recording was admitted as evidence, Marc's attorney had protested, insisting his client hadn't known he was being recorded, that he was just showing off. But New Jersey was a one-party consent state, so the recording was admitted. Now, with the trial just a few months away, Marc's attorneys were scrambling to find anyone who had something nice to say about their client.

They seemed to be having a very hard time. Even Cush was silent.

"Hello, anyone home?" The side gate opened, and Brenda poked her head inside. "Is it too early for visitors?"

"You know you're welcome anytime." Jill gestured for Brenda to join them. "Coffee's fresh and so are the cider donuts. Would you like some?"

"Absolutely." Brenda entered the yard carrying a cardboard box, fresh from the printer.

Ellie scrambled to her feet. "Are those the flyers for tonight?"

"The very ones." Brenda rolled her eyes. "Talk about cutting it close."

"I'll get to work on putting them together." Ellie scooped up the box and eyed the contents. "Is this enough, do you think?"

"There's another box in the back of my car," Brenda said with a sigh. "I'll bring it in. Lemme just catch my breath after the encounter with the printer."

"That's okay," Ellie said as she headed inside. "I'll take care of it."

Brenda called her back. "Oh, wait. I almost forgot: Ryan said to tell you the website for the show is ready. He linked the page to Billy's new retreat. Billy said he hates it."

"Awesome," Ellie replied, completely unflustered. She'd grown used to Billy's mercurial nature and there was no one better at managing his moods. A moment later she called from the kitchen, "I'll bring you out some coffee."

Brenda called back, "Thanks, doll."

Jill and Brenda sat in companionable silence for a while, listening to the comforting sounds of Ellie rummaging in the cabinet for a mug, pouring coffee and adding cream. She emerged a moment later with a sturdy mug glazed in shades of ocean blue, then retreated back to the house to finish her work.

"Is this one of mine?" Brenda cradled the mug in her hands. "Feels like it."

"It is," Jill said. "We get all our best stuff from your studio sales."

Brenda sipped her coffee. "Speaking of…" She gestured to the building that sat on the second lot, next door to the cottage. "Big day for you. Are you excited?"

"Kind of," Jill answered weakly. The truth was she'd had butterflies for weeks now and they were getting worse.

To her surprise, Brenda laughed. "I was a wreck before my first show." She placed her coffee on the side table and rose from her seat. "Best solution is to meet it head-on. Let's go over."

They followed the sandy path from Jill's yard to the gallery and pushed open the side door to enter. Work on the building had just been completed. It was a little smaller than Jill's cottage—tiny by city standards, but perfect for Dewberry Beach. She and Brenda had sat on the committee to design the space and found that they worked well together. The floor was made from reclaimed wood, the walls white shiplap, and bright spotlights shone on the artists' work. The space was open to everyone and the calendar was filling fast; tonight was opening night.

An exhibit of Jill's photography would be the first showing.

Inside, Jill paused to breathe it in, to savor the moment.

They'd finished the display the night before, and even now it didn't seem real. The walls were covered in her work. The collection was titled "The Off-Season" and all the pieces were from Dewberry Beach.

In the quiet, Jill padded barefoot around the gallery, remembering when she'd taken each one.

Rose hips from the vine Betty had trained to grow around the slats of her white picket fence. The dusting of beach sand on the grass and a tiny drop of dew on the rose hip, frozen overnight and reflecting the soft pink of sunrise.

The dog who loved to chase driftwood was there too. Emerging from the surf with a weathered gray stick in his mouth, his eyes bright with joy as he brought his treasure to his owner.

There was the tidepool too, and the fishing trawlers, the Fish Shack and the woman who wrapped overstuffed lobster rolls. A delivery driver pulling out a bundle of newspapers from his truck for the newsstand. A baker from Mueller's prepping in the early morning, kneading dough in a cloud of flour. And fishermen setting the day's catch on the dock, the fish stacked neatly on ice as the great trawlers idled in the background.

"You should be proud of yourself," Brenda said softly.

"I kind of am," Jill answered. It was better than she'd ever imagined.

The bell jangled above the front door, indicting someone had entered the gallery. Doors were rarely locked at Dewberry Beach.

"Hello?" an older woman's voice called. "Is anyone here?"

Jill walked to the front of the gallery, intending to gently remind the woman that the show was scheduled to open later that afternoon.

But she stopped when she saw who it was.

"Mrs. Brockhurst?" The woman was dressed impeccably, in a cashmere overcoat, black leather gloves, and a bright silk scarf tucked into the collar.

At that moment, Jill realized what she herself was wearing and felt a flush of embarrassment. She tightened the tie of her bathrobe and hoped her bare feet would go unnoticed.

Mrs. Georgiana Brockhurst seemed to notice none of it. Instead, she just smiled.

"Please forgive me for showing up so early," she said finally. "I know it's shockingly bad form, but I wanted to make sure." She pointed to a photograph on the far side of the gallery, the one image that had not been taken at Dewberry: the bridal portrait Jill had included in her portfolio so long ago. "Has that piece been sold?"

The image didn't fit the theme of the exhibit, but Brenda had talked Jill into including it. She said it was the photograph that had started it all. Jill looked up in time to see Brenda leaving the gallery, the side door gently closing behind her.

"No," Jill managed. "It hasn't been sold. Nothing has."

"I know the exhibit isn't scheduled to open until this evening," Mrs. Brockhurst finished smoothly. "I understand and I hope you'll make an exception, because I'd like to buy it."

"You would?"

"Yes." The woman frowned. "I made a mistake not hiring you last year for Libby's bridal portrait, and that decision has always bothered me. My reasons were valid, but it felt like a missed opportunity. I'm sorry not to have taken a chance when you came to see me that day. I wanted to tell you that."

Not trusting her voice, Jill simply nodded. After a moment she was able to swallow past the lump in her throat. "I'd like to give it to you."

Mrs. Brockhurst's refusal was immediate. "Absolutely not," she scoffed. "An artist should never give away her work. I *will* settle for a sold sign though, firmly affixed to the wall there. So I can be sure the photograph is mine. And I'll come back later when you're officially open. Thank you for letting me barge in now."

Jill glanced outside at the long black car parked along the curb, a uniformed man waiting beside it. Surely she hadn't planned to drive back to Summit?

Jill called her back. "Would you like to come inside for some coffee while you wait?"

To her surprise, Mrs. Brockhurst laughed. "Oh, honey, it's okay. I'm going to visit Wim Ivey. Pretty sure I'm gonna surprise the hell outta her."

Jill was so stunned at the drop in facade and the New Jersey accent, she felt her mouth fall open.

At that, Mrs. Brockhurst laughed harder. "Wim and I go way back. We worked Atlantic City back in the day. She was a psychic, did you know? Had an act with a crystal ball and everything, but that's a story for another day."

After Mrs. Brockhurst left, Jill returned to her cottage. She stood on the back deck and looked out over the ocean, watching waves break against the jetty, pushing foamy water across the sand and filling tidepools along the shore. Further out, an ocean tanker crept along the horizon, and a trio of seagulls swept across the blue sky. Despite the shaky start, she'd come to love Dewberry Beach. She'd found a home here and imagined Aunt Sarah and Uncle Barney would be pleased.

"Jilly?" Ellie called from the kitchen. "Phone for you—it's Danny. He wants to know what time to pick you up for dinner before your show."

Smiling, Jill went inside to answer the call.

A Letter from Heidi

Thank you so much for choosing to read *The Girl I Used to Be*. If you enjoyed it and want to keep up to date with all my latest releases, please sign up at the following link. Your email address will never be shared and you can unsubscribe at any time.

www.bookouture.com/heidi-hostetter

Isn't it funny how the smallest encounter can grow into something so much more?

The main character for this story, Jill DiFiore, was a brief mention in *The Shore House*, the wife of a secondary character and that's it. In fact, she didn't even make an appearance at the party her husband hosted. I thought it was odd, but lots of my characters are odd. When *The Shore House* ended, Jill's voice got louder. She told me she had a story of her own and it was time to tell it. So I let her talk. Turned out she had a lot to say, and *The Girl I Used to Be* is her story.

For me, it was wonderful to return to Dewberry Beach, this time in the off-season. In October, the small shore town takes on a whole different look. Summer guests have left, their vacation homes shuttered until Memorial Day. The off-season on the New Jersey shore is every bit as beautiful as it is in the summer, but now the focus is on a community coming back together as daily life for residents falls into an easy routine. Instead of fireflies and sparklers and crabbing off the pier, there's hot tea and spice cake and catching up with neighbors you've only managed to wave to in the busy summer months.

Jill comes to town unexpectedly and doesn't intend to stay long. She has plans for her life and they don't include Dewberry. But the New Jersey shore works its magic, and the results are unexpected. I hope you liked the story—and the ending—as much as I did.

My next book will be set in Dewberry Beach too, this time with a different family and different circumstances to address. I look forward to visiting the shore again and I hope you'll join me.

I hope you loved reading *The Girl I Used to Be* as much as I loved writing it. If you did, would you mind writing a quick review? It doesn't have to be long, and I'd appreciate it. Reviews make it easier for new readers to discover my books for the first time.

If you want to contact me directly, that's great too—I love hearing from readers. The Facebook links for my Author Page and Reading Group are below. Or, if you'd rather just hang out and see what I'm up to, that's okay too. My Author Page has the latest news. You can also find me on my website.

My Author Page on Facebook:
AuthorHeidiHostetter

My Reading Group on Facebook:
www.facebook.com/groups/636728933179573

And my website:
www.heidihostetter.com

Warmly,
Heidi

Acknowledgments

Once again, I'd like to thank the talented team at Bookouture for helping to shape this story into something wonderful. To my insightful editor, Kathryn Taussig, who can always see the story, no matter how murky the first draft. To Kim Nash and Noelle Holten, who make launching a book look easy when I know it's not. And to the authors in the Bookouture Lounge, you are inspiring and I'm glad to know all of you.

To my sister Heather, for the crash course on points of real-estate closings and zoning laws. To my brother John, who answered every one of my construction questions, though I'm sure he screened most of my calls toward the end. To my writing group, whose weekly Zoom meetings got me through 2020. Eight years, you guys, can you believe it? Ann Reckner, Heather Stewart-McCurdy, Laurie Rockenbeck, Sandy Esene, and Liz Visner—you're the best.

I'd also like to thank Kelly Dwyer, whose insight and suggestions helped bring this story to life. I'm grateful.

And my most sincere gratitude goes to my readers. Thank you for reading and thank you for reaching out to tell me how much my stories have meant to you.

It is my honor to write for such an engaged audience.

Made in United States
North Haven, CT
06 October 2022

25054885R00157